THE SHADOWS WE KEEP

SHADOWS AND SECRETS DUET
BOOK 1

CINDY DAWSON

Copyright © 2023 by Cindy Dawson
All rights reserved.
Cover Art by Cindy Dawson & K.M. Mixon
Interior Design by K.M. Mixon
No part of this book may be reproduced in any form or by any electronic or mechanical means, including information storage and retrieval systems, without written permission from the author, except for the use of brief quotations in a book review.

All people, places, and scenarios inside this book are works of fiction; they are entirely works of the author's imagination. Any similarity to real-life persons or scenarios is a coincidence.

For all my readers that bloom under a firm hand. You know who you are.

AUTHOR'S NOTE

The Shadows We Keep is technically a dark romance. However, I'd say we're more in the gray area between contemporary and dark romance. Regardless, there are darker themes and explicit scenes throughout and this book is intended for an adult audience.

See my website for a full list of trigger and content warnings: author-cindydawson.carrd.co

PLAYLIST

I Want It – Two Feet
Cracks – Flux Pavilion Remix
Don't Blame Me – Taylor Swift
Who Is She x The Perfect Girl – Xanemusic, NVBR
Dark Horse – Sleeping At Last
Rosenrot – Rammstein
Sinner – Dezi
A Girl Like You – Machine Gun Kelly, Travis Barker
I Want It All – Cameron Grey
Sad – Bryce Savage
Can You Hold Me – NF, Britt Nicole
My Type (Little Attitude) – Bryce Savage
Better – Emma Remelle
Shackles – Steven Rodriguez
Scorpio – Pour Vous
Are You With Me – nilu
Apartment – Bobi Andonov
Silhouette – Pushloop Remix
Do It for Me – Rosenfeld

Power Over Me – Dermont Kennedy
Lilith – Ellise
MIDDLE OF THE NIGHT – Elley Duhé
Mind Games – Sickick
Do you really want to hurt me? – Nessa Barrett
All The Things She Said – Ponette
NFWMB – Hoizer
Dirty Mind – Boy Epic
Gimme Love – Rosenfeld
Scars – Boy Epic
Bad Moon Rising – Mourning Ritual, Pere Dreimanis
Him & I – G-Eazy, Halsey
Nails – Call Me Karizma
Wicked as They Come – CRMNL
Find You – The Phantoms
Can You Keep A Secret? – Ellise
No Rest For The Wicked – Klergy
See You Bleed – Ramsey
Give – Sleep Token
Crazy Girls – TOOPOOR
Switchblade – Neverwaves

PROLOGUE
KEIRA

I Want It – Two Feet

The grinding of coffee beans mixes with the whistle of the steaming milk as the barista assembles my latte. Customers bustle about the small space, picking up their morning dose of legal crack or relaxing in one of the oversized leather chairs near the windows.

"Keira," the barista calls and I snag my drink from the counter, peering around for an empty seat. One in the back corner opens up.

Perfect.

I sag down, my limbs heavy with exhaustion from working an overnight at the airport. I should have gone straight home and gotten some shuteye, but the nagging in the back of my mind to see if there were any updates online had me shuffling to the coffee shop around the corner from my place instead.

Reloading the bookmarked page on my browser, his timeline still looks the same. It's killing me. He's posted nothing in weeks. My nails are bit down to the quicks. I'm going through serious withdrawals, and I need another hit. Just something small to take the edge off. I click from his page to his best friend's, although it's been hard not to notice the distance growing between them over the last couple of months. Can I blame him, though? Not when he's been through something so tragic.

It's another dead end. The last post with them together is from weeks ago. Someone else connected to him online has to have something. His dad, strike two. His mom? I don't have high hopes since she usually keeps things picture perfect and high class.

Fucking rich people.

Dear god, why does one woman need so many photos of her perfectly manicured garden? It's not like she's the one that tends to it. Just as I thought, another dead end. I slam my laptop shut and shove it back into the messenger bag at my feet.

He's absent from socials and hasn't checked in to the online support group. For the first time in years, I'm feeling the miles between us like they're actually there. He was the last piece of the puzzle I had to cling on to. If I can't find him again, I truly am alone. The dark thoughts of years past filter through my mind. There's nothing left holding them at bay.

I race for the door and push it out, heaving in a lungful of air, clearing out the heaviness that started setting into my chest. My vision clears, the little black dots around the edges fading slowly. I push through a group of kids getting off the bus, stopping at the corner.

A right, and I'm a few blocks from home and only minutes from crashing into my mattress. But if I take a left in the opposite direction, I can do a lap and check out his family's building. They have a mega mansion in California and an industrial modern apartment in Brooklyn.

Oh, to see how the other half lives.

My body decides before my brain can even contemplate the options. My subconscious saw the flash of his face, and my feet followed. I'm not sure why I do it. They've never stayed here before. Anytime I've seen their trips to New York online, they're held up in some swanky hotel in Manhattan overlooking Central Park.

I stop across the street and lean up against the red brick of a pizza parlor, taking in his building. Scanning the tinted windows, I realize how obnoxiously out of place this remodel is against the traditional brownstones.

But that's when I see him, coming around the corner, hoodie pulled up, boot laces dragging along the pavement. A whoosh of air leaves my lungs, and my hands grasp the rough brick ledge behind me.

He's here, across the street, closer to me than ever before. My world tips on its axis. An hour ago, I was jonesing for a bite of information on his whereabouts. For once, the universe is on my side.

Following his strides with my gaze, I survey every inch of him. The black hoodie drapes from his frame, but his jeans hold tight to his toned legs. I know underneath he's coated in inky designs. The once country club going, prep school jock is gone. In his wake stands the mysterious man in black across from me. He enters the building, disappearing behind the tinted door.

He's here.

I don't know how long I've lingered, but my feet ache and my palms are scratched raw from the rough exterior of the building. I give up on the hope that he's coming out soon. Turning to head back in the direction I came, a for rent sign in the window snags my attention.

I duck inside. No one sits at the counter, but a jovial voice with a thick Italian accent calls from the back. A gigantic mountain of a man comes around the corner with flour coating his shirt. "What can I get you?" he asks.

"Who do I talk to about the apartment for rent?" I throw a thumb over my shoulder in clarification of my question.

He takes me in. I probably look rough since I've been up almost twenty-four hours because of my minor detour on the way home. I must pass his inspection because he finally answers, "Boss isn't in right now. Should be back this evening. Can you come by then?"

"Yeah, I can make that work. Do you know which apartment it is?"

He points up to the ceiling. "Third floor, faces that monstrosity of a building across the street." He visibly cringes.

I like him. That's perfect. If I can swing it, I can keep better tabs on him if he's done away with socials.

"Great." I extend my hand across the counter. "I'm Keira." He wipes his tan paw against his shirt and takes mine tightly. "Can you let your boss know I'll be back later? I'm looking for a place as soon as possible."

"Sure thing." He nods in confirmation, and I head back for the street, looking down at my watch. It's already one, by the time I get back home I'll only have enough time for a quick nap before I'll need to get ready for work again if I want to stop here before my shift. Tonight's going to suck.

"Rent's $1,300 a month. You pay for everything. There's a clause in the rental agreement that you have access to the pizza parlor downstairs. My family owns the business and the building. You get two slices a day. Don't abuse it." His seedy stare rakes down my body and I bristle inside. Unwanted attention isn't anything new for me. I've been deflecting it for years.

I quickly do the math in my head. It's twice what I'm paying now, but I'd have the space to myself. No more sharing a bathroom with two other roommates and their weekly guests. It's not great, the paint is peeling, there's a stain in the bedroom that eerily resembles blood. But if I'm tight with things, I can probably make it work. Plus, if I take advantage of the free pizza, I won't have to buy groceries.

"Do you have an application I can fill out now?" I ask. He pushes the packet of papers across the kitchen counter where we've ended the tour. I look it over. Nothing out of the ordinary pops out at me, so I fill it out and hand it over.

"When can I expect to hear from you?"

"A day or two if you get it." He looks over the information and ushers me toward the front door. It's a long shot, but I had to try.

<u>Two Days Later</u>

My back hits the hard mattress on the floor with a thud. I'd planned to get a frame for it eventually, but when the place you live in is nothing more than a place to lay your head and wash up, what's the point? Six hours of sleep in a manner of three days has not been enough to keep me going. My eyes fall closed the moment I turn to my stomach and hitch a leg up into my favorite sleeping position.

Buzz....Buzz...Buzz

Consciousness slowly creeps back into play. My hand fumbles around on the floor next to my bed, looking for the offending party that woke me. By the time my fingers wrap around the edge to snag it, the buzzing ceases. *Of course.*

As my eyes adjust to the bright screen in the dim room, I see a missed call from an unknown number. Usually, I'd leave it because the only numbers that show up unknown are solicitors and scammers, and I refuse to waste my time with either, but the voicemail icon pops up, stealing my attention.

"Hello Keira, this is Marco, the landlord you met with the other day. I was just calling to let you know that we have approved you for the apartment. My father wanted me to tell you the rent for this unit is only $800 and that includes all utilities. Please stop by Luigi's as soon as you can to sign the lease agreement. I'll leave it at the front counter with Sal."

Holy fucking shit, is this really happening? An entire apartment to myself for not much more than I pay for this dump with two other people. That $500 difference changes everything. I jump up and look around my dilapidated room. There's not much here for me to pack up. My small crate shelf holds all my clothes and shoes. A small collection of the odds and ends perched on top, while a stack of books I still need to return to the library sit next to it.

I take it all in, my room is depressing. But when you grow

up without a permanent address, it's hard to break the mindset that you're not staying long. Although now that I'm about to move again, it's convenient. Rolling to my feet, I throw on some clothes and pack my bag for the day. I'm relieved today is my day off. If I can get over to the pizza shop, fill out the paperwork, and get it to Marco, maybe I can move in later today or tomorrow before I go back to work.

I haven't told my roommates I'm moving out, but seeing as we're on a month-to-month lease, and I've already paid this month, I'll tell them tonight and leave them to figure it out. It's officially not my problem.

I luck out when I step through the pizza shop's door and see Marco at the front counter; I didn't expect that he would work in his own restaurant. He appeared the type of guy that did the bare minimum and expected the rest to be handed to him.

When his eyes lift from his phone, his gaze skirts up and down my body. I'm in my usual attire: skinny jeans, oversized hoodie, and combat boots. There's not much for him to take in, but that doesn't stop his eyes from glowing with lust. What a pig.

"Ahh, there she is, our new tenant. You ready to move in?" His saccharine smile sends shivers down my spine. I'll have to keep a wide berth with this one.

"That's what I was hoping to figure out from you today. Once I fill out the paperwork, when can I move in?"

"As soon as you sign on the dotted line and hand over your rent, I'll give you the keys."

I do as he says, filling out the paperwork and signing my life away. Well, for the next year at least. I dig through my heavy shoulder bag for my wallet. It's bulging with the entire contents of my savings account I drained in order to afford double rent this month. I drop the bills to the counter. "Hope cash is fine?"

He nods and tucks it into his jacket pocket, pulling free the jangling keys and dropping them in my outstretched palm. "Need me to walk you up?" he asks.

"No, I think I remember. Thanks though. I'm going to head up now and see what all I need." He points to the interior door to the side of the restaurant that opens into the small entrance alcove for the apartments.

"I left a card with my information on the counter. Call if you need anything." The emphasis doesn't evade me, but I pay it no mind. The more attention, positive or negative, you give a man like Marco, the harder he grips on to a possibility.

The front door creaks open, bumping against the wall. When I move into the space further, I'm shocked to see furniture in the living room. A couch and coffee table fill up most of the space. They're nothing new, obviously second hand but still in decent condition. It's the oversized plush chair off to the side that pulls my attention because it looks new.

What the hell is going on here?

The thought of going back down to the restaurant and dealing with Marco face to face dulls my excitement of the day. Maybe I can just text him? His card rests on the counter next to a packet of the rental lease. Drawing out my phone, I type in his number and save it to my contact.

> Hey Marco. I just got into my apartment. I think there might've been a mistake. There's a bunch of furniture in here.

> No mistake, welcome to the building.

WELL, I guess that settles that. I'm not one to look a gift horse in the mouth, but life's never dealt me a helpful hand that didn't have strings attached. Walking through the rest of the apartment, proves the same results, a bed frame and nightstands that weren't there the day before. A full dresser nestles against the one available empty wall. My mind races as the logical half of it can't catch up to a reason behind the unexpected furnishings.

But when I turn around and take in the floor to ceiling windows that look out to *his* building, I can't find a reason to care. My feet move me to the glass. The sun shines brightly, filling the room with a warm afternoon glow. I'm sure anyone who had the inclination to take in my apartment from afar would have a clear view. Curtains are at the top of my list.

I wasn't so lucky in my quest to suss out his apartment's floor the other day as I stood outside, but the wonderful thing about being a road's width away is I have all the time in the world. If it takes befriending someone in the building to gain access, so be it.

ONE
HARKIN

Flux Pavilion's - Cracks

One year later...

Full, heavy clouds litter the jet-black sky. The impending storm is rolling in faster than they'd predicted, and we need to get down the mountain before the rain falls. Gripping my keys tighter, the bite of the teeth digs into my palm as her footfalls follow behind me. The gravel crunches as we round the trunk of my car.

"Just get the fuck in," I snap.

"I wasn't ready to leave. And you can't drive. You've had too much to drink." Her whining grates on my nerves. I hate this side of her. The drunk party girl that never knows when to quit until her tongue is down someone else's throat.

Ignoring her, I swing the driver's side door open and stare through the tinted windshield, right as the first fat plop of a raindrop hits the glass. Fuck.

"I'm sorry." Her demeanor switches as she falls into the passenger's seat, rubbing the chill from her exposed skin. "I didn't mean to."

I sigh. She never means to, yet somehow, it always happens. I'm tired of it. Tired of the constant, accidental cheating because she can't help herself once the booze or the drugs race through her system. If I didn't love her as deeply as I do, I could walk away, but that isn't us.

At that very moment, the sky opens, rain pelts against the car. The roads are going to be a nightmare as the water collects on the asphalt and runs downhill.

"It's fine. Put your seatbelt on."

She curls into a ball, pulling her knees to her chest. I twist the knob up, the heat blows in her direction, and I shift into drive. The roads are slick, glossed over with black streams. Thankfully, there's no one else on the two-lane road coming up the mountain at this hour. I grip the steering wheel tight as the tires shift over the solid white line indicating the very narrow shoulder.

Twenty more minutes. Twenty more minutes and we'll be back on flat ground and my anxiety might subside.

"What's that?" Alina murmurs, pointing forward in front of the car.

I don't see it until it's too late. The tree's down across the whole road blocking our path. My foot collides with the brake, shoving it to the floor but with the water quickly rising, the tires lose traction and the car fishtails out of control. We stay on the road sliding from one side as I over correct and try to slow the car down, but it's no use. The car's pointed straight for...

JOLTING UP, I clutch the cool sheets around my waist. My body drips with sweat and the smell of it permeates around me. *God Damnit.* The dream rocks me as visions of that night swim through my head. But not the actual impact. Not our last moment together. The doctor said that was a normal trauma response. The brain's way of protecting itself from the horror of the accident. But his scientific bullshit didn't help the fact that within minutes I'd lost the one thing I'd loved most.

I need to shake this off or it'll haunt me all day and the last thing I want is a repeat on my flight to California. That right there was easily the cause of the nightmare resurfacing after so many months without one. Back home, back to where it all happened. Where my parents expect me to act as though I didn't take the life of a girl they expected me to marry and have two-point-five kids and a dog with.

They're the only ones, though. Alina's parents wanted to press charges. To test my blood for drugs or alcohol, because that would have been a better reason for the tragedy instead of the rain. I understood their need for restitution for the crime committed against their only daughter. But when you're the son of a business mogul, it's hard to make a case stick.

Throwing the bright white sheets to the floor, my muscles strain as I climb from the bed. Stretching every which way to loosen the pull of them. The ache in both knees means it's going to rain or maybe it already is by the dull look out the half-covered windows. A shower should set things right.

The hot spray cascades down my body, the bass of Flux Pavilion's, *Cracks* streams through the speakers in the ceiling. Alina's face pops into my head again. Tugging at my hair, my forehead falls to the stone tile.

"Fuck!" I grunt, feeling the emptiness inside me just as present as the day I awoke in the hospital to the news about Alina. I guess the shower didn't do the trick this time.

Stepping up to the fogged mirror, I swipe my hand back and forth against the condensation, clearing a distorted view. Vacant eyes glance back at me, the dark circles under them a physical sign of my restless night. The man staring back at me sees every little thing that's changed in me since her death.

The dark ink covering most of my skin camouflages the scars left behind by multiple surgeries to place bones back where they belong. The nose rings, the only viewable piercings passersby know about. My onyx hair's grown out, the stubble against my chin longer than what's deemed respectable. I'm not looking forward to the outright gawking from the people back home, especially my mother.

The alarm beeps with confirmation that it's set. I heft my duffle bag over my shoulder and head for the street. The weather's dreary as usual for this time of year. If I'm lucky, I'll miss the rain and get to California where the weather is bound to be better than here in New York. Stepping out on to the street, I signal for a taxi. I'd take the subway, but I don't have time to make the switches necessary from my place in Brooklyn.

My move to New York was the last straw for my parents, as if the steady growth tattoos covering my skin, pill popping, and alcohol abuse weren't enough of a red flag that my head wasn't on straight. I spent years spiraling into the dark abyss of depression, feeding it with anything that would numb my pain. I needed to get out of that town, where every turn reminded me of her. Where the friends we shared overburdened me with their love and support, then eventually drifted away at the sight of the mess I'd become.

There was nothing keeping me in California. I was no longer the carefree teenager, raised with a silver spoon shoved so far up my ass I couldn't walk right. That privilege had always been second nature, nothing to think twice about. But after the accident, when the only consequences I faced were an aching body, damaged mind, and broken soul, I couldn't stand it any longer. When I'd finally hit rock bottom, overdosing on the same shit I'd fought with Alina over time and time again, I packed my stuff and left. The last thing I took from my parents was the apartment I live in now.

The taxi pulls up to the curb in front of me. A small hand reaches past me for the yellow handle as I tug to open the door and slide in. I look over and freeze as recognition sets in, but it's not possible. I shake my head, trying to expel the image of Alina in front of me. This isn't happening. My mind is finally snapping. Maybe I should have toked up before heading to the airport to take the edge off today.

"Umm, I need this taxi," she says.

Her raspy voice makes it sound like she's just waking up from a night out and needs a glass of water. I don't respond, instead I continue staring at the golden eyes that are all too familiar.

"Look, I'm late for work. I need this ride," she says again.

Her brashness brings me back to reality, Alina never would have talked to me like that.

"Hey lady, I called this taxi. I know you saw me standing here on the curb waving my hand in the air. Don't act like you did the same. This is my ride and I'm running late for my flight." She stops her huffing at that.

"Where are you flying out of?" She doesn't have a New York accent. I can't help but wonder where she came from.

"JFK." I throw over my shoulder, climbing into the cab. When I reach out to swing the door closed, her big bag thrusts between us, keeping the door ajar.

"Scoot over." She urges and pushes against the side of my body with her slight frame. But I don't budge.

"What do you think you're doing?"

"So, turns out we're both going to the same place. I'm

headed to work at JFK. We might as well share a cab and split the fare; it won't be cheap."

I think about her proposition, not that the money matters. "What the hell? Why not?"

The door shuts behind her. She leans forward against the partition to tell the driver where we're heading. The hem of her black shirt rises and the hint of a purple swirl against her skin draws my attention down. Unfortunately for me, she catches my stare.

Her icy gaze bores into me. "It's a thirty-minute drive. Try not to be a fucking creep, would you?"

I smirk at her bite, the girl has sass, and it's caught my attention. Not in the typical *fuck this bitch is crazy* way, but like a magnet that pulls out the inner asshole in me and makes me want to spar with her. The fact that she's a carbon copy of my dead girlfriend has very little to do with it. Or so I keep telling myself.

"So, what takes you to JFK?"

"Work." Her uninterested tone makes it clear she doesn't want to chat it up with the rando she's sharing a car with.

"Yeah, I gathered as much from your introduction."

She scoffs. "I work at the airport."

"Uh, huh. Got that too. Want to expand on that?"

"Why can't you just be like any other normal New Yorker and sit there, shut up, and stare like a zombie at your phone? I'm really not in the mood to make small talk."

I nod. Her message received loud and clear. I pull out my phone, skimming through the unread texts that I've ignored for the last few days, emails that went straight to the trash folder. Finally, ending up scrolling through my photos.

I had to double check. Maybe it's just my mind's weird way

of connecting with this person. Maybe she doesn't really look like Alina's doppelgänger. Unlocking the hidden folder I'd moved all our photos to months before, I open one. Alina's spread out on my bed in nothing but my tee shirt. Her hair was a mess, thrown haphazardly across my pillows as she smiled up at me.

I examine her every feature, then glance sideways at the woman sharing the bench seat with me. Their noses are both thin and straight, a small slope up when you see them from the side. Golden brown eyes the color of fall leaves, with tiny flecks of green. I figure it'd probably freak her out too much to stare that closely to tell. Their lips are both full and round. How could this be?

Alina didn't have any family outside of California, so they couldn't be related. I try to pinpoint the differences. Where Alina's hair was long and blonde, professionally highlighted to cover her natural brown, this girl has deep brown hair with a slightly red tint that only shows through when the light hits it. Alina's skin was golden brown, but in California, that's most of the population who spend any amount of time outside. But this stranger is pale, skin lightly dotted with freckles.

I look over again to compare. This time, our eyes meet, and my fingers quickly turn off the screen of my phone.

"Baggage," she mutters.

"Excuse me?"

"I work in baggage claim," she reiterates.

Oh, so now she wants to talk. It's about time. Sitting in a taxi, next to someone you don't know in an awkward silence, could only last so long.

"Where are you headed?" she asks.

"Back to California."

"Ah, I had a feeling you weren't from around here." She smirks.

"I'm just visiting. California that is. I moved to New York almost a year ago," I confirm.

"Still a transplant. You can't really call yourself a true New Yorker until you've been here a few years, at the very least."

"How about you? You from New York?" There was a deep-seated need to know more about her budding in the back of my mind.

"For the most part, yeah. Not necessarily the city, but I've been here long enough."

"I'm Harkin." I hold my hand out to her. She stares down at it, inspecting before she takes it into hers.

"Keira."

I hold on to her small hand, covered in big silver rings. Each one a unique design. One looks like a saying's inscribed through the metal, but it's too small to read without bringing it up to my face. I run my thumb over them without a second thought as she stares down at our joined hands. Hers pale and small, engulfed in my tattooed one that seems to swallow hers whole.

"JFK. That'll be $52.50." The driver's declaration that we'd arrived pulls us apart, and I'm not ready for the wave of ice it causes through my body at her loss.

"Have a safe flight." She parts ways with a few simple words and no look back.

TWO
KEIRA

Don't Blame Me – Taylor Swift

I slam my bag down on the conveyer belt, not bothering to remove the items that are supposed to go through screening separately. The machine beeps and my bag comes back toward me. The security guard looks me up and down as if I'm an idiot.

"You need to remove any electronics and place them in a separate bin."

I roll my eyes. John never cared. It's not like they can't see exactly what's in my purse with the machine, anyway. It just makes their jobs easier, while making mine more difficult.

I'm covering Jasmin's day shift this morning, which I'm already late for. And this middle-aged woman with a stick up her butt, who doesn't know me from a hole in the wall, is making it worse.

Fucking figures.

I pull my phone and my small tablet from the bag, shoving them into the empty bin next to it. I look up, her judgy eyes watching my every move. I raise an eyebrow, and she nods. Pushing both through the x-ray machine again, I step forward through the metal detector and am finally permitted to enter the employees only entrance.

God, I hope today doesn't continue down this shitty path. Sprinting through the office and down the hall, I clock in at my airlines booth and step up to the computer. The bag check line is backed up, wrapping around in the lobby. There goes that hope.

"Hey, what's up with you?" Bonny asks as the last bag hits the belt.

"It's been a morning. And you know me, my ass is not used to being up this early. I work the night shift for a reason. Remind me never to cover a morning shift again." Not to mention, my dumb ass decided it was a great idea to share a cab with the guy I've been watching every spare moment I've had while simultaneously hiding from for the last year. The moment his eyes met mine, I should have apologized and walked away, but instead, I insisted we share a cab to JFK. I tried being rude, hoping it'd rub him the wrong way, and he'd ignore me, that didn't work.

"Girl, you're acting like it's the crack of dawn, its ten am."

I shrug. "Same difference. I'm usually still sleeping at this hour." I laugh it off.

"Go get some coffee. We don't have another boarding for at least an hour. And when you get back, you can tell me what's really going on."

I stare her down, unimpressed with her ability to catch my bullshit. That's what happens when you work with the one person who is a walking lie detector test. "Want your usual?"

"Of course." She smiles sweetly, then heads for the other side of the floor.

There's only one coffee stand on this side of the airport before going through security to get to the gates. Thankfully, it's good and airport staff receive a hefty discount with their employee badge. I order our coffees and take the long way back to the bag check area. Sipping away at my black iced coffee, I see him across the way, standing in line for security, that same stupid bag hanging off his shoulder.

After all these months, I can't believe we finally ran into each other. I was running so late; I hadn't noticed it was him hailing the cab. Not that I cared about stealing it from someone who'd obviously been the one to call it to the curb.

Eleven months, thirteen days, and ten hours. That's how long I avoided running into Harkin Greyson.

I knew the moment he set eyes on me it was game over. There was no way he wouldn't be able to put two and two together. It didn't matter that I was pale and had dark hair. Or that my nails weren't done, and my face wasn't coated in makeup. If I hadn't been in uniform, I'd have had a bit more to play down our likeness. But the truth was, I look just like her. And I know it.

It's so undeniably obvious that he had to realize it too. His eyes penetrated mine the moment they lifted to see who was trying to steal his cab. I'd fucked up. The recognition was as clear as day on his face as he internally battled to make sense of the situation. How was his dead girlfriend staring back at him? Well, it was pretty simple when you'd grown up knowing the truth and not living a lie.

His eyes shift across the walkway littered with people. He can't see me standing against the pillar hidden in the shadows. My petite frame is a bonus for disappearing in crowds. But that doesn't stop my heart from racing as I watch him wait for his turn through security. He seems like he's looking for something or someone. Maybe he isn't traveling back to California alone, but he doesn't have any friends here.

I don't take my eyes off him, studying the way his tall frame cascades over the family in front of him, his leather jacket and combat boots in hand for easy processing. The designs cover every inch of naked skin on full display. I desperately want to inspect it up close and in person instead of through a screen. But that isn't happening. Not today, not any day.

I turn and finish the long route back to the desk and set Bonny's coffee down, water lining the top where the ice has already melted.

Shit, how long had I been standing there?

"What the hell took you so long?"

I cringe. Apparently, it was longer than I'd thought. "Long line. You know how it is." I try to brush it off. But again, human lie detector.

"You're so full of shit. We've only got twenty minutes before the next flight starts collection, so you better spill. And you better not leave anything out."

I blow out a long breath. Where the hell do I even start? And how do I come up with a believable lie for the stuff I can't tell her?

"Okay, so you know that guy I met online through that grief chat room a while back?" She nods in confirmation. "Did I ever tell you he moved to the city?" Her eyes grow with shock and slight annoyance that I'm just now telling her this.

"You mean the guy from California? Why'd he move all the way here?" she asks.

"He wanted to get away from his family. Away from the

area and the people who reminded him of the accident, I guess." I'd told her about Harkin and what he went through. But I wasn't honest about how I knew.

"Okay? So, what about him?"

"I ran into him this morning on my way to work. But he didn't know it was me." I tread lightly. This is where it could get messy.

"Wait! I'm confused. How'd you know it was him, but he didn't know it was you?"

God, she always knows the questions to ask that I don't want to answer. I let out a slow breath, quickly putting into place a cover story.

"He told me his name one time after group, even though it's supposed to be anonymous. But we just kind of had this connection from the start. His username was Calibred275, so it was easy to assume that's where he was from." I let out a slow breath. "His full name and state, plus what I'd learned about the accident, made it easy to google him. I just hadn't expected him to be from a well-known family."

Her hand shoots out and grabs my arm. "Wait, wait, wait, how famous are we talking here?"

"You probably wouldn't know him, but his dad is this huge business mogul. He owns a bunch of commercial real estate. He uses some for his own companies but then leases the rest out to other big businesses. The man's loaded." She whistles in understanding.

"So, it wasn't hard to find pictures of him once I knew that. I found his socials next, and that's why when we both reached for the same cab this morning, I about peed myself."

"Okay, first off, who knew you were Veronica Mars? Actually, now that I think about it, you do kind of look like her, with dark hair. And second, you know that sounds like a meet cute in a rom-com, right?" She laughs and I smile at her joke.

The sound of raised voices drift toward us. The baggage belt my empty coffee cup is resting on moves away from us.

"Saved by the belt." I sigh in relief that our story time is over.

THREE
HARKIN

Who Is She x The Perfect Girl – Xanemusic, NVBR

Stepping out into the California sun is like standing in front of an open oven on broil. The heat radiates from every surface and instantly makes you sweat. It's been less than a year, but I've acclimated to the seasonal swings of New York's weather. The oversized, blacked-out SUV stops next to me at the curb. I'd planned on Ubering to my parent's house, but I guess that wasn't on their agenda.

"Mr. Greyson, welcome back," the giant bald security guard donning a black suit greets me while taking my bag.

I nod my acknowledgement and make my way into the back seat. The entire flight had been a parade of memories of Alina. The stranger in the cab doing nothing to help how my morning had started, if anything making it worse by shoving me down the rabbit hole my phone had become.

I pull my headphones out. "So, are they home?" I don't have to specify who I'm referring to.

"No sir, they are out of town this weekend for a charity auction. They're expected home Sunday evening."

I could pretend be surprised, but I'm not. They knew I was coming to visit, or we could call it what it really was, a check in to make sure I hadn't completely faded away in New York. Apparently, they'd been concerned enough to warrant this unnecessary trip, but not enough to be here when I arrived. Oh well, one and a half fewer days I'll have to spend with them. Come Monday morning, my ass will be back on a flight to New York, and I'll be back on my daily grind.

The ins and outs of my day that got me back on track without their help. Shocking that all it took to kick my ass into gear and off drugs was the space two thousand miles awarded. The near radio silence on my life in New York didn't stop my dad from pushing me anytime we got together to join the family business. It didn't matter that my body's covered in head to toe tattoos. Or that I technically didn't hold a college degree, even though I could out code any Ivy computer science graduate. He'd find use for me somehow. Shit, knowing how he dealt with his business, he'd probably use my computer skills for some sketchy business dealings. But I didn't need his business backing me to use my skills. I did just fine on my own.

We ride up to the gates that section off my parents' estate from the rest of the mansions in the area. Stepping out of the SUV, I scan the front of the sleek, modern home. It hasn't changed except for the landscaping near the front window, but I have. Where I didn't use to think twice of the blatant display of wealth, its bold statement irritates the shit out of me now.

The front door swings open before I can approach. A well-dressed older woman in sensible shoes greets me the same way baldy had at the airport. I don't mean to be rude; I just can't bring myself to care enough to interact with them. Nodding, I pass her and head down the hall to my room.

Dropping my bag on the neatly made bed. I shuffle through it until my hand meets the cold metal of my laptop tucked safely among the soft clothes. There was no way I was checking this baby through baggage claim. My whole life revolves around this damn thing.

Speaking of baggage claim, I want to see what I can dig up on taxi girl, Keira. I honestly wondered if I photoshopped one of Alina's photos with dark hair and lightened her skin color if I could reverse image search for her.

But first, where had she come from? I didn't see her as I left the building to hail a cab, yet she'd been right there as soon as I tried to get in. Pulling up the security camera feed for my building, I push through hours upon hours of footage until I have all four views synced up to the right time.

I watch myself exit the building and step up to the road, but she's nowhere in sight. Seconds pass as my eyes flip from each small box dividing my screen. She must be somewhere; I know for a fact I hadn't imagined the whole situation. I'm not that fucking messed up in the head. Then it happens. She pops on to the screen in the bottom left corner, meaning she would have come up from my left on the street. That's something, or at least I want to believe it is.

If she'd been late for work, it meant she'd likely been rushing from her place to get out to the street. It's possible she could have been at someone else's place, but I don't want to think about that possibility. That realization is jarring. This girl's consuming my every thought, even if she is for all intents and purposes, a stranger.

I have a name, a place of work, a general direction on where she lives, and that she looks like my dead girlfriend. It isn't much, but I've worked with less before. I watch the video footage on repeat, slowing it down to play frame by frame, looking for any little thing that might give me another bit of information about my mystery girl.

The California sun dips low through my west-facing window. The sunsets are different on the west coast. I'd give California that. Tall buildings don't diminish the golden red glow that spreads across the sky.

A knock at my door pulls my aching eyes from the screen for the first time in hours. "Come in."

"Sir, will you be needing something to eat from the kitchen staff? They didn't prepare a meal but can make you something."

Glancing at my wrist, I realize that the only thing I've had today was thanks to the airlines in-flight snack. "No, it's fine. I'll go out and grab something. Are the car keys still in the garage?"

"Yes sir, but I don't think..."

"It's fine. My car should still be here." He nods, his hesitation showing behind his professional demeanor.

Thai take away and two Redbulls later, I'm ready to dive back in. Halfway through my Pad See Eiw, I have a new angle to work with. JFK has to have an employee register somewhere online. Baggage claim narrows it down slightly, but the airport hosts around seventy different airlines. I could cross reference her first name easily enough. Keira isn't exactly your traditional American name.

"Gotcha." I smile at the screen as her work badge photo pulls up. Keira Fitzpatrick. Baggage Claim. Delta airlines. Home address and phone number listed. Dividing the screen, I type in the address on file. It's nowhere near my place and from the outside google view it looks like a bodega. Possible, but not likely. Irritated with the setback, my fist collides with the desk in frustration.

There has to be something else I'm missing. I work through my normal list that any amateur coder would know. My screen runs through the pre-programmed algorithm I added her information to. Time; I'll just leave it running and give it time.

Standing from my hunched position, my knees creak from the sudden movement. I really shouldn't have sat all night after sitting all day in the cramped airplane seat. I interlock my fingers and raise my arms straight over my head. Leaning left to right, my obliques strain against the stretch. Twisting side to side, my vertebra pop one after the other as my spine realigns. I could go for an alignment at the chiropractor.

I have to get my head off this girl. I feel myself being drawn into focus. A focus that isn't smart to hyperfixate on. But her face won't leave my mind. Where Alina was light and airy, this girl was rough and filled with sass. Maybe this is a second chance the universe is throwing my way.

FOUR
KEIRA

Dark Horse – Sleep At Last

It's been four days. Four days of worry and wonder, anxiety, and desperation. I slide the dark heavy curtains over just enough to peek out across the street, his place sits pitch black. I wish I knew how long he was going to be in California for. If this was a year ago, all I'd have to do was check his Facebook and there'd be a post about it for the world to read.

That's not him anymore, though. His socials are dead. The only updates coming from tagged post and photos, most being grossly offensive memes. The radio silence would kill me if I didn't have the perfect view right into his home. His apartment takes up a huge portion of the third floor in the southeast corner. Must be nice to live in Daddy's building.

My tiny, outdated apartment stands across the street from his east side windows, three floors up from the pizza parlor.

The apartment building belongs to the owner of Luigi's, but his skeezy son is the only one I deal with lately. If I wasn't determined to live in this exact location, I wouldn't put up with his constant come-ons and wandering hands. If only it was the worst I'd ever had to deal with. It isn't, not by a long shot, which means I've had zero issue skirting his advances on the regular. Always keeping in mind to do so playfully and without aggression, less he tells his father to evict me from the rent control box that's prime real estate in Brooklyn.

The sweet aroma of marinara wafts through the vents. My apartment constantly smells like I'm oven baking freshly made pizza. I love it. If I wasn't on my feet eight hours a day lifting thirty-two and a half pound suitcases, over and over, all day long, I'd actually have to think about working out. But because I am, I take full advantage of my allotted daily pizza slices offered in the rental agreement.

I have to be at work in just over an hour. The night shift starting at nine p.m. is perfect for me. Heading down the dimly lit hallway, I avoid the discolored linoleum and keep my head down. The locked door swings open and a wave of heat from the oven hits me.

"Hey Sal." I nod to the chef as he wields pizza dough like a flying shield up in the air, rotation after rotation.

"Hey Darlin', you eating tonight?" His endearment doesn't bother me. We've built a close bond over the last year. He feeds and watches over me like a hawk, while keeping a tab on the shop.

"You know it. Couldn't miss my Monday usual. Can you throw it in the oven for me?"

"On it." He winks and begins topping the dough.

Stepping around the counter, Marco—said skeezy son—sits

at the counter, eyes downcast at his phone. I keep my distance, waiting for Sal to bring my pizza out.

I slink into my regular booth in the corner, back to the wall. My unobstructed view is the same as my apartment upstairs. While at this level, I can't see into Harkin's place. I can see the front door and who comes and goes. The street is busy, but the entrance to his building remains vacant.

"Pepperoni, pineapple, and pepperoncini." The paper plate with two steaming slices sides in front of me. "You know that's not real pizza, right?" Sal eyes my favorite combination. "When ya gonna let me make you a slice of real Italian pizza?" he pleads.

"Sal, this is perfect. Sweet, salty, a little kick. The perfect trifecta."

He mutters something in Italian under his breath, motioning the sign of the cross in front of his chest. Shaking his head, he makes his way back to the kitchen.

Turning the volume up on my headphones, I jump back into the video I was watching, while enjoying my non-Italian pizza. I check my watch, chewing up the last delicious bite.

Shit I'm going to be late for work if I don't head out soon.

The bell chimes again, distracting my worry when my gaze moves to a tall figure stepping out on to the sidewalk. I'd know that frame anywhere. Dark blue denim paired with a leather jacket strides across the street, a giant pizza box tucked to his side.

He's back.

Fucking finally.

I felt off kilter with him, gone; not having the reassurance of his lights on at night. The guy never closes his shades all the way. A patterned glow of rainbow colors reflects off his windows. Creating a light show, nightly. Specifically for one or so I like to tell myself anyway. Work is going to drag now that I have a reason to come home.

In my own little world, celebrating my man's return to the city, I'm rudely interrupted by Marco, tapping my shoulder. "Hey Keira, why do you insist on eating over here by yourself when I'm all alone at the counter? Don't you want to keep me company?" His pitiful, fake puppy dog eyes do nothing to guilt me into wanting to spend any more time with him than I already have to.

"You know I have to talk to people all night long at work, Marco. I just try to enjoy the brief silence I get when I can." I smile up at him, hoping he doesn't prod any further.

He smiles at me, reaching for a loose hair dangling in my face before pushing it behind my ear. I try to keep my body still as a shiver wracks through me.

Total fucking creep.

"Do you know that guy that just came in here?" His scowl pulls his dark, bushy eyebrows down toward his nose.

"Uh, I have no clue who you're talking about." I shrug, hiding my interest.

"Well, he seems to know you. He was a little weird if you ask me. Might want to keep an eye out when you're coming home in the morning. Anyway, he left this for you." Marco slides a white note card across the table and picks up my trash. I smile my thanks and snag the paper from the table, hiding it quickly in my purse.

It's eating at me to rip it open and read his words, but I can't do it now. Not with Marco staring me down from the front counter. I give him an unenthusiastic wave and head out the door for the subway. My eyes scan across the street, up to the third floor, where his windows leave little to the imagination.

Then I see it. It's quick, just a blur really, but I know in my gut it was him. He's watching me.

Well, this is new.

The streets are sparse of people at this hour. The odd couple heading out to dinner or businessmen coming home late from the office. My commute to work is preferable to my morning commute home when the only people out and about are true morning people.

Yuck.

The doors slide close on the subway. My music stops at the end of the *Dark Days* playlist I found on Spotify. I hit shuffle on my liked songs, needing the comfort of familiarity before I dive in. When Hozier's soulful lilt fills my ears, my anxiety wanes as I pluck the white note card from my bag. My toes tap rhythmically in my Docs as my fingers trace around the edges of the paper.

In three, I'll turn it over and read whatever he left me. In three… two… one.

Did you miss me?

I read it over and over in my head, mouthing the words slowly as I process. Of course, I missed him. He was gone out of my sights longer than any other time since he moved to New York. The note he scratched out is messy with slanted handwriting. I want to know his game. Why leave the note and not just come up to me at the table?

The speakers announces my spot as the same thing flashes on the reader board lining the roof. I stand, gripping the pole to my right, the metal cools my palm, the note card stuck in between.

"Please tell me we can go out this week?" That's the first thing out of Stace's mouth before I can even put my stuff away.

"Damn girl, no hi, hello, how are you?"

She slaps my shoulder. "Oh, shut up and answer me."

I give her a quizzical look, kind of an oxymoron there, but she doesn't catch it. I love Stacey. She's the only person in this damn city I'd choose to spend my free time with. She's my complete opposite. Tall, blonde, bubbly, and extremely extroverted. The girl could make friends with an on-duty Queen's Guard. But somehow, we mesh. In hindsight, it's probably our mutual love for sarcasm, strong drinks, and shit talking.

"What'd you have in mind?" I ask.

"You know the new bar that just opened down the street from your place?" Stace says excitedly.

"No? How do you know about something in my neighborhood? You don't even come down there, except to hang out with me."

"You are so clueless, I swear. They just had a huge opening. It's all over. Apparently, it's pretty risqué." Her eyes light up like a kid on Christmas morning.

She eyes me up and down. "Oh, and there's a strict dress code."

I roll my eyes at her clear judgement of my typical fashion choice. Stace shrugs and turns to move over to her desk. I'm sure I've got something hidden in my closet. If not, I guess I'll be borrowing something. Fingers crossed, it'll fit. We might be the same size, but we are so not the same height.

The flow of travelers is steady tonight. The redeye flyers are usually single people or people with young children hoping that the late hour will help them sleep through the entire flight. There's a certain quiet that comes with working at the airport at night. It's calm, giving me plenty of time to obsess over the note burning a hole in my pocket.

Why now? Does he know?

FIVE
HARKIN

Rammstein - Rosenrot

She left the pizza shop and hasn't come back. I watched that slime ball from the counter slink his way over to her table. He lingered a little too long for my liking as his fingers brushed against hers, handing over my little, white note.

My worn leather chair squeaks as I readjust to face the street. I count the flickers of the neon Luigi's sign across the way. It might be just after five in the morning, but this time of year, it's still an inky black outside. By the time I reach an even hundred, a slight frame dressed in head-to-toe black types in the passcode for the apartment entrance next to Luigi's.

I'd bet my unused trust fund that it's her. I inspect the building window by window, as if it'll tell me more, but she's vanished into the dark like a shadow. That is, until the smallest sliver of light peeks through the bottom of dark curtains in the apartment right across from mine. It can't be.

My eyes don't leave the narrow seam, my only possible connection to her. And then in a blink of an eye it's gone.

What am I doing?

I'm crossing a line, violating her privacy even more than digging through her online footprint. But I can't seem to scrape up a single fuck to give. When I glance at my computer screen, her small profile picture is a beacon in my dark apartment.

I tell myself to get up, that I should get some sleep. At this rate, it'll only be a couple hours before I have to start on a new job I took last week. Instead of heading into the bedroom and taking an extended nap, I make my way to the kitchen.

Pulling out the coffee, I line the upper chamber and fill it to the rim with dark roast grounds. When I flip the switch, it hums as the water heats and drips to the pot. The aromatic brew fills my nose. Here's to hoping a caffeine boost is all I need to get through the next twelve hours.

I haven't pulled an all-nighter in months. But as I watched her stuff my note into her bag and take off at breakneck speed, my brain wouldn't shut off. I wanted to know if she'd seen me, or if she knew who the note was from. I craved her answer to the question, though I wasn't all too sure why I'd asked it in the first place. Hour after hour passed as I sat waiting for her to return.

It would have been easier to set up new cameras, besides the ones that already littered my apartment. But I didn't want to watch her second hand on the screen. Instead, I made myself comfortable. Well, as comfortable as you could get when sitting in the same chair in the same position for over eight hours.

THE SHADOWS WE KEEP

I realize as I finish the last sip of my coffee and reach over for the pot to refill my mug that she'd likely been at work. New York is New York and there are bound to be people around regardless of the time of day. I hate the idea of her traveling to and from work at odd hours. I never take advantage of the private car my parent's continue to keep on hand in the city, even though their visits are few and far between. But I want her to use it.

I want to know where she's going and when. I want to vet the damn person driving her, and know the car won't break down—like what happens occasionally with the subway. If only I could gift it to her somehow, without it being weird—or her knowing who it came from.

I pause as a harebrained idea forms in my mind. Maybe it's the lack of sleep, and I'm becoming slightly delusional, but it could work.

I have her email from her work file and what do I have to lose?

The worst that could happen: she'll think it's spam and send it straight to the trash file.

Snagging my laptop from beside the leather chair, I move to the kitchen island and plop onto the metal stool. Picking through the company's website, I steal their logo and affix it to the top of my email. I type up my draft, making up a dummy no-reply email address, throwing in a couple stock images and a link to the "giveaway" sign up form.

By the time I'm through and scan over the email one last time, a smile tugs at my lips. It's ridiculous how easy it was to do this. It might be well below my typical standards, but this is personal, not business. And she'll be safer, anyway. Without a second thought, I click send and snap my laptop shut.

The metal, artistic clock against the opposite wall tells me it's already six and I have a meeting up town at eight. The third cup of coffee finally kicks my body in to gear and I can feel it pumping in my veins. If I don't burn some of it off, I won't be able to focus when we sit down and discuss software analytics.

My laptop might be my lifeline, but that doesn't mean I let my skills dictate my appearance. My fingers are talented against the keys of a computer, but they're even better with a pair of throwing knifes, or anything sharp really.

Heading for the gym, I open the glass cabinet lined in black velvet and take out my working knives. They're not the pair I always keep on me, but I'd rather not send those flying into the wood post. Those I'll save for a special occasion, like a body—if ever necessary.

The cold metal against my skin is so familiar, an extension of my hand that allows me to whip them free and hit target after target. It doesn't matter if I'm standing still or working through the choreography that mimics an attack. The knifes thwack against the solid wood dotted with markers, always meeting their intended targets.

Thirty minutes later, the sweat drips down my body and I'm slightly out of breath. Rammstein blares over the speakers. If it wasn't for the soundproofing I did in this room, my neighbors would hate me. Reaching down, I pick up my discarded shirt, swinging it over my shoulder. With the knifes put back in their case, it's time to shower and get to my meeting.

Out on the street, I pause before heading for the subway. Looking up, I can barely see anything as the sun reflects off the black windows of the building. But her curtains are still shut. If I'm lucky, they'll be in the same position by the time I get back, and she'll still be in there.

I sit in the conference room of Black Meg Tech—a small app developing company I've been running analytics for trying to help them see where they're hemorrhaging money every month. I've got a couple of ideas, but as I lay them out for their CFO, he isn't listening. Instead, he's shaking his head in denial, but the number trends don't lie.

"Sir, I'm sorry to be blunt about it, but this app needs to go. It's not bringing in nearly as much money as it needs to keep up with what you're putting into it."

He stares down at the papers I've placed in front of him, eyes skimming over my fully detailed report. His face scrunches his eyebrows in concern as he finally runs a hand down his face. "You found nothing else we could off-load to make up for it?"

"No sir, nothing that would make a notable enough difference in the time frame you need," I tell him.

"Very well," he says.

He doesn't say thank you. He only stands, gripping the rolled-up report in his hand and heads for the door.

You're welcome, asshole.

If these kinds of jobs didn't allow me to live in New York on my own dime, I'd have given them up months ago. After a meeting like that, I need a drink. I look down at my phone. Okay, maybe not a drink, considering it's only noon. But my body doesn't realize that since I've been up for over twenty-four hours.

It's going to take me forever to get back to Brooklyn from here. The sidewalks are packed with people on their lunch breaks, taking the couple minutes they're allowed to themselves. I swerve in between men in their three-piece suits and women in reasonable heels.

If we were playing Where's Waldo, I'd be Waldo. It's no wonder the security guard patted me down a little longer than necessary. My look screams *does not belong*, but that's on them. I do half the work for twice the pay by freelancing, and I haven't had to give up my leather jacket for a suffocating blazer.

By the time I make it back on to my street, it's one thirty. That's late enough for a beer, at the very least. Strolling down the sidewalk toward my favorite local burger joint, a notice catches my eye.

This block's been cleaned up. A rope extends down the street from a heavy red wooden door outlined in gold. A faint beat thuds rhythmically, but I can't make out the song. As I close in on the top of the rope, a bouncer walks out, and the music rises.

"Hey man, is this place open yet?" I ask.

He eyes me. He's taking in my appearance, judging whether I'd be a good fit for this place. "Yeah, opened last week."

I nod and keep moving, my mind on a frosty beer. I might just have to check it out; could be a good place to meet up with clients depending on their vibe. Since this is Brooklyn, that's always a crapshoot.

"What'll you have?" the bartender asks as I sit.

"I'll take a Lambo Door, if you got it." He gives me a *'you've got to be kidding, right?'* look before setting the can in front of me.

"Anything from the kitchen?" he asks.

"Burger, Fries, side of BBQ sauce."

He jots it down on a pad and disappears around the corner. The dual screens above the bottles of booze plays ESPN sports highlights on one side and the news on the other. Neither interest me. Bringing the can to my mouth, the cold, fruity bitterness touches my tongue, and I swallow down half the can, flagging for another while I wait on my food.

My phone vibrates against my thigh. Digging it out from my seated position is a bitch. I stand, grabbing it and readjusting to sit again. A notification flashes from my lock screen. A new email forwarded from the dummy account I set up this morning.

An anxious grin reaches my lips.

Please tell me she took the bait.

A few clicks later, I have confirmation. I didn't take her for someone who would enter a random giveaway online. While a private car might sound appealing to most in the city, it's not always worth the hassle of Taxi-crowded streets.

The bartender sets the plate of greasy goodness in front of me with my next beer. I'll get back to her tonight.

SIX
KEIRA

Sinner - DEZI

"If you don't hurry up, we're going to be late!" I yell from my living room couch to Stace, who's still getting ready in my bedroom.

"Girl, it's a club, not a movie. Chill," she sasses.

'It's a club, not a movie,' I mock back, rolling my eyes.

"I saw that." Stace stands in the doorway, hands on her hips, eyebrows raised.

"Whatever." I laugh. "You want to pregame?" I stand, heading for the kitchen, pulling out the bottle of vodka from the freezer.

"Do you have anything to mix with that?" She eyes the bottle warily.

"What are you, forty? Take a pull and stop being a little bitch."

Yanking it from my outreached hand, she twists the cork

free with a pop and tilts the bottle back. Five seconds pass before she takes a breath and gives me a death glare.

Touché.

I copy her, but limit myself to a couple of seconds. I might have a great tolerance, but Stacey's got six inches and thirty pounds on me. It sucks to be tiny sometimes.

"So, how do I look?" She twirls in slow motion. "This is the only thing you had that fit right!" Stace did a little digging into the dress code, turns out my closet was more suited to their tastes after all.

I whistle a catcall. "That dress looks better on you. Hate you." I fake a pout.

The silky black slip dress lays perfectly over her tall thin frame, hitting mid-thigh. With her velvet thigh-highs and lace stockings sticking out, she's sex on a stick. I look down at myself.

"Don't you dare do that. You look hot. Every guy's teenage, wet dream."

That's what I'm afraid of.

On my small frame, it's hard to not look like I'm dressing out of my sister's closet. But I don't think the club would let me in wearing my favorite ripped skinny jeans and black hoodie.

The black-laced corset bodysuit pairs perfectly with my leather mini skirt that laces up the sides, showing off my ink. On my right side, an exotic garden of flowers and greenery cover my ribs, down to my right thigh. Two snakes slither between a skeleton's eyes from my hip to my knee on the left. It's the reason I bought the skirt in the first place. If you're going to spend thousands of dollars on ink, you might as well show it off occasionally.

This outfit is so far out of my comfort zone. I'll have to be wasted before I can relax and let loose tonight. And that's the whole point of us going out.

We both take one last swig from the bottle before I pop it back into the freezer. Down the hall, we stop to check our makeup one last time in the mirror. You'd think with an outfit like this, I'd choose something natural. But my eyes are smokey, my liner thick, and my lips bold. She said the club was erotic; I should fit right in. Swinging my leather jacket over my shoulders and shoving my ID and credit card into my bra, I'm ready to go.

The line to get in is down the block, but Stace doesn't stop at the back. Interlacing our fingers, she pulls me past the pissed potential patrons. I tilt my head down, avoiding eye contact as she steps up to the giant man they've hired as a bouncer.

Still having to lean up, even though she's wearing five-inch heels, she places a kiss on both his cheeks. "Robert." She flirty smiles at him. "You working all night, or are you going to come in and find me before I leave with someone else?"

This fucking girl, I swear.

"You better fucking not, or you'll regret it." He smacks her ass and tilts his head toward the dark wooden door. They engraved a crest of some sort in the wood, the hollow parts flickering with gold paint. She looks over her shoulder and winks before we step through into the darkness.

The music is different, a combination of EDM and metal. It blares from the overhead speakers and mixes with the ones near the stage viewable when we exit a long hallway onto the main floor. A bar stretches across the entire left side of the building. Bottles of every kind of alcohol line the wall on three tiered shelves against a mirrored backsplash.

Small platform stages at different heights, some with poles

or metal cages, litter the dance floor, professional dancers fill them, gyrating in thongs with fishnets and pasties, leaving very little to the imagination.

The dance floor takes up most of the space, but tall tables to our right give people a place to take a break and refresh. They're all taken with people chatting and getting a drink. I look up and find a grated catwalk above. It's thin but offshoots to different areas where the floors are clear. I stop in my tracks. Dark booths paired with interesting leather-coated benches...

Oh my god, is that a Saint Andrew's Cross?

Metal catches and reflects the flashing lights from the floor below, and that only confirms my suspicion.

Tugging on Stace's hand, I pull her ear to my mouth. "You said erotic, not sex club."

She shrugs her shoulders... *shrugs*.

This bitch.

Don't get me wrong, I'm not a prude by any measure of the word, but a heads-up would have been nice.

We stop in front of the bar and order four shots of vodka rimmed with sugar and garnished with lemon. Better to keep on track with what we've already had. After a few minutes, they all hit me, and I'm ready to lose my jacket and hit the dance floor. I scan the way we came in. I didn't notice a coat check.

I peel off the leather and flag down the bartender who made us our shots. I slide a twenty across the bar on top of my jacket. "Hold this for me." I yell over the music.

He looks me over, eyeing the lace of my bustier and no doubt the ink across my chest, and winks. I smile back at him and turn to find Stace already on the floor.

"I can't believe you brought me here," I yell in her ear as our bodies bounce and shake to the hard music.

"It's just a dance club. You can't get upstairs without a membership or an invitation from a member. The glass floor is just for ambiance and show. Gives the exhibitionist exactly what they need." Her Cheshire grin tells me she's got a plan up her sleeve and if she doesn't achieve it tonight, we'll be back here next week.

Stace grabs my hips, grinding against me, arms around my shoulders. Her height, plus her boots, has her towering above me. As I flip my hair out of my face, I catch her eyeing a couple of guys across the floor sipping on their drinks leaning against a table.

She looks back down at me, left eyebrow raised and a smirk asking for permission. I wasn't really looking to go home with anyone tonight, but it has been a while and what's a one-night stand on a girl's night out?

I shrug and a genuine smile crosses her face.

Poor bouncer.

If he really wanted to go home with her, he should've known better than to let her loose in here.

Her hands slide seductively down my waist as she turns me around to face the guys who haven't taken their eyes off us. She's got her prowling strut on as I'm pulled behind her. It's not like we need to hurry. They're obviously interested.

As we near the tall, round table, I take them in. They're dark club, five drinks in kind of hot, but not exactly my type. The guy on the right is tall, probably six three. His short cropped blond hair, big blue eyes, and tan skin, screams boy next door. His clean-shaven baby face doesn't help, and honestly makes me wonder if he's even legal.

No, thank you!

Lucky for me, he's already got an arm wrapped around

Stacey's waist and a hand splayed across her ass. He's bold, I give him that.

His friend reaches out for my hand and pulls me in closer so he can talk directly in my ear. "Hey gorgeous, I'm Ryan." He pulls back, looking down into my eyes. Now, he's a little more like it.

"Keira."

He squeezes my hand and drops his own to rest on my waist. "You Irish then?" His dark eyes twinkle mischievously.

"Could be," I reply, shrugging the question off.

"You going to let me buy you a drink?"

I check over my shoulder and see Stace and the boy next door are gone from the table, but they're not too far on the dance floor.

"Sure, let's go."

His big hand shifts from my waist to the small of my back, guiding me through the crowded club. The music has shifted from heavy metal to something sultrier. My body immediately responds.

I stop midway to the bar and Ryan looks down at me, his thick, dark lashes covering confused eyes. I grab for his hand and pull him toward one of the raised platforms. Unlike the single pole stands, a thick box holds this large cage up.

I push Ryan against the shining metal, his devilish grin encouraging my rough movements. The music flows from the speakers, controlling my hips, and I press my front flush against his. There might be a height difference, but when it comes to dancing—and sex, it always works in my favor.

His fingers graze lightly down my arms and bring them to wrap around his neck. My fingers automatically dig into his thick auburn hair and pull. His cock grows hard against my stomach.

So, he likes it a little rough.
I knew he was more my type.

I'm so into the song and the way it feels moving through my body that I don't even care when his hot tongue traces down the side of my neck, right to the sensitive spot where it meets my shoulder before he bites down.

My body surges into his as he places an open mouth kiss over the assaulted area and sucks, soothing away the sting. His shameless desire sends tingles straight down my spine. His cock grows harder against me, and I can feel my arousal against my thighs as my body rubs against him.

Who said the exhibitionism was only for upstairs?

I turn my body quickly, my arm reaching backwards hooking around his neck. Before pulling his mouth to mine. He's quick to growl his approval into our heated kiss. He nips at my lip, and I can't help but mewl. It didn't take long for him to find my weakness: a bite of pain with my pleasure, and I'm bound to drop to my knees.

My free hand reaches behind me. While the grinding of our bodies is doing a great job of rubbing him off, my hand can do better. I keep my body timed to the beat of the music. If anyone looked over, all they'd see was a couple taking advantage of the extra dark space beneath the platform stage dancing.

I feel a nip to my ear before his husky words hit, "If you keep this up, I'm going to take you in to the bathroom and bend you over the sink."

I slow my moves and remove my hand.

He chuckles darkly. "How about we go get that drink?" I nod and step away, cooling down the instant we lose contact.

What the fuck was I thinking?

SEVEN
HARKIN

A Girl Like You – Machine Girl Kelly, Travis Baker

I watched her through the window tonight; one of the rare occasions she'd left her curtains open. She and her friend danced around the apartment, trying on outfit after outfit before they were ready to go out. I should have left it at that, but the way her delectable small curves looked in the tight skirt and barely there lingerie, left me no choice.

She couldn't go out in that without protection. I knew how guys would look at her when she sauntered out onto the street. It wasn't her fault; she wasn't asking for it. But most men were dogs that couldn't be trusted to handle their baser instincts. I needed to follow. Which led me to the same club I'd passed on the street the other day. Lucky for me, I'd looked into it later that day and decided a membership was too good to pass up.

So, here I am, in their top tier, members only section,

watching over the girl who's taken over my ability to think straight.

And it's a good thing I am, because what the fuck was she thinking?

I didn't miss the way her hand slid around her body behind her back. The way he immediately sank into her touch left little to the imagination. I sip my whiskey and adjust my dick to a comfortable position. It might not have been me her sinful body was pressed up against, but witnessing it was enough.

The glass floor really is the perfect way to show off from the second level of the club, but it's even better for watching what's unfolding underneath. The tall backed, velvet couches hide each member from another section. I reserved an empty booth since I knew I wouldn't be using any of the equipment, at least not tonight.

My grip loosens from around the corrugated knife handle when they step out of the darkened alcove and walk toward the bar. I point the tip to my thigh, applying just enough pressure that the sharpness digs into my dark denim without puncturing the skin beneath.

Spinning the knife back-and-forth calms me as his hand finds her lower back, guiding her away from the dance floor toward the bar.

"Another whiskey, sir?" A sultry voice comes from my left, and my gaze swings from my girl below. The waitress's eyes heat as she takes me in, but I'm not interested. I switch my empty glass, ice clinking against the sides, for the full one she offers from her tray. Reaching into my pants, I snag a couple of bills and hand them to her with a note.

"Do me a favor, darling." She quickly nods her approval, eyes wide with hope. "Give this note to the short, dark-haired girl down at the bar over there for me." I jut my chin in her direction and drop the white note card on her tray.

Her face falls.

"Uhm, I'm not supposed to leave the members only area." Her irritation rises at my dismissal.

"You're actually supposed to do as I request, as I'm a member of this club. Don't forget that."

Her chin dips with embarrassment. She knows I'm right. I had to pay a hefty price to get in here, but it'll be worth it in the end.

She scurries away from my section, and I watch as she basically runs across the dance floor to the bar.

Whispering in my girl's ear, she hands over the little white note, then gestures in my general direction. I don't flinch because I know she can't see me from the ground floor. The man she's with turns around with her drink and she quickly hides the card in her bra. Sneaky, sneaky, my little dark one is.

My phone vibrates, pulling my attention from downstairs. A notification from my system running an information sweep back home. Her work's database gave me enough to do a basic search online, but all I got was a couple online profiles for different social media accounts. All it did was pique my interest further.

So now I'm looking deeper, public records, birth certificate. Maybe she's got a marriage license out there. The notification tells me I've got something, but the file won't transfer to my phone. I'm desperate to get out of here and find out what it is, but I won't leave her in his hands. I don't know where this innate need to watch over her and protect her has come from, but I can't ignore it.

Standing, I shove my phone back in my pocket, finishing the last swig of my whiskey before heading for the stairs that lead down to the first floor. I scan the crowd from my bird's-eye view, figuring it'll be easier to locate them up here, but she's gone.

Fuck.

I take the stairs two at a time, heaving my thick leather jacket on to my body and pulling the fabric hood up. I slam my hand down on the bar. "The girl that gave you her jacket? She come grab it yet?"

He looks down under the counter and his eyebrows crinkle.

Fucking hell.

"She must have had someone else grab it for her." He shrugs and gets back to taking drink orders for two blondes at the other end of the bar. I swear to God if she left with that fuckwad, I'm going to lose it.

Watching her with the random stranger unlocked something primal within me. The burning rage that roared to life the moment they tucked into the dark alcove under the cage, left my fingers itching. I wanted to rip her from his clutches, and use my blade to slice off the fingers he dare lay on her. The dark image sends my moral compass spinning wildly. She's cracked something open inside of me, and it doesn't look like I'll be shoving it back anytime soon.

Heading for the exit, I pass the hall for the bathrooms when a tall blonde in a short black dress catches my eye. Her friend steps out of a doorway and my chest relaxes as she follows right behind her. The blond guy her friend's been with all nightstands against the wall across from the women's bathroom. His friend is nowhere in sight.

Keira lifts on her toes and pecks a kiss on her friend's cheek, whispering something quickly in her ear before heading in my direction. I drop back into the crowd, waiting for her to pass me. Once she does, a magnetic pull drives me to follow her home.

The frigid air hits as I catch the heavy door seconds before it closes all the way. I'm a few paces back, but she doesn't stop in front of the club for a cab, which would be a complete waste of money considering we only live two blocks down. But at one in the morning, it'd still be a safer bet.

She hunches into herself as the wind whips down the street, but her stride never slows. One block to go, she stills. I tuck myself against a barbershop's sign that protrudes from the side of a brick building. Her face is cast in shadows as she checks behind her, but the street is empty. She waits just a little longer before running across the street to her block.

Slowly lurking behind her, I see Luigi's neon sign light up her body as she stands typing in the password for her walk up. I wait in the recess of the building next door until the click of the lock slides free and the door closing pulls me out of hiding.

My hand rushes out to stop the door from shutting all the way. I peer down the dimly lit hall. The linoleum floor is stained and scuffed to hell from years of wear. As I make it to the stairs, I notice they're covered in a hideous pea-green, paisley carpet runner.

This place looks like its last update was in the seventies and no one's bothered to clean it since then. My body heats with anger as I climb the stairs floor after floor. It's not abnormal for New York to have walk-ups, especially in smaller buildings. But the paint is peeling where it's not stained from greasy fingerprints. I can't believe she lives in this dump.

The stairs stop on the third-floor landing, and I hear a jingling to my left. Peering around the corner, I see her three doors down before she gets the door unlocked and steps inside. Waiting a beat, I weigh my options: continue down this obscure path, or turn around now, chalk this up to a mental anomaly, and leave the poor girl alone for good. A deep breath brings with it the realization that there's no choice to be made. The latter is the only answer for our situation.

I count the doors as I pass by, making sure I've got the right one before I drop to a knee and press my ear to the door. There's no shuffling from the other side. Sliding my tension wrench and pick from my pocket, I quietly force the pick to the back of the lock before applying pressure with the wrench. Within second I hear the click and twist the handle; the door pushes open.

I stop it before it gets too far and strain to hear her inside. Another door slams and the soft melody of music plays muffled through the apartment. I step through the front door, twisting the handle as I slide it closed, making no noise as it latches shut.

I creep quietly down the hall on my toes, praying this old ass building doesn't have squeaky wood floors. No such luck. Just as I get to her living room, I can see her bedroom door is open. My foot stops as the floorboard gives, and the sound is deafening. By the grace of whatever is holy, her shower turns on at that exact moment. My shoulders fall and I let out the breath I'd been holding.

The little clothing she had on is littered across her bedroom floor, a direct path to the bathroom. The tight leather skirt that clung to her pale thighs is nearest the door. I step over it, noticing her bathroom door is cracked open just enough that from this angle I can see the small, square mirror is partially fogged already. I take the smallest step to the left to catch the shadowed silhouette of her naked body through the glass enclosure. Heavy drops drag down the fogged surface, revealing a fraction more of her to me.

The song changes to a gravelly female voice against a backdrop of sensual instrumental chords. The lyrics catch my attention as her muffled voice sings along. They're dirty and exactly what I want to be doing to her body.

Jesus, what is she doing to me?

Her hand slaps against the glass and a breathy moan fills the room. My cock twitches at the thought of strolling in there and shoving her body against the steamed-up glass before driving home into her tight center, but it's not time for that, yet.

I shift my body away, tearing my eyes from the bathroom and notice my white note lays discarded in a pile of black lace, the bodice that cupped her small—but full—breast. Plucking it from the pile, I read the message, debating if I should let her see it after all. But something twisted inside wants her to know I was there, watching, waiting, and… claiming her as mine.

I slide it onto her nightstand, message down. The dark wood and clean space make the card the focus The water's still running as I look around her room, taking it in. It's messy, but only with clothes. There are no keepsakes or clutter. The room is decorated minimally, with only her bed and a pair nightstands with a simple lamp.

Anyone could live here. There's no personality. The walls are empty. There's no pictures of her and her friends. Rounding the corner from the living room, I see she doesn't even have takeout menus secured to the fridge.

A pile of unopened mail covers the counter that separates the kitchen from the living room. Her place is so small she doesn't have a table to eat at, only a little bar area. Flipping through the papers, I find it's mostly junk, but a personalized letter grabs my attention. I shove it into my back pocket and pull out another white card.

I scan the counter for a pen to leave a second note for her to find, but she's got nothing. The white card looks plain to the naked eye, but it's my business card for those who know how to view the heat activated ink.

I pull open the drawer in front of me and luck out with a fine tipped marker. Popping the cap off, I jot down my thoughts and hide it in her mail. Maybe she'll find it... Maybe she won't.

The water switches off, and the bathroom door creeks. I pull up my dark hood and creep back down her front hall to the door.

Without turning around, I reach behind me, twisting the lock out of place and the handle slowly to pull the door open. I step through and close it just as slowly, ensuring my clean exit. Shoving my hand in my jean pockets, I skulk down the staircase, back out onto the sidewalk and cross the street to my building.

I ascend the last step before my building's entrance, my hand rests against the cold mental handle as I pause turning to glance at her windows. Her thick curtains are closed, but that slight glint of light passes underneath. This is only the beginning for us, my little dark one.

EIGHT
KEIRA

I Want It All – Cameron Grey

The soft towel clings to my damp body as I flip upside down to dry my hair, ringing out most of the excess moisture. The alcohol is slowly wearing off and after that burning shower and my self-given orgasm, I'm ready to climb into bed and pass out.

Shuffling to the kitchen, I quickly grab a glass from the cabinet and the pitcher of water from the fridge. The aspirin clinks against the plastic bottle as I shake three into my hand before popping them in my mouth and washing them down with a swig of icy water.

I trudge toward my room, but the sweating glass in my hand pauses halfway through its journey to my mouth. I squint in confusion, eyebrows crinkling before my head tips to the side as I inspect the front door.

That's strange, I could have sworn I locked the front door on my way in. Flipping the lock and turning off the kitchen lights, I brush off the situation.

Falling asleep at the perfect extent of intoxication makes a drastic difference to your morning wake up. Too drunk and you're bound to get the spins as soon as your head hits the pillow and your eyes close. Not enough and you miss the blissful heavy sleep that makes you feel like you slept for years, waking in a different century.

I drop my towel and climb into bed, dragging the heavy blankets over my body. Reaching over to turn off the light, the note the cocktail waitress at the club handed me catches my attention. What the hell, I know for a fact I didn't put that there. It's eerily placed, perfectly center on my nightstand, not tilted one way or the other, but perfectly aligned with the sides and the front.

I slide it to the edge and slowly lift the corner to see what's written underneath. My skin pebbles with goosebumps the moment the words come into view.

You let him touch what's mine.

It shouldn't rattle me. I knew the moment she placed that white slip of paper in my palm, not trying in the slightest to hide her sneer, it was from him. A replica of the note from the pizza shop, but with a new message. I slipped it in my bra, not knowing where the rest of the night would take me. Even though I'd come close to letting Ryan fuck me right there on the dance floor after I cleared my head, I knew I didn't want to invite him back to my place.

He was good looking, but I wasn't worked up enough. Getting myself off and passing out sounded better than a possible lousy lay and an awkward morning. I'd forgotten about it on my walk home, as the liquor in my veins set in, and sleep called to me. I'd undressed without care, wanting to wash off the slight scent of Ryan that lingered on my skin.

So how the actual fuck had this little white card ended up on my nightstand?

I lie on my back, holding the card up in front of my face, reading his thick script repeatedly. Before I know it, I push my covers off and I'm standing against the wall, pulling the bulky curtains back just enough to peer out into the dark.

His apartment is dim, backlit from the kitchen, the lights near the floor to ceiling windows turned off. Where my windows are always veiled with curtains to block out prying eyes, his are on full display for anyone who cares to take notice. Which I take full advantage of on the regular.

The soft fabric grazes against my naked skin, my nipples pebbled against the frigid air. The high back leather armchair he occupies sits a couple feet behind the center window. His lengthy form is nothing but a shadow for my eyes. His body's relaxed, leaning back, legs spread wide. My core tightens as I envision him sitting there watching me.

Then a slight movement on the left catches my gaze. Straining my eyes against the darkness, it becomes clearer. His hand moves slowly up and down in his lap, stroking what I can only imagine is his hard length.

Tracing my fingers down between my breast, they graze softly against my flat stomach before my breath hitches as I circle my clit. Gripping the curtains with my free hand, I pull as the euphoric sensation rises in my core as I work by body into a frenzy.

As much as I want to close my eyes and relish in the high, I can't tear them from the dark shadow across the way. The longer I stare out into the dark, the clearer my erotic live performance becomes.

His movements get faster, his free hand reaching down to cup his sac. What I wouldn't do to be on my knees in front of him. To be the one pulling the pleasure he's feeling from his body. Slickness coats my inner thighs. I push harder against the bundle of nerves, causing a zing of pleasure to rush down my spine to my toes.

My breathing picks up and I moan out his name as the wave of pleasures crests and sends me over the edge. My legs buckle, I grip the curtains tighter to catch myself except my weight is too much for them and the clips pop one after the other, pulling free the fabric as it falls to my feet.

In all the commotion, a quick movement pulls my attention from the mess at my feet. His head snaps up and I swear his eyes meet mine. His body jerks in the chair as his fist slows and his body slouches. I realize that while my room is dark, the red tint from my lamp is silhouetting my figure for him.

I should move, pick up the curtains and cover myself, but everything in my head is telling me to let him get his fill. We're at an impasse of voyeurism meet exhibitionism, and I'm almost regretful that I got the perfect show, while he got nothing.

He stands, tucking himself away, and steps toward the glass. Drawing up, he presses his palm flat against the window. So close to the window the darkness from outside hides his features in shadows, but his piercing gaze doesn't stray from my direction.

I turn, giving him my back. Walking slowly, my hips sway to the beat of my own seductive song as I twist the knob on the lamp, plunging my room into total blackness.

THROWING my arm across my eyes, I groan my displeasure.

Why is it so damn bright in here?

My head pounds and my stomach revolts. I strain my dry eyes open into slits and smack my parched mouth. *Jesus, I feel like shit.* Slowly rolling toward the assaulting light, I'm reminded of the night before and the curtains that pile on my floor.

I want to pull the comforter over my head and ignore the daylight hours, but my bladder protests. I finish up in the bathroom, wiping my hands against the damp towel from my shower the night before. Pulling my blood red silk robe from the hook on the back of the door, I cloak my body in the light fabric and pad toward the kitchen with one thing on my mind.

The delicious sweet, nutty aroma of my pour over coffee fills my body with the slightest bit of energy before I've even had a sip. There is something so meditative about making my morning coffee.

As the precious drips of liquid slowly fill my favorite oversized mug, I snag a few more aspirin from the bottle on the counter, placing them next to my mug so I can take them in a couple of minutes.

The pile of unopened mail stares up at me mockingly. I swipe through it lazily. Junk. Junk. Bill. More Junk. And then it happens again. The little white card falls free from in between the flyers for local businesses. I don't have to move it to see his next message to me.

He shouldn't have touched what's mine.

A smile creeps onto my face. It shouldn't please me, but it does. I've wanted him longer than he'll ever know. Before she was dead. Before he moved to New York. Before I'd had the experience of being next to him in an enclosed space, hearing his deep voice.

But this isn't enough. It isn't me he wants. It's only the reminder of her that spurs him on. I finger the thick card stock, wanting to put it with my other two notes from him. I grab my steaming cup of coffee, palming the card against the mug to carry them both to my room while I pop my pain pills.

Curling up at the top of my bed against the wall, relaxing into the softness while sipping on my life water, I look down at his card again. Except this time, it's not only his sharp handwriting, I see. A design of some sort spans the background. But it's slowly disappearing the longer I stare at it.

What the hell?

And then it's gone.

I blink slowly.

Was I seeing things or was there really something else there? What if it was another message from him? That thought spurs a desire in me to figure it out. I think back to a couple of minutes ago. What was I doing that could have made it change?

Taking another sip of my coffee, it dawns on me. The coffee, I had it up against my hot coffee cup. I slap the card against my coffee mug, a little too forcefully, and the liquid sloshes spilling down the side and over my hand.

I pull the card away quickly; heaven forbid I ruin the secret message or distort his handwriting. But the faint outline of the logo is back.

Yes! That's it.

The heat from the mug makes the image viewable to the naked eye.

My coffee's cooling by the second. Instead of trying again, I shove the empty mug on my nightstand and run to the bathroom with the card in hand. Dropping it to the counter and pulling open the vanity drawers, I dig to the bottom where my rarely used hair dryer lies in a tangle of cords, covered in broken makeup powders.

Yanking it free, I shove the triple prongs into the wall and shift the settings to light and hot. Flipping the power to on, I pin down the card with one hand and focus the warm air from the hair dryer onto the card. Slowly but surely, the logo displays again, but it's not just the logo that reveals itself. It's a boxy QR code shows too.

Dropping the hairdryer still running into the sink, I sprint into my room and snag my phone off the charger. Making it back to the bathroom, the card is once again all white but for his thick scrawled handwriting in the center.

I apply more heat and pull up my phone's camera at the same time. Zooming in on the card while I wait for it to recognize the small QR code under the logo in the bottom left corner. I hold my breath, not sure if this is going to work, or if I'm getting my hopes up for nothing.

Seconds tick by.

I zoom out and zoom back in. I manually focus on the area and keep the hot air streaming against the card, not letting it cool for a moment. I'm about to give up when it finally registers on my phone, and I tap on the link.

The website pulls up, but there isn't much to find. A black page with a white password bar sits in the middle. I check the URL, but it's just a mix of random letters and numbers. It makes no sense.

God damnit, all of that for nothing.

If only he'd left me a password, but nothing about his messages seems remotely password like. But fuck it, I'll try anyway. Stabbing away at the keys, they tap quickly as my anxiousness rolls through me when I hit enter. An error page pops up automatically. I slap the counter and sigh in frustration. Clearing out the password bar, it hits me. I've got two other cards.

Storming through my apartment, my work bag hangs from the wooden hook in the hallway. Pulling it down, I turn it over and the contents thuds against the wooden floor. I shove it around until that little white card catches my eye and I snag it up.

Tripping over my feet, I seize the lone card from my nightstand and drop back into my bed. Two more cards, two more possible passwords. The card from the bar strikes out. I pull a deep breath in through my nose and type in the last phrase: **DID YOU MISS ME?**

The screen goes black. Nothing happens for so long that I think it turned off or broke. I hit the power button, but the screen is still backlit. What the heck. Tapping the page repeatedly with no display, I finally give up.

NINE
HARKIN

Sad – Bryce Savage

"I'm sorry, I just can't do it. Tell her parents I've got something important for work going on," I snipe at my mother. It's not her fault, she's just passing along the information. I can't go back and face everyone, especially not on the anniversary.

My weekend trip was short enough that I didn't have to worry about running into anyone, but this would be walking straight into the firing squad's line of sight. Even if half of them believe it wasn't my fault, that still leaves half of Barton undecided.

"Harkin." Her tone is sharp, I can imagine the little vein protruding in irritation on her forehead. "How are you ever going to change people's minds if you just keep running from this? If you just…"

But I'm there to cut off the thought before she can finish it,

"No. Just no, Mom. I'm not coming. I won't be there. And I don't care what the town thinks of me for moving away. What did they expect me to do, sit around and morn her forever?"

Her small huff is all I get in response before the line goes silent.

My phone whizzes across the room, smacking against the back of my gray leather couch. I pull at the roots of my hair; the pinch of pain releases the pressure building inside.

I've tried everything in my power to ignore this week. To brush it off as just another week this month, keeping my mind busy with work or my body focused in the gym. I was so close, but then she called.

A ping from my laptop on the jet-black marble table across the room breaks my internal spiral. Swiping my finger across the scanner, the page displays. My frustration dissipates as she steals my focus. The corner of my mouth pulls up in a smirk. I can't help it.

She did it, my smart, smart girl.

How disappointing it must have been for her to get the page to go through, only for it to be nothing she could see.

But that's all I needed to gain access to her phone. A virus programed to release once she entered that passcode into the QR Code website designed just for her. The car service is great for tracking her whereabouts during the work week and monitoring her. But this gives me full location access when she has her phone on her.

Opening the location program on my computer, I watch as the little red dot pings on the map and then zooms in. Switching over to satellite view, I squint in confusion. What is she doing at Evergreens Cemetery?

If only it wasn't on the other side of town. I'd never make it at this time of day before she left. The cemeteries website is useless; It doesn't have a directory of its plots, but there might be another option.

A quick google search leads me to a website where people can add information and photos of graves they've visited. Mostly, it's used for historical and ancestry information, but not today. I filter it down to Evergreens, depleting the results by over half. That's still a lot of information to look over.

Searching specifically for graves with Fitzpatrick included drops it again. There's a handful of options. Some dating back way too far to be likely. Which leaves me with two—Sean Fitzpatrick or Claire Fitzpatrick. Sean Fitzpatrick, born September 23, 1968, died October 11, 2015. Beloved Brother and Friend: is all the headstone reads, but no mention of a wife or children.

Maybe he's an uncle?

Moving on to Claire Fitzpatrick. The small, dark stone has a border with moss. It's not as nice as Sean's, or as detailed. The only information it bores is born January 14, 1982, died July 04, 2005. All that tells me is she died young. Local burial, possible local obituary. But that's not what comes up in a google search with just her name and the date of death.

Something I never expected pushes through the search results to the top of the google page. A dreadfully outdated web page that doubles as a transcription for the local police scanner. That's not what catches my eye. The black and white photo shows windows busted and shattered to the ground, police tape blocks the public from entering from either side of the street.

Officers mill about, frozen in movement, while one crouches at the entrance. A white sheet lays over a dead body, only a glimpse available from his viewpoint, not mine. The title of the article to the right reads: *Tragedy Strikes at Willie's'* in big, bold lettering. It skims over the incident, nothing of importance noted. It's the website creator's follow up entry that has exactly what I need.

> Our beloved local diner Willie's was shot to pieces last week.
> Closing the only place to get great pancakes in the neighborhood.
> But the true loss was the young life of Claire Fitzpatrick,
> a 23-year-old single mom.
> Our sources tell us her eight-year-old daughter was present.
> Her mother selflessly saved her life by stopping two bullets as she fell to the ground.
> They transported the young girl to the local hospital and treated her for minor cuts and scrapes.

THERE'S no mention of who did it. Only a theory of a gang getting even with a drive by, but that was never confirmed. A twenty-three-year-old single mom with an eight-year-old daughter, dead. If Claire died in 2005 and her daughter was eight, that'd make the daughter twenty-three-ish now. The timelines match up. This has to be who Keira is visiting at the cemetery today. My body sags into the hard kitchen chair.

Jesus, my poor girl.

I slam the computer shut with a thud. The kitchen chair clangs against the hardwood floors in my escape to the gym.

The glass knife case clatters open as I violently pull free my throwing knives to let out the aggression rising in me.

It's too much. Too close to the anniversary. Too much death. The cold metal calms my racing heart slightly as a trickle of sweat runs down my temple. Throw after throw, the sharpened metal glides from my fingers to meet their marks against the wall until my hands are empty. The whomping in my ears matches the quickness of my heartbeat as my chest heaves. My mouth runs dry from exertion.

I pick them out one by one as the last blade stacks in my hand. The heaviness breaks my illusion of calm, and my mind wanders back to what this week brings.

Fuck this, I need a drink.

The bell above the door dings as I push it open. Music from the speakers drum in the background as conversations drown it out. The dark bar top hides the metal stools lined neatly underneath, few people choosing to sit there during dinner when a full dining room is available.

The stool's feet scrape against the stone floor as I drop onto it and wave down the bartender.

"Double, Jack. And keep them coming." I drop a hundred on the counter and he nods his understanding. Three rounds down and the conversations around me have dulled. The drum solo of a 90s rock song moves my toes on their own as I keep time with the beat of the music.

Doing my best to numb my mind, another glass filled with amber liquid sloshes down in front of me.

"I can't believe you won that giveaway. I didn't get an email from work. God, I wish I had a personal car to drive me around the city whenever I needed." The whinny voice behind me is annoying as hell.

But it's the response that freezes me in place while I strain my ears.

"Do you really read your emails, or do you just select all and delete them?" Her muffled laughter has me sliding my gaze to the mirror behind the bar, giving me a perfect view of the two of them.

"Ugh, that's not the point. If they wanted us to read a company email, they should have sent it to my work email. It's not fair." Her friend from the club pouts.

Her eyes light at her friend's misfortune. "Life's not fair, girl. Maybe it'll be you next time?" She laughs.

I sit for hours, eyes glued to the reflections in front of me, zoning out completely to my surroundings, except for their conversation, that is easy enough to hear with how loud they are. A quick tap on the bar drops my gaze. "You want anything else? I'm closing out my shift."

I shake my head and slide him a twenty. All thoughts of wasting away the night belligerently drunk lost the moment I heard her voice. He shakes his head slightly, untying the black apron around his waist.

"They're drinking mules," he shoots my way as he pockets the twenty.

"That obvious, huh?"

"Only to me, you haven't moved since they sat down a couple of hours ago. Your eyes haven't left the mirror, and you didn't finish your last drink after downing three earlier back-to-back."

I dip my chin to him in understanding.

A tall blonde saunters behind the bar, switching places with him. "Hey Darlin', what can I get ya?" she purrs in a thick southern accent, eyelashes batting away.

"Two mules and send them over there." I quickly tip my

head backwards to the table behind me.

Her flirty demeanor slips, but she must be used to brush offs because it quickly shifts back into place as she moves around behind the bar to make the drinks.

"Nothin' for you, though?" Her hands move quickly, mixing the vodka with lime juice and some carbonated liquid. That looks disgusting.

"I'll take another whiskey, neat."

"That's more like it." She winks and refills my glass before taking the two copper mugs over to the girls. I don't shift, but I can see the conversation happening behind me. Their heads jerk in my direction. I don't turn around, instead I hold my glass up high to the side in silent salute.

The bartender rounds the corner and into my view, her eyes cast behind me to the side. A delicate hand wraps around my bicep. The long pink nails are a dead giveaway that it's not my girl. Craning my neck to the left, I glance down at her hand with my eyebrows raised before trailing my eyes up her body to her face. Her bronzed cheeks heat to a pale pink as I don't shift, adding a leer at her touch for good measure. She picks up on my mood, pulling her hand away quickly.

"I, uh, just wanted to say thanks for the drinks. My girl could really use it today."

Her girl? No, my girl. And why does she need it?

"Well, then maybe she should be the one to come thank me then." My gruff tone offends hers and she sways backwards a step.

"She's not really the peopling type," she concedes.

I nod and turn back to the mirrored bar, dismissing her from my side.

Her heels click against the stone floor. "What a dick!"

I laugh to myself. She wasn't even trying to hide her sentiment. My girl giggles and the surrounding air lightens with her amusement.

"Strike out?" she asks.

"He said you should go thank him." Her friend bites out and throws back the rest of her free drink before slamming the mug down on the wooden table.

I quickly throw a couple of bills down on the bar and head for the door before she can get to me.

Another time. Another place.

But not yet.

No, not yet.

TEN
KEIRA

Can You Hold Me – NF, Britt Nicole

"Hey mom." I pull my knees to my chest, wrapping my arms around them and laying my head back onto her headstone. The cemetery's empty on this side of the park. Not that there's usually too many people wandering about on a Tuesday afternoon.

"So, I know you never wanted me to know about her, but I do, and now you're both gone. Today's the anniversary of their accident, and I know I have no right, but I can't help but want to march over to his apartment and shove my way inside to comfort him." I pull in a deep breath and my chest heaves against the many layers of clothes I had to put on to make sure I could sit out here and not die of hypothermia.

"He's all alone and never has people over. He rarely goes home. The guy barely leaves the house, at least not when I'm home. Which I guess could mean he leaves while I'm at work... sorry; I'm rambling." A raven flies high above my head, circling as if it's sensing death throughout the area. Even if it's decomposing six feet below.

"But I can't do that, can I? He doesn't know who I am, other than some rando from a cab ride." Sighing, my mind wanders as I take in the surrounding graves. They're all the same. Nothing much ever changes here.

"It's just not fair that she got him. She got everything. The big house, the luxurious life, two parents that are still alive and loved her until the day she died. She got the full high school experience with lots of friends and a social life." Just thinking about all the ways her life was picture perfect has my blood boiling. I'm fuming, my fists clench, knuckles turning white as the blood circulation cuts off.

"I love you, Mom, but why did I get the struggling single parent? Why did you have to be a hero and die that day? Why did I have to get shoved into that malicious group home?" Wetness coats my icy cheeks as my voice cracks, my despair bleeding out in thick droplets.

A door slams in the distance, and I quickly swipe under my eyes and jostle myself to standing. Lifting my fingers to my mouth, I place a kiss against them, dropping it onto her headstone. "Love you. Thanks for listening to me."

THE BLACK SUV that's been carting me around for the last few weeks stops in front of Luigi's. My stomach gurgles. I throw my thanks over my shoulder to James as I climb onto the sidewalk and slam the door behind me, making a beeline for the pizza parlor's door.

"There she is!" The boisterous Italian peeks out from behind the brick fire oven. His huge stature would intimidate anyone with eyes. But his close friends know what a teddy bear he really is. "You come to get your favorite pie?"

I step up to the counter and he meets met there.

"Your special, please." His worried eyes meet mine; he knows where I've been all afternoon. When I pull out my wallet, he shakes his head at it, reaching under the counter and pulling open the mini fridge hiding there. Two bottles of frosty beer clank on to the countertop before he takes each one and jams the tops against the counter's edge, popping the metal caps off before handing one to me and taking the other to the back of the kitchen.

"Your pizza will be done soon, hon."

I shuffle over to my favorite table, the Luigi's Pizza sign reflecting off the smooth windows as the light outside diminishes. I drown in the salty bitterness of the cold beer, chugging until it's empty. The smell of fresh fired dough and melted cheese makes my mouth water. Sal slides a plate of greasy goodness in front of me. He traces my empty bottle for a full one and I thank him for his unwavering kindness.

Soft Italian music keeps me company as I enjoy the one good thing to come from today. The fresh gooey mozzarella mixed with the rich tomato sauce, topped with the earthy basil, is exactly what I needed after today's visit to talk with Mom. The traditional Margherita pizza would be nothing without their award-winning sauce.

And then *he's* there, waiting at the counter. I slink down in the booth, my jeans sticking to the plastic covering. The obnoxious noise is deafening. I squeeze my eyes shut in embarrassment. When I finally brave opening them, he's looking right at me. His piercing gaze is unwavering; even when Sal comes out again to take his order How do I know this? Because I locked my eyes on his, like a missile on target, when they very well shouldn't be.

Some sense of reason comes back to me, and I drop my gaze down to the empty plate on the checkered table. The perfect excuse to escape, but I'm not fast enough. His powerful presence sits across from me, but I'm not ready to break the bubble of uncharted territory between us.

Maybe he doesn't remember?

"Keira, right?"

Fuck me.

"Yeah. Taxi stealer, right?" I finally look up into his deep eyes. A half-assed smirk brightens his face a smidge and I know right away today's weighing on him.

"If I recall, you're the one who tried to steal my ride."

"Semantics. It worked out better in the end, anyway, don't you think?" I pause, taking in his scruffy face and the deep-set purple under his eyes.

His pupils enlarge, and his chest inflates.

"For splitting the fair," I press out, not sure if he's mad about the incident.

He whispers something under his breath I can't catch since Sal drops a full box of pizza on the table with a thud.

"You need anything else?" Sal's eyes catch mine and quickly shift over to Harkin.

"No, I'm good. Thanks, Sal."

Sal nods and heads back to the kitchen, checking on me one last time before he disappears behind the oven.

"Hungry?" I jut my chin at the large pizza box between us.

"Meal prepping for the week." He smiles at me. A full white smile.

I roll my eyes, but the reality is, I probably eat pizza more than he does.

"You must come here a lot if the cook is looking out for you?" he inquires.

"You caught that, huh?" I question.

"Yeah, I live upstairs. Sal keeps me fed most nights and likes to keep an eye on me."

"You guys related?"

I look at him dumbfounded, pointing at my basically translucent skin. "You ever seen an Italian this pale?" Raising my eyebrows in questions "No, my Irish roots run deep." I laugh.

He flips open the pizza box, settling into the squeaking seat in front of me, a look of expectance and question in his eyes. My cheeks grow warm under his bold exploration, my body coming to life from the attention I've craved for so many years in the safety of my mind. In the darkness of my bedroom, at night, with my hand, the only thing making the fantasy playing through my head come true.

"What?" My voice comes out shy, which is new for me.

"You look like someone I used to know."

My blood runs cold at his statement. I pick at the dried skin along my cuticles under the table, as nervous energy dances an Irish jig in my gut.

"Oh?" I squeak, not knowing what else to say.

It's not like I can be like, *oh you mean your ex-girlfriend. AKA my sister. My twin.*

But he doesn't expand, and I don't pry further. I don't think I could take him talking about her, especially today.

"Do you live around here?" I play stupid. I don't want him to pack up and leave or stop the timber of his voice from filling my ears. Building the first genuine connection we've ever had.

"Across the street." He smirks, thumb pointing out the window to the black stone building across the way. The neighborhood is splitting down the middle. Half still belong to the old neighborhood—the families that emigrated from their homelands to start a new life, bringing with them a mixing pot of cultural diversity. While the other looks like his renovated building across the street, updated to attract a millennial generation—with their love for overpriced iced coffee and microbrewery IPAs. They've flocked to Brooklyn, and it's slowly changing the charming divergence that once was.

I chuckle at him. "How's your fancy new loft?"

He cringes at my jab and drops the pizza he's been devouring back into the box.

"It was a necessary sacrifice; I promise you that." He pauses, the silence between us thickening until he can't take it any longer and breaks. "So, Keira, what do you do when you're not working at the airport? Do you like to dance?"

I stiffen in surprise, not sure if I should show my hand or play it close to the vest. "If the vibe is right." I give him a small smile.

His continued questions don't dig deeper than the surface. But mine want to. I want to ask him how he's doing today. If he's thinking about her. About their accident. I want to know what he does all day, shut in his loft. I have a million and one questions I've always wanted to know the answers to, but could never ask.

"I'm closing up, kids," Sal's deep voice calls from the back, shocking me from the trance I've been in since Harkin sat down.

"I'm gonna go," I stammer out, snatching up my bag, quickly sliding out of the booth. My feet don't make it far before a jolt of heat shoots up my arm from his hand wrapped around my wrist. I stare down. His tan fingers, covered in black ink, contrast perfectly against my pasty wrist.

An image of that same hand wrapped around my throat flashes through my mind. A blush creeps into my cheeks. Shaking the image free, I peer up at him through my lashes. A small smirk sits on his face.

"You were just going to run off?" His thumb soothes over my sensitive flesh, back and forth. It should be comforting, but my body doesn't get the message. I'm on pins and needles, dying to flee, but desperate for a minute more of his time.

"N… No… No I just needed to get going," I finally spit out, biting my bottom lip.

Jesus, get a hold of yourself, girl.

His free hand reaches up, thumb pulling my lip free, but it doesn't leave my face. My body's burning, core tightening, the tingle between my legs making me want to squirm to relieve the building pressure. I can't help it; my thighs shift anyway, drawing his gaze to the apex of my thighs that rubbed together.

His pupils darken and his breathing shallows.

"If you run, I'll have to follow," he says, his crooked grin showing a playfulness that doesn't reach his eyes. Any other girl would take that as a threat, but I'm hoping it's a promise. Strong footsteps come up behind us and I unwillingly pull from his touch.

"Let me walk you up?" he asks.

I bite my lip again, the pinch of pain centering me to this moment.

"She'll be fine, kid. I'll make sure of it," Sal says over my shoulder.

Harkin's jaw stiffens, his dark gaze shifting from my face to Sal. "I think she can speak for herself." His tone is forceful, leaving no room for sarcasm.

The air thickens with toxic masculinity, chests puff, heights lengthen.

For fuck's sake.

"You know what, boys? I think I'll walk myself." I turn on my heels and head straight for the side door that leads into the stairwell for my apartment.

Let them have their pissing contest. I don't have time for it. The door slams shut, and the quiet surrounds me as I make the climb up three flights of stairs home.

ELEVEN
HARKIN

My Type (Little Attitude) – Bryce Savage

Last night was like coming home—if home was a person and not the place I abandoned faster than it took for Alina's life to slip away. Sitting across from Keira in the tiny pizza parlor was refreshing. After a day of wallowing in my self-pity, I stumbled across the street, sobering at that sight of her hunkered down in the corner.

We chatted about nothing, but I'll hold on to it and replay it like a famous scripture. The minutes ticking away to hours when we were forced from our bubble of sanctitude. If I didn't already know that Sal treats her like a daughter and nothing else, we would have had a much different conversation after her hasty departure. Her sass eased my irritation, and I made it extensively clear to Sal that I would be around from now on.

Seeing her concealed apartment with the sliver of light peeking through under her curtains offered the reassurance I needed to know she made it home safe. It wasn't two minutes after I walked back into my apartment that I'd stripped down, my cock ridged against my abs, begging for relief. The steaming water splashes against my back; my hand grips hard around my swollen member, while pictures of her biting her damn lip fill my head. The heat from her earlier stare confirming what her body obstinately betrayed. We may have only met a couple times, but I affected her in the most devious way. She can try denying her body the urges now, but I won't have it that way much longer.

THE REPLAY of last night clears as my fingers pick up speed. I punch in the code I need to reveal the secrets I'm being paid big money to find and share with my employer. The things I've found while sleuthing through the electronic information are mind-blowing. People think they're doing a bang-up job hiding behind elementary passwords. I don't ask questions about the content I find, my program identifying the keywords or phrases necessary in the data stream.

My phone pings beside me on the table.

> You got it yet?

IT'S ALWAYS the men who have no clue what I really do that demand results right away. They wouldn't know a security program from a virus download if I painted it in big red letters in an email to them.

The search runs across my computer, pulling up screen after screen with hits. It'll take hours to go through the results and pinpoint the pertinent information for my report. But I'd rather sit here in my home office than clock in to a nine-to-five working for some mediocre manager. Freelancing keeps the money rolling in and my hands clean of the reality behind the information requested.

> I told you to give me a week. You'll have your package then.

I TYPE BACK to the anonymous number and drop my phone back on the desk. It pings back right away, and my irritation grows. But it's not a text notification staring up at me. I open the map app. The little red dot that floats across the city streets as the black SUV drives her around. I have just enough time to slide on my shoes, snag my keys from the counter, and head out the door.

With the app still pulled up on my phone, I time my stride to reach the front door of the building just as the SUV rounds the corner two blocks down. Jolting across the busy street, I startle as a cab's horn blares in my ears. The driver throws his arms in the air and silently screams at me from inside the car. I flip him off and keep moving, my sights set on the car that's now idling against the curb.

I slow as I round the hood, eyes downcast on my phone like

I'm out moving through my day, like every other New Yorker in the area. My shoulder checks the back passenger door, halting my progress. The door swings in and a muffled curse meets my ears. Her irritability of my carelessness intended to be shared. But as she finally looks my way, finishing her pleasantries with the driver, our eyes meet and her crass demeanor shifts.

"Harkin?" The pleasant surprise in her tone only enhances my smugness about our time together.

"Keira." My eyes rake down her body. The tight, leather leggings cling to her short, toned legs. Her creamy skin peeks through the cropped A Day to Remember band T that's sliced to shreds.

"You know, I didn't expect a girl like you to have a personal driver in the city." I'm being a dick; I know it. But watching her squirm under my judgement is too delectable to miss out on.

"I don't have a driver." She slams the door and steps into the middle of the sidewalk. I give her a questioning look. "Well, I mean, obviously I do. But I don't pay for it." Her weight shifts back and forth on her feet, her bag slung over her slender shoulder.

Well sweetheart, that doesn't make you seem any less high maintenance.

I don't fill the silence building between us. Instead, I wait to see if her rambling need for me to understand continues.

I'm not surprised when it does and she says, "I won it."

Her shoulders deflate at the truth, but not from embarrassment. No, my girl doesn't want me to associate her with the typical crowd that prefers unnecessary expenses like private cars. She's too proud, but not stupid enough to refuse the luxury. And that benefits me because now we're here and can finish what we started last night.

"Well then, lucky you, I guess." I smile at her, and her eyes light up at my attention.

"Were you heading home?" she asks, shifting the large bag she clutches close to her body. My eyes zone in on the strap, digging in against the delicate arch of her shoulder. Red lines bloom along the edges of the worn leather, marring her unblemished skin.

"I was going to get something to eat. You hungry?" Her eyes drop to a thin, silver watch adorning her wrist. The street light glints off the metal, filling my imagination with scenes of her trussed up to the wall, very different silver bracelets sported on both wrists.

"Were you planning on going far?" she asks.

"Just around the corner to that new pho place."

"Okay, I should still be able to make it then." Her agreement urges me forward, slipping my fingers under the strap of her bag and pulling its weight off her.

"Allow me." My freehand slides to her lower back, ushering her forward toward the restaurant.

We're seated at a small table in the back corner. The hostess drops the laminated menus before taking our drink order.

"So, big plans tonight?" I didn't miss her comment earlier.

"Not really, just a couple of friends getting together for a band over at Gypsy's."

"Oh? Who's playing? I haven't been over there in a while. Tell John the bartender you're a friend of mine. He'll take care of you tonight."

Curiosity sparks in her eyes.

"He'll just know who I'm talking about? There has to be a handful of Harkins in the city that go there." She laughs, and the lightness of it inflates my mood.

"I guess you'll just have to see. So, is that your scene? Underground rock music?"

Her nose wrinkles. "Scene? No. Do I like live music, yeah. I'm just not picky about the genre. I'm as likely to go see rock as I am to find some new folk band."

"Ahh, a music connoisseur, then?" I tease.

Her eyes narrow at the friendly jest. "Definitely not." She finally cracks a smile and laughs. "I like live music. The inconsistencies of the feedback, the truth of the singer's voice, nothing marring it like you get with streaming."

"A purest. Now that I can respect." I finish with a wink. A sweet blush creeps slowly across her chest and up onto her cheeks.

I wonder where else that lovely color lies.

The food is quick and delicious. That's one thing I was happy to not have to give up when I moved from California. There are just as many hole-in-the-wall places as there are fancy restaurants. You're never lacking options here.

My phone pings, and pulls my attention away from the conversation. I ignore the nuisance quickly, but not before Keira pushes out of her seat, the chair scratching against the linoleum flooring.

"Shit, I lost track of time. I really need to go," she says, while digging through that ridiculously oversized bag when a wallet pulls free.

"It's on me." I drop a couple of bills to the table and swipe the wallet from her hands, plopping it back into her bag. "Let me walk you out and hail you a cab."

Her big golden eyes stare up at me.

"Thank you." Her chin tips ever so slightly.

"You know what? Maybe I'll just walk. It's really not that far." She halts just outside the door and turns toward me.

"It's probably best if you take a cab. You can never be too safe out here," I remind her. If James wasn't off tonight, she'd be using his services.

"Are you busy?" She worries that bottom lip, pressing it tightly against her white teeth. I'm catching on to her nervous tell.

"In general, sweetheart, or now?" If she really wants to know, she'll have to be a bit more specific. Her slender fingers fidget with the watch on her wrist, twisting it back and forth.

"Uh, now. I was wondering if you wanted to come to the show with me. It's casual; my friends won't care. And you could say hi to that bartender friend of yours," she blathers on.

"I wish I could, but I've got a work thing I have to get to."

Her eyes fall to the ground and her shoulders slump. She projects her emotions so clearly without even noticing.

My finger skims along her chin before nudging it upward gently for our eyes to meet. "Another time," I promise. "Music with you sounds way better than the reports I've got to get finished sitting on my desk back at my place."

She hits me with another small chin nod. Always so agreeable, but it's met with a strain I'm familiar with.

A honk pulls us apart.

"Let me see your phone?" I request.

She pulls it quickly from her pocket while the cab idles at the curb.

It's unlocked. I pull up her call screen and type in my phone number, pressing call. My phone vibrates twice in my pocket before I end the call and hand it back to her. "Save it. Text me next time you're headed out to see something. I want to be amazed." I drop a quick kiss to her cheek, the heat from her skin searing my lips.

She opens the cab's door, sliding in quickly. I knock against the front window, motioning for the driver to roll it down. I hand over the fare for her ride and note the cabby's name and cab number, memorizing it. The look I give him ensures he'll know better than to try anything with my girl.

Two taps on the roof and they're pulling away. The last glimpse I see is Keira, face lit from her phone's screen. Two seconds later, my phone vibrates again. Drawing it from my back pocket, I look down at the text from an unknown number.

> You have no idea what you just did. ;)

Her shy, anxious demeanor seems to melts away as soon as she's away from me and behind a screen.

TWELVE
KEIRA

Better – Emma Remelle

The bouncer scans my ID, not looking twice to make sure I match the picture it displays before he hands it back and nods me inside. The band isn't playing yet, but music roars from speakers lining the small stage at the front of the grimy bar. Gypsy's is one of the last places around here that hasn't sold out to attract a certain crowd into their doors. They've stayed true to what they do, cheap, standard booze and good live music.

I scan the mass of people filling the tiny space, but my eyes don't land on anyone I know. I push my way through to the bar. An older guy with a bald head and leather vest wipes water spots off glasses before stacking them against the wall behind the bar. A younger kid with the same dark eyes and thin lips meets me as I step up to order.

"What can I get you, sweets?" He taps in front of me.

"Is there a John that works here?" His eyes narrow and they search my face.

"Who wants to know?"

"Just a friend of Harkin's. He told me to tell him something."

A sly smile tips his lips. Giving away exactly what my gut was already telling me.

Who does this kid think he's fooling?

"Oh yeah, and what's that?"

My brain freezes. It's not like I can just flat out tell him what Harkin said to me. He'll think I'm looking for free drinks. Not that I would turn them down, but I'm not expecting it.

"Just that he might stop by tonight is all," I finally get out.

"You want something or not?" His flirtation from earlier gone.

"Whiskey."

The short glass is placed in front of me, the dark amber liquid sloshing against the sides as he pours two fingers. I drop a ten on the bar and snatch up my drink, downing half the glass. A harsh slap against my ass jolts me forward, the sting spreads down my thigh. I spin around so fast the whiskey meshes with the movement, whirling my head as my anger heightens at the assault. But I should have known.

Flowing blonde hair and a wicked smile greet me. "You dumb bitch." I chuckle. "I almost swung at you."

"You would have hit me right in the tit from your vantage point." We both bust up laughing at the truth. Her natural height, plus the stiletto boots she's sporting, just exaggerate our height difference, especially since I'm wearing proper foot attire in a place like this, converse.

"What are we drinking?"

"Whiskey." Her nose scrunches up at my drink of choice. "Well, I never said you had to drink it you fool."

Spinning back around, her arms drape over my shoulders and her chin digs into the top of my head.

"Hey John," I shout down the bar, and his head whips in my direction. I smirk at my victory.

Got you, sucker.

He flashes me the bird before finishing the drinks he's working on for another customer and heads in our direction.

His eyes ignore me completely, taking in my beautiful blonde friend who's currently draped over my back like a koala.

"John, Stacey. Stacey meet John."

Her hand shoots out to shake his, but he brings it to his lips instead. It'd be funny, but shit like this happens almost every time I go out with her. The girl could easily be a model, but her looks are the last thing that matters to her. It's why I love her so much.

"What can I get you ladies?" John's flirtation is turned back up to eleven.

"Whiskey again for me. Jack, not Jim this time." My snotty half-smirk irritates the shit out of him by the looks of it, and satisfaction glides through me.

"How about for you, beautiful?" he asks.

It's like night and day watching him interact with us. If I didn't know any better, I think he was gracing the stages of Broadway.

"Vodka Soda and two shots of tequila with salt and lime," Stace orders.

"Oh shit, you're out to cause trouble tonight," I shout over the music, glancing over my shoulder to check the stage as the thrums of a guitar sound check in the mic.

She drops a wet, sloppy kiss to my cheek.

"I'm going home with him tonight." She giggles in my ear.

I pat her hands that are practically groping my chest.

Of course she is.

We throw back the tequila shots, the burn a welcome numbing in my veins, the limes bitter against my tongue. I entangle our fingers, swiping my whiskey and pulling her away from her conquest to the floor, getting closer to the stage where the band is almost ready to start.

"Did anyone else end up wanting to come out tonight?" I yell in her ear as we make it to the front. It's easy enough for me to sneak through the crowd with my compact frame. And as soon as guys look Stace's way, they part like the red sea.

"Nope, just me and you." She hip bumps me but instead of our hips meeting, hers hits my ribs and almost sends me stumbling in the other direction.

The band starts up, and the music rains down on us. The volume's deafening but worth it. A deep base pounds against my chest. Their lead singer screams into the microphone. The lyrics fade as my drinks set in, and my body moves to the rhythm.

They break halfway through their set and I'm in desperate need of cooling down. Sweat trickles down my spine. My leather leggings cling to my body. They'll be a bitch to take off tonight, and if that wasn't the case, I'd be heading for the bathroom. But I'm also not stupid enough to stand in line for the next twenty minutes trying to make it in there. Stace heads in that direction, regardless.

I trek toward the front door in search of air that isn't heavy with humidity from all the bodies cramped together. The door swings open, the bouncer still seated on his stool—ever the lookout. His expression doesn't change, just like the queen's guard. Gathering my hair in my hand, I pull it up, exposing my neck to the cool breeze that swirls through the night air.

Digging in my bra, I pull out my cell, wiping the screen against my shirt to dry away the collected moisture. I'm eager to see if he texted me back. I'm disappointed when the only notifications I have are a few texts from Stace to let me know she was on her way and updates from my social media account.

I take in a deep breath, filling my lungs with fresh air—well as fresh as you can get when you're in the middle of an overpopulated city. My limbs are heavy with alcohol. I might drink on the regular, but that doesn't matter when you're only five foot two. It sets in quick and doesn't leave for hours. I spin and rest my back against the grating brick wall. It scratches my exposed skin, but it's cold and my body temperature hits a comfortable point.

I fix my eyes on the small screen in my hands, his number displayed in bright blue. It's closing in on midnight, but I know the likelihood of him being awake is high. That man never sleeps, at least from my observations from across the street. He said he had work, but who works at this time of night?

That's ironic considering my shifts run through the witching hour, but that's a different story. Before I register what I'm doing, I tap on his number and my phone displays the video call. It rings, once, twice, three times and just as I'm about to select end, the screen turns black, and then his face appears.

Shit.

My brain finally catches up to what I just did, but I can't back out now. His deep, cerulean eyes drive straight into mine. His dark hair is messy around the edges. He's shirtless and seated up against what seems to be a headboard. Black ink spreads across his chest in detailed outlines of flowers surrounding a beautiful woman, ruminant of a goddess I'm not familiar with. I'm staring, analyzing every little detail pixilated on my phone's screen.

"Keira." His rough voice washes over me, pulling me from my examination.

"Yes?" I don't know what else to say. I don't know why I even pressed the call button at all.

"Are you still at Gypsy's?" His tone is direct. He sits up, limiting my view to only his face. And while his face is beautiful, I miss the dips of his abs that I desperately want to run my tongue down. My core tinges at the thought and I shift against the wall.

"Keira," he says again, but my mind is wandering in a completely different direction. It's hard to focus when he was so perfectly on display for me seconds ago.

"Mmm," I mumble, my imagination running away with me. Images of his sculpted chest scored through with red slices from my nails as I sit on his cock and ride him hard. His stomach taught as pleasure wracks through his body. His head thrown back, lips telling me what a good girl I am for pleasing him so well.

The fantasy builds a pleasurable throbbing deep inside my core. My chest heaves, and I try to catch my breath. My nipples harden against the smooth fabric of my shirt. The thin material cut to pieces, doing nothing to control their sharpness against my growing arousal.

"Sweetness, are you going to answer me or just stand there?" His deep tone is sensual and not helping with my current predicament. I focus on ignoring the pulse between my thighs.

"Yes," I puff out, gaining a molecule of clarity.

"Yes, you're still at Gypsy's?" His brows turn down in seriousness.

"Yes, Harkin," I snark, the alcohol feeding my boldness. I'm feeling feisty, my irritation rising that he turned down my invitation, but he's obviously not working.

"You lied." My hand flies up to cover my mouth, the accusation spills out.

"And what did I lie to you about?" One eyebrow quirks this time, his face sculpting into a handsome portrait that I want to capture and display on my wall.

"You're not working." I pout.

The crowd from inside grows loud and music fills the air again, pulling my attention away from the serious man in front of me.

"I didn't lie, sweetness. I was working earlier. I promise you that."

"Keira." My name sounds across the sidewalk. My eyes shift from the mesmerizing view at the tips of my fingers. My head whips toward the call. And Stacey stands in the club's doorway, arms waving for me to head back inside.

"Goodnight, Harkin." I smile at him and hang up, shoving my phone back into my bra for safe-keeping.

"Who were you talking to?" Stace questions as my body settles against hers. We make our way toward the stage but choose to stay closer to the back of the club, standing closer to the bar, where tables outline the crowd.

"Just a friend." I shake my head, trying to throw her off the trail.

"Want another drink?" she asks but doesn't wait for my answer before her hips are swaying as she gallivants back to the bar.

I shake my head, knowing she'll get exactly what she wants by the end of the night.

THIRTEEN
HARKIN

Shackles – Steven Rodriguez

Her call fades to black. Someone distracted her as she said goodbye to me. I'm up out of bed and walking toward the closet, pulling on my black jeans, and throwing a tee shirt over my head before tearing my leather jacket from a hanger and shoving my arms into it.

John should have been keeping an eye out for her, but apparently all he was worried about was pouring her more drinks than she needed.

From that call alone, I could tell she was beyond the point of feeling tipsy, shifting very close to being wasted, and I just can't have that. My front door slams behind me, my boots picking up speed as I choose the stairs over the elevators, not willing to wait for its arrival. I'm quick to get to the curb in front of my building, hand waving in the air, trying to hail the cab.

It's creeping past midnight, but this is the city that never sleeps and that includes paid transportation. I jump in the cab, rambling off the address—when I probably could have just given him the name of the bar and he reset the fare counter. My knee bounces as nervous energy courses through me. I keep the screen of my phone lit, hoping she calls me back but knowing she's likely back in the bar listening to the music.

"Can you hurry!" I shout to the driver and he startles, but the car accelerates, throwing my body backwards against the seat. Within minutes, we're pulling in front of the bar. A couple of people stand in groups along the sidewalk smoking. Matt guards the front door of the bar looking bored out of his mind. He nods me in, recognizing me right away.

It's dark outside, but the bar is darker. My view's hindered by the blinding stage lights and fabricated fog for the performers.

Then I hear it.

Her laugh somehow cuts through the roaring crowd. My gaze shoots straight to where she stands at a high table with her friend Stacey, the same blonde from the club last time.

They're not alone. A small cluster of grimy concert goers huddle with them around the table full of shots.

Jesus Christ.

I halt my progress, shifting my path over to the bar where I can see John staring in the same direction I just was. His jaw is tight and if I hadn't just gotten off the phone with him; I'd think he had his eyes on my girl.

"Did you have to give them a tray of shots?" I shout to him, leaning over the bar and slapping his hand in our typical greeting.

"Bro, her friend is relentless. Plus, I'm trying to take her home tonight."

"Anything happen?" I ask him, my curt tone a marker for my current mood.

"Nah, I've had an eye on them. Those guys are harmless. Plus, they just got there when you walked in." He nods to the girl's table. "Well, maybe not for long." His eyes darken at whatever is going on behind me.

My stride carries me across the floor in seconds before I pull up behind her and wrap an arm around her waist, my hand flattening possessively against her stomach.

She contracts in surprise, trying to pull free of my hold, but I only tighten my arm and settle her closer into my body.

I dip my mouth to her ear. "Is this what you wanted?"

The eyes around the table focus on us as she gasps but relaxes against me. Her fingers settle against my hand and trace lightly against my skin.

Her eyes meet mine across her shoulder, her pupils dilate as her chest rises and falls in a staccato rhythm.

"You came?" Her words are a ghost of a whisper in the bar. But I can read the meaning from her lips.

"You think I'd leave you to the wolves after that call? The look in your eyes was enough to have me bounding from my bed." She turns in my hold, her arms wrapping around my neck. Her small body molding against me. Each curve settling against my ridged planes.

"I didn't mean to call." Her eyes dance with mischief.

"Don't lie to me, sweetness. We both know that was no accident."

"But I've been drinking. I didn't know what I was doing." Her smile illuminates her face even against the blackness of the bar. Her beauty is my beacon in the dark.

"Drunk actions are sober thoughts, little one, or didn't you know that?" I tsk.

Her body pulls against the boundaries of my arms, trying to break free from me.

"K! Who is this guy?" Her friend finally butts in, a little too late for my liking. Keira spins, her ass settling against me. I groan in her ear, and she pushes back harder, wiggling slightly too.

What a little minx.

"Stace." Her tone soothes her worried friend. "This is Harkin." She pauses, swiping a shot of God knows what from the table and throwing it back before I have a second thought to stop her. My grip against her waist tightens, and my mouth finds her ear again.

"That's enough for you, little one." I bite down against her earlobe, and she shutters against me.

"Remember that guy I told you about?" she asks.

Her friend's eyes find mine over Keira's shoulder, her stare intense as she takes in our bodies entangled in each other like longtime lovers. Slowly, it shifts from one of concern to one of giddiness as something dawns on her. She shakes her head, throwing it back and laughing. I'm confused by her reaction, but maybe she's just as drunk as my girl.

Keira's hand sneaks out onto the table again, reaching for the last full shot glass. But my fingers wrap around her wrist, tightening to stop her movement.

"Have you not had enough?"

She peeks at me over her shoulder, rolling her eyes at my controlling inquisition, turning back for the table and trying again.

My fingers snap up to her chin, wrenching it back to my gaze. "Did you just roll your eyes at me, little one?" Her body stiffens against me at my sharp tone.

Her eye dart across my face, searching for a shift in seriousness, but she won't find one. As I watch her breathing pick up with realization, my grip loosens, gliding down her petite throat that I can already see, collared and lovely. My fingers brush lightly against her exposed collar bones. Her body relaxes as they continue tracing along the rips of her shirt where the milky skin shines through. The overcrowded room of the bar falls away, leaving us to our own exploration.

A soft moan escapes her sweet lips. My eyes dart to the offender, waiting for more.

"And if I did?" Her cheeky delayed response catches me off guard.

I'd forgotten about my question as my hands wandered across her body. It's so easily distracting, and I could let it slide, but the glint in her eyes tells me she doesn't want me to.

"Come with me." I slide my hand into hers and yank her away from the table. Her friend calls after us, but with the way John had his sights set on her earlier, I have nothing to worry about. Her feet stumble under her, tripping her body against mine. Snaking my arm around her waist, I pull her warmth against me, dragging her along to the empty office I know is in the back of the bar.

Pushing open the door, I shove her—not so lightly—into the vacant room. It's dim, the only light from a small lamp in the corner towering over a leather chair.

"Harkin, what are you doing?" She stumbles over her feet, catching herself against the desk.

"You call me in the middle of the night. Tease me with those beautiful, lust-filled eyes. Stumble off the call. Make me worry. And then roll your eyes? And you wonder what we're doing in here?"

Her body straightens. The alcohol running thick through

her veins, she sways, catching herself against the mahogany desk.

I stalk toward her. Her body retreats, stopping when she's flush with the desk. Nowhere to go. Her knuckles turn white against her grip. Boxing her in, I take in her state: eyes dilated, skin flushed, breathing rapt. I smile down at her.

"Tell me what I should have done, little one?" Her eyes close, and I lean in to rest my forehead against hers, her chest bursting in quick flutters against my shirt.

Those big golden eyes stare up at me through thick black lashes. Her nose nuzzles against my own.

"I'm glad you came," she confesses before her lips collide with mine.

My mind blanks, thoughts of punishing her attitude forgotten. I'm too wrapped up in the searing heat radiating from our joined lips. I dive in deeper, pushing apart the seam of her full lips and slipping my tongue inside. She must be drunker than I thought because the sting of alcohol is potent on her tongue.

I grip her narrow waist, lifting her body and dropping her to the top of the desk. Her legs wrap around me, and I'm pulled against the junction of her thighs. I thicken against her heat and thrust forward. Her guttural moan encourages my hands exploration down her sides, landing on the band of her leather pants.

I pull away, taking in a deep breath, bringing clarity to my brain. "Tell me why you called, sweetness?"

I lick against her lips, teasing our joining, but controlling the pleasure. She whimpers against me but doesn't answer. My finger traces along the band of her leggings, dipping through the tightness as I push through toward her core.

Her wetness coats my fingers. No barrier meets my assault.

The slickness pulls me down and her hips widen, giving me permission and access all-in-one.

"Tell me to stop, little one."

Only a whimper answers my pleas. I have no self-control now to stop myself from plunging deeper into her heat. I need to feel her on my skin.

"Harkin."

My name–a plea on her lips—spurs me on as my fingers rut in and out. The tightness squeezes me, throwing me down a warpath to bury my cock deep inside her and feel the same. I curve my fingers forward, rubbing a spot that makes her cry out my name in a broken whisper. My lips find hers, pressing deep, nipping and sucking, pulling every moan and sigh inside me before it escapes for anyone else's ears.

"Harkin, please," she whines, making my fingers pump harder, her cunt pulling me deep.

"Tell me what you want, little one." Her walls flutter against my fingers. Her arousal dripping down to my wrist. I want to drive myself deep inside her, fill her full of my cock until her eyes never roll in my direction again. But the way she's clinging to me seconds away from falling apart, beautiful, and free, I can't stop myself from driving her toward the edge. I need to watch her fall apart in my hands.

My lips surge forward, capturing hers. Biting and pulling, nipping, and sucking, until her breath is uneven, and her cunt has a vice like grip on my digits. She pulses around me and then her head throws back, her throat beautifully displayed to me.

I bite down, sucking the slick flesh in with a tight nip, soothing away the pain with a warm lick and a sweet kiss. Her breathing slows. My fingers pull free. Bringing them to my lips, I lick her juices and she tastes just as sweet as I imaged.

"Fuck," she huffs out.

Her naughty mouth doesn't give up, even with the pleasure I've just given her. I shouldn't have. She should have been punished for the excessive drinking—and especially for the eye roll. But that's all over now. My mind is blissed out and my cock raging against the teeth of my zipper.

Her chest bounces, deep breaths pulling in as she regains awareness of her surroundings. Her slender fingers dig sharply into my shoulders as her eyes find mine and a shy smile pulls at her lips.

"Was that my punishment?" Her sassy satisfied smirk should irk me, but the taste of her cum still on my lips makes that hard; it makes me hard.

Her dainty hand pushes against my chest, trying to make space between us, but I'm not ready for her heat to leave my body. Instead, she closes her thighs, shoving me back inch by inch until they're closed. I drop into the chair in front of the sturdy desk and heave a sigh.

"That was definitely not your punishment, sweetness, and you know it."

FOURTEEN
KEIRA

Scorpio – Pour Vous

My heart races as I fail to catch my breath, and he just sits there on display in the sandy-brown, leather chair. His toned arm reaches up, pushing those skilled fingers through his dark locks. Thick veins run down his forearm, black ink overlaying his exposed skin. Only small sections along the surface are empty, allowing an understanding of the detailed illustrations.

I can't believe that just happened. It shouldn't have. He's basically a stranger. I might know way too much about his life from what I've gathered over the years online, but he's met me fewer times than the amount of fingers he just had inside my pussy. That didn't seem to factor in his decision to waltz into the bar, steal me away from Stacey, and shove me in this random room.

My brain became mush as soon as his hands grazed my

skin to pull my body against his. The whiskey and tequila mixing with his intoxicating scent. Now that there's some space between us, the haze in my brain is lifting enough that I can enjoy the buzz from my drinks.

"Are you just going to stand there staring at me?" The timbre of his irritation is palpable, and it pisses me off. I didn't ask for this. I might have made the mistake of drunk calling him, but that's exactly what it was: a drunk call.

I straighten my clothes and push off the desk, taking a step closer to his relaxed form. His body and his words giving off two very different vibes. There's no hiding the thickness of his manhood against his thigh. My mouth waters at the possibility of tasting him. His lap shifts, a rough hand strokes against his length. My eyes shoot up from their ogling. The ache between my thighs he just quenched back with a vengeance.

"Actually, I think I'm going to go find Stacey." I turn on my heels and hustle for the door. The cold brass of the handle feels like ice against my heated skin. The music pulses through the wood, but as soon as I crack it open, it pierces against our seclusion.

A quick thud above my head slams it shut and I'm violently whipped around. We're back to the same stance as before, my brain short circuits. He smells like the woods after a rainstorm. Which is ironic, considering there isn't a forest within a hundred-mile radius.

"You should let me go." I study him. The sharp jaw, a crooked nose that looks like it's been broken once or twice, his thick kissable lips, but it's his eyes that hypnotize and soon I'm no better than Alice falling down the rabbit hole.

"I don't think I can," he mutters against my neck, taking an audible sniff of my dewy skin.

My hands lie flat against the office door behind me,

pressing harder with every moment that passes, as the urgency to feel his skin against mine grows. But I won't allow myself the pleasure. I know if I do, we won't leave this room. I won't go find Stace—who's probably wondering where the hell I disappeared to.

"Harkin." His name tumbles from my lips as I take a deep breath. I can tell from his hard stance I'm the one who needs to make the next move. "I'm going back out there." My right hand reaches back out for the handle, but his skin is already covering it. Electricity shoots through my arm, straight to my core. The ache for him growing as his warmth seeps into me. He moves and the door behind me shifts me even closer against him.

"Then we better go, little one." His gaze spears through me.

I rethink the necessity of leaving this room and heading back into a crowd, but he's already pulling me out into the narrow hallway that leads back to the main bar. I press on to my toes to get a better vantage point for finding Stacey. Her bouncy, bright blonde hair isn't anywhere in my eyesight.

"Do you see her?" I shout to Harkin.

His head shakes no, pulling me along again. He parts the patrons with ease, shoulder checking everyone, not giving a second thought to their response. We make our way to the bar on the other side of the building. He pulls me forward, settling my body against the bar and his body against mine, arms caging me in, creating a buffer between anyone else around us.

He waits a couple minutes before John heads in our direction. John's eyes meet mine and his head shakes slightly before he bro nods to my personal bodyguard.

"Have you seen her friend?" Harkin leans in, our bodies might as well be glued together at this point. My ribs dig painfully against the bar's edge, but I ignore it. Instead, focusing on the fact that his cock is still hard, and I can feel every inch against my backside.

I wiggle my ass and throw my arms up, reaching behind me to wrap my hands around his neck. My fingers lace in his thick hair. I've completely forgotten why we're standing here at the bar. My fingers tighten, pulling on the soft strands. A deep groan reaches my ear.

The music feeds my buzz, my hips refusing to stay still. Closing my eyes, I lose myself to my surroundings. I'm at the perfect point of drunkenness, all inhibitions abandoned, no signs of nausea or the spins. I don't want this moment to end. But my blanket of heat is gone, my safety cage removed and my eyes spring open.

"She's gone." Harkin's face is back in view. I don't remember twisting in his direction, but here we are.

"What?" I shriek.

"John said she left about fifteen minutes ago, she tried looking around for you, but couldn't find you." He ends with a smug smile.

My vexed eye roll is automatic. It doesn't dawn on me until his eyes harden and the smile falls.

Guy's got a serious aversion to disrespect; the funny thing is it makes me respect him more.

I drop my eyes to the floor in a silent plea of repentance. I'm not even sure why I did it. In one breath, I'm trying to get away from him, defying his sharp tongue. In the next, this dire need to please him devours me.

A gentle finger tips my chin up. The sudden movement sends the dotted, colorful lights spinning and then it all fades to black.

THE WARM SUMMER sun tightens my skin. Thick blades of dense grass tickle my limbs. The heat radiates everywhere, and I can feel my temperature rising. I have that feeling of when you wake up in a closed-up tent too late in the morning. I've always related it to an earthly like state of hell. Kicking at the air, something wraps my legs, causing resistance and the panic sets in.

My body jolts ups, eyes flying open but still hazy from dreams of summer fields. I glance at my surroundings. Nothing is familiar and I'm hit with a thunderous pain behind my right eyebrow.

Great, a hangover.

To no doubt go along with a night full of regrets. But you can't really regret what you don't remember, right?

I heave in a deep breath and search for my cell. I check the nightstand, but there's nothing there that's helpful to me other than the time: eleven fifteen.

Throwing my legs off the mattress and flinging the clean white sheets back, I notice I'm in a tee shirt—not one of mine, but the well washed, soft, cotton, oversized, male kind. A faint smell of pine clings to the material—and a pair of silk panties. Which is odd considering I wasn't wearing any the night before.

My feet thud against the cold, wooden floors and when I'm up-right the shirt falls to mid-thigh. There's nothing in here to tell me whose bedroom this is. Maybe I went home with a gentleman who put me to bed in his guest room.

I press my ear against the door, but nothing sounds from the other side. Creaking it open just an inch, I peer out into a hallway. Generic landscapes line the cool, tan walls. No portraits to help jog my memory.

I tiptoe toward the end of the hall. The open concept living and dining room sits across from a spacious kitchen. But it's the wall of windows to my right that finally gives me some bearings. I have a clear view across the way to my apartment building, even through the tinted windows.

Harkin.

As quickly as his name manifests in my mind, his body appears around the corner in the kitchen. He doesn't notice me across the room. I take the advantage and watch him as he effortlessly glides around the kitchen island, making coffee, stirring something in a pan, and flipping bacon.

I went home with Harkin last night. Small flashes of the bar play in my mind: a call on the sidewalk, a girl's night hijacked, an abandoned office. My cheeks heat at that last memory. It's all flooding back to me. But for the life of me, I can't remember anything after we stepped out of the secluded space and severed our first intimate experience.

He stops in the kitchen, typing away at his laptop on the counter between two plates. The music switches from a song I don't know, to Rockwell's Iconic hit: *Somebody's Watching Me*. My eyes leap from his fingers to his face and his eyes are in fact watching me now. My breath hitches. I should move further into the room, but my feet are cemented into the floor.

"I'm making breakfast. But I guess by now it's really brunch." He turns his back to me and it's the first time I realize he's shirtless, gray sweatpants hang low on his hips. Just like his arms and chest, the black and gray ink covers his entire toned back. This time, instead of a goddess haloed in lotus flowers, a thick skull with two wicked snakes intertwines their bodies to cover his skin. The two pieces are the epitome of life and death, and it makes me wonder if it's symbolic of his life.

I haven't responded to his statement; I've simply become a statue to decorate his living room.

"Keira? You going to come in here and eat with me?" His tone is light and playful. He's obviously not battling a crippling hangover headache.

I shuffle slowly toward the kitchen bar where he's laid the two plates piled high with breakfast food. I thank the gods above that the fusion of smells in the air isn't harsh on my stomach. Two small, white pills sit next to a glass of orange juice and a mug of coffee. A carafe of cream and a jar of sugar are next to the black sludge that I'm putting all my cards on to bring me back to life.

I mix them in, giving the mug a quick swirl with my spoon before throwing back the pills and taking a long sip of the glorious drink. Only then, do I slide onto the barstool and make eye contact with the man of the house.

"Harkin?" I want to know how I got here and why I'm with him and not Stacey.

Oh my god, Stacey.

Thoughts of what could've happened to her spring to the forefront of my mind.

"Cell phone!" I all but shout. The small, black device slides against the marble countertop in my direction. The screen already lit from the movement.

Shit, five miss calls and enough text notifications to nest against each other. Oops.

I'm too hungover to deal with her right now. Shooting off a quick text to let her know I'm alive, I set my phone back on the counter face down and slouch in my chair, lifting the coffee mug and inhaling the delicious aroma wafting from it.

"How am I here?" My eyes peek over the cup, shielding my small smile from him.

"We took a cab."

"You know what I mean, Harkin, why am I here, and not at home?" My mug clanks against the counter, a sign of my growing irritation.

His eyes pierce mine, but his features remain cool. My blood heats—or maybe that's only the coffee doing its job. I've noticed it doesn't take much from him for frustration to grip me. He's as infuriating as he is delectable. He leans casually against the counter opposite the island, his legs crossed at the ankles, those damn sexy V muscles every girl melts for on full display.

"Well, let's see: Stacey ditched you at the bar, you passed out before we could even get out the front door, and I didn't think it would be a smart idea to walk ten blocks with an unconscious body in my arms. I didn't know how to get you into your apartment or which one it even was. And last but not least, you were so drunk I couldn't get any answers from you. So rather than leave you at the bar to fend for yourself—which you couldn't have because, again, unconscious—I had no other choice but to bring you here." He kicks off the cabinet and stalks toward me, dropping his elbows to the island so we're only a mere foot away from each other now. "Is that a sufficient answer for you?"

I'm shocked into silence, a rarity for me. I want to be mad, but it seems the only person I should be mad at is myself, or maybe Stacey, because that bitch was the one to go get the last tray of shots. I knew those were a bad idea, but the look on his face and the growling in my ear sparked a rebelliousness I haven't felt since I was a teenager.

"Thank you," I mumble under my breath.

His dark eyebrows raise in question but he says nothing.

My fingers interlock in my lap, my thumbs running over one another in anxiousness. "Thank you," I tell him again, this time clear enough for him to hear. Our eyes stay locked across the counter as he shifts to push away.

I think he's making a break for the bedroom when he rounds the corner of the island to stand behind me. My stool swings around and our knees bump before mine settles inside his stance. His muscles were too much of a distraction before; I missed the black metal bar bells pushed through each nipple, during my drunk facetime call. They're easily camouflaged against the dark ink. But now, they're right at eye level. My immediate, impulsive thought is to lean forward and take one into my mouth before pulling, just to see what sound he'd make.

His throat clears, and I crane my neck back to reach his eyes. "You shouldn't drink that much." His even tone tells me this is less of an opinion and more of a cold, hard fact.

His hand reaches up, the backs of his fingers trailing lightly across my cheek before he presses a stray hair behind my ear. I've just rolled out of bed, completely hung over, so I'm sure my hair is a wild mess. And that's why it falls forward again into my face once his fingers are gone. But the gesture was sweet.

"I usually don't, but I also don't need a babysitter, Harkin."

His palms drop to my exposed thighs, fingers digging into the flesh. He's trying to keep his composure, but it's slipping—just like his fingers up my thighs.

I tighten my quads, trying to pull them together, but he's stronger and they don't budge against my efforts.

"Do you know what could have happened to you?" His husky whisper is filled with distress.

His concern satiates the deep-seated need I've had stirring within me for years to be wanted by him. Years of obsession and daydreams are slowly unraveling and becoming my reality.

His hands draw me out of my head and back to the closing distance between us. My core tightens when the tips of his fingers disappear under the oversized tee shirt I'm drowning in. My breathing stops as I wait for the sensation my body's craving, but it never comes.

His eyes are watching me. Every little sliver of reaction my body has to his, gives him a clue how much his presence affects me. I realize I never answered his question, shaking my head no. I hope it's enough to break the tension stewing in the air.

His palms slide up another inch before disappearing completely. A sharp nudge presses against my clit, shooting tingles through my limbs. The pressure shifts, gliding across the silk covering my pussy. A moan escapes my throat. His fingers still, but he leaves them teasing near my entrance.

"Tell me, did you call me on purpose? Did you want me to show up? Were you trying to tease me?" He whispers each question into my ear. His hot, wet tongue traces the shell of my ear before a tight nip captures my lobe. He pinches my clit at the same time, and my legs jolt together. This time I only want to quench the need he's kindling, not halt his pursuit.

I huff my frustration. His hand is now trapped tightly between my thighs, his fingers nestled next to my heating core. His struggle to free them only causes more friction, forcing me to groan. I bite my lip to stifle the sound, but his lips quirk up in understanding.

"Answer the questions, sweetness. Don't deny us both what we want."

"I don't know."

His knuckle pushes forward and my hips surge against his assault. I'm seeking more relief, but he's teasing me. And he stops dead when my body moves against him.

"I think you do," he quips.

My body is so wound up, I'm desperate for a reprieve.

"Yes!" I shout before my mind can process the agreement.

His lips capture mine in frenzy. A truthful answer for an ounce of bliss. I like this game. His tongue soothes mine where I've drawn blood in my struggle not to give into him.

So much for that.

My back shoves against the edge of the counter, my legs spread open, wrapping around his waist, pulling him in to settle tightly against my heat. His rough hands grip my hips. We're skin-to-skin, but not where I yearn for it.

His mouth traces my chin, his morning scruff rough against my sensitive flesh. He moves south, leaving sharp bites along the way, sucking in harshly. He's determined to leave a mark, but I don't care. I'd let him mark me all over, if only to let the world know I belong to someone. I think the tee shirt will stop him. But why would it? He easily rips it over my head and throws it to the floor behind him. I'm exposed. Nothing left on but my tiny silk thong.

His lips quirk to the side in an amused smile. "We match," he says, before his lips capture the sensitive piercing, sucking and nipping with a renewed fervor. It pops free, and he drops to his knees. My ankles unlatch from around his waist and my thigh settles on his shoulders as he pulls my ass forward.

FIFTEEN
HARKIN

Are You With Me - Nilu

My knees dig into the hardwood, but the pain's forgotten as soon as I inhale. Her scent is heady. I run my nose along her damp slit through her silk panties. I bite down on her tiny bud, and her body jerks against my face. The barrier between my tongue and her cunt has to go. Slipping my hand behind my back, I pop the button to free my knife and trace it up her calf.

Her body shivers at the cool metal, and goosebumps rise on her skin. The flat of my blade makes its way to her inner thigh when I notice the marks, faded with age, but raised nevertheless. My blood boils instantly at the possibility that someone made these marks in an area that's only exposed in intimate situations.

The tip of my knife traces the oblong shapes, but I don't press down hard enough to draw blood—even though I want to. I want to mark them as my own, take away whatever memory she holds when she looks at them, replacing those thoughts with what's about to come—her.

I drop a kiss to one side and then the other, realizing it's not just her right side, but both. The marks are in the crease between her thigh and pussy, well-hidden–even in a bikini.

"What are these?" I whisper against her skin. Licking the ridges and watching her breathing pick up. Her toned thighs tighten. I look up into her heated gaze. She's so far gone into bliss she doesn't answer me.

"Don't make me repeat myself, little one. I thought we were past that."

Her body stiffens at my tone, not her typical response to my demands.

Her body retreats. She catches me off guard and pushes off the stool, moving past me in a blur. Her feet pound against the floor like she's running a marathon. I stalk after her. If she thinks I'm letting this go, she's got another thing coming.

I fling the bedroom door open. It crashes loudly against the wall. Puffs of drywall flitter to the floor in its wake. My eyes scan the room, but nothing moves; she's nowhere in my sights. The slam of the ensuite around the corner gives her away.

I pound on the wood. "Keira, open the damn door."

I don't get an answer, instead the sound of water cascading against the stone starts. My pounding ceases. It's no use. I reach up, tracing my fingers along the trim of the bathroom door until they meet thin metal.

I shove the skeleton key into the lock and twist. It clicks out of place and the knob turns with ease. I push the door open, expecting to see a wet naked Keira in the shower. Instead, she's slumped in the corner, knees pulled to her chest, head resting against them. Her eyes bore straight in my direction.

Tears flow freely, her eyes rimmed red, matching her cheeks. But her gaze doesn't meet mine. It looks right through me. Not into the bedroom, but she's somewhere else completely. My anger melts into concern as I approach her spooked form.

I drop to my ass in front of her, separating my legs as far as they'll go to pull her into me. She doesn't move, but she doesn't resist. I pull her head against my chest, running a hand against her mess of hair.

"Come back to me," I whisper to her and drop a kiss against her temple.

Her body trembles, but I tighten my grip against her skin. It's then I realize she's practically naked. I lean to the left and snag the plush white towel hanging from the warming wrack. Wrapping it around her shoulders, I pull it closed at her chest. Her face is still downcast, ignoring everything happening.

"Keira." I'm pleading with her to look at me. "Tell me." I tighten my tone back to the demanding man she's used to surrendering to.

The shaking calms, but a slight tremor continues to pulse between us. Her eyes sweep up from the ground, finally landing on my own, I lean forward and capture her lips. Trying my best to coax her back to life; back to me.

"It's not a big deal. Don't worry about it," she murmurs.

"Let me decide what I should be worried about." I try to lighten my voice, but based on her reaction, I don't succeed.

"Men, always sticking their noses where it doesn't belong," she mutters under her breath. "Why can't you all just ignore them?"

Now it's my turn to stiffen. It's a slap in the face when she references her past relations while we're tangled together in each other's arms. I'm in denial that there was anyone before me, and I plan on making damn sure there's no one after.

"I'm not other men," I declare. "Tell me what happened, little one, and put my worries to bed."

Her head shakes against my chest.

Why won't she just tell me?

Nothing that comes out of her mouth could be worse than the horrific images bombarding my imagination.

"Foster care is no joke," she admits.

My arms automatically tighten around her. The millimeters separating us disappear now that she's on my lap, straddling me. I knew the reality of foster care was a possibility for her when I read the article about her mom, but hearing it fall from her lips tears through my soul.

I say nothing, waiting for the silence to break when she continues, "I was only eight...." She pauses and shifts, dropping her chin. Her red-rimmed honeyed gaze is hypnotic. I'm drawn to her, like an idiot moth to a flame. Desperate to hear the rest, so I hang on to every word. "I was only eight when I watched my mom die. She stepped in front of a blaze of bullets when we were leaving a diner near here."

I know all of this, but there's something different about hearing it from her perspective and not from some rando in a basement that's got a hard on for tragedy. My hand rubs up and down her back, the fabric of the towel soft, but her skin is smoother. I wish there wasn't a barrier.

"It was always just me and my mom. I never knew my dad. I never got the chance to really ask her, since she'd always brush off my questions when I tried. As I got older, I wondered if I had grandparents or aunts and uncles, but she mentioned no one. We never spent time with other people. I can't even remember now if she had boyfriends or friends." Her shoulders heave as she releases a sigh.

"I guess there really wasn't anyone because the police couldn't find a next of kin. They placed me with CPS that night. The women who worked through my paperwork kept telling me I'd get adopted quickly. I was young, a girl, and pretty. She repeated those words over and over until I finally tuned her out and fell asleep in her office."

"When I woke up, it was to her shaking me, pulling me from the seat and shoving me through the door toward a man with gangling limbs and stringy hair. I remember a feeling washing over me while I stood there in front of him like something bad was—" She stops mid-sentence, new tears dripping down her rosy cheeks. Her breathing is even, her eyes are on me, yet they leak without her knowledge.

"It did, not even twenty-four hours after he took me to the all-girls group home they had momentarily assigned me to. It didn't happen to me, but that night after lights out..." She pauses, shivering even though the room is hot and humid. "The door to my new room that I shared with a handful of other girls creaked open. I was lying on my side, counting backward from one-hundred, trying to fall asleep, but it was pointless being in an unfamiliar place. The light from the hall was blinding against the pitch black where we were trying to sleep. The old flooring groaned under his weight. I didn't dare move. His shadow was huge. I wasn't sure if it was him or a demon roaming the night. But then my mattress dipped from the opposite side. You see, there were five of us in the room, but only two beds and one mattress thrown on the floor. The youngest girl was nice enough to give me her space on the bed, but at that moment I was wishing she hadn't. My whole body stilled when the mattress moved. I held my breath once the antique, iron bed frame started moving and squeaking rhythmically. The girl behind me, I couldn't recall her name yet, cried, but he muffled it. I'll never know what actually happened because I didn't move, I didn't turn around, I didn't say a word. I just laid there. I was only eight, and I knew whatever was happening mere inches from me was wrong."

I shift her weight, lifting us from the hard bathroom floor, and walk us back to the bedroom. I sit on the edge of the mattress, settling her again on my lap. Her thighs grip my waist and I want to climb inside her, erase all the horrible memories from the inside out, but she hasn't even gotten to the reason behind the scars on her inner thighs. I still my wandering hand, calm my racing heart and nod for her to continue.

"I was at that house for sixty-seven days. His visits didn't happen every night. There were five other rooms with just as many girls in them. He made his rounds, switching from one to the next, never visiting the same room two nights in a row. After I'd been there a few weeks, the mattress dipped behind me."

She squeezes her eyes shut, scrunching her entire face, as her breathing becomes labored. The deep tremble pulsing through her body shakes her small frame in my hold.

Every fiber of my being is burning with rage at what she just insinuated. I'm fighting with my logical side that knows I can't flip my lid. But the need to hunt him down and make him suffer tenfold for what he put her through surges within me. I make a mental note to do just that when the time comes.

I stash the those thoughts deep down because she needs me calm and collected, here to hold her as she relives one of the most traumatic times in her life, that I stubbornly pushed for.

My finger finds her lips pushing softly. "Do you want to keep going?"

Her head gives a small shake and some of the tension releases between us.

She's right, the marks aren't what I thought at all. I never would have associated them with something that she went through at eight-years-old.

She blinks at me, the tears have stopped running down her cheeks, but the haunted look holds fast. I drop my forehead to her chest and pull her in tightly, flopping back against the bed. The towel is long gone, discarded on the bedroom floor.

She settles against me, burrowing into my chest, and I wish we could stay like this forever. After a few minutes of nothing but our matched breaths filling the quiet air, she shifts, interlacing her fingers and splaying them flat against my chest under her chin, looking up at me.

"I did it." Her rich eyes fixate on my face. Her words don't register at first. I'm lost to what she's referring to until my confusion clears. My question in the kitchen, the stupid question shaped by my fury. The shortsighted invasion into her past that I wasn't ready for.

"Why?" It's a dumb question, but it slips out anyway.

Why did I let the burn of alcohol numb me or use the sting of needles to steal my pain after the accident.

"I needed a release. When the grief and hopelessness felt like it was swallowing me whole from losing my mother. Losing the only person who'd ever loved me, cared for me. When the agonizing torment of that night settled on my soul, even though I didn't fully comprehend what was happening, I needed a release." The pain in her explanation is palpable all these years later.

"I snuck through the kitchen drawers one afternoon when I

was on dinner prep. In the back of a junk drawer was a red BIC lighter. I'd seen him use one just like it to light the menthol cigarettes he chained-smoked. I tucked it into my waistband and ran to the bathroom. When I slipped inside and shut the door closed behind me, I pulled it free and flicked the wheel quickly. The flame blazed before my eyes, drawing me into a trancelike state before it burnt my finger, pulling me back to reality. I did it again, until the heat became too much, and the metal burnt my thumb on purpose. That burn calmed something in me, so I did it again. Only the next time when the pain hit my finger. I pulled it away and pressed it against my skin. It sizzled and the smell of burnt flesh was nauseating, but I learned if I left the lighter against my thigh until the heat dissipated, my body transferred my overwhelming internal pain."

Her weight shifts against me; she's relaxing. And the tension building in me lessens. Shoving my hips up, I flip her body underneath mine so I can look down on her. She's beautiful, broken, but so strong, and I want to consume every inch of her.

"Is he still alive?" I need to know. Her eyebrows pinch together. "The man from the group home," I coax.

"No." She doesn't elaborate, but her pupils dilate. A tinge of disappointment spikes at her news, but I still plan to dig further into that time of her life so I can find out what happened to him.

Her eyes wander down my face, and further still, and my gaze follows. Her delectable curves are on full display beneath me. Her breathing hitches at my blatant perusal and I smile down at her.

"Tell me, sweetness, should we start where we left off in the kitchen?"

SIXTEEN
KEIRA

Apartment – Bobi Andonov

What the hell was I thinking? Spilling all my dark secrets, well, almost all of them. I've never hidden my scars; I've never cared what anyone thought about them. Guys I've slept with have asked, but it's easy to brush off when you're already naked and can redirect their attention. Girls, on the other hand, were the ones who would look at me with understanding in their eyes. We didn't need to have matching scars to have matching pain.

I trace my foot up his calf to his thigh, hooking my leg around his hip before I pull him down on top of me. His face is a mere inch from mine. My tongue darts out and licks across the seam of his lips and then we're back to where we were before.

A moan breaks from the back of my throat. He's settled

between my thighs, thick and hard, pushing against the thin material separating us. I rock forward, creating a tantalizing friction. I'm desperate for more; without the barrier. His lips trail over my skin, heating it with every new touch.

Snaking my hands in the tight fit between our hips, I pull at the elastic of his sweats, easily shoving them down his legs. His legs are kicking, trying to set themselves free, but it doesn't happen. He sighs, frustration building when he rolls off me, losing his weight and heat throws me into a shiver.

He yanks the pants off, tossing them to the floor like they personally offended him. I stifle a laugh, sucking my lips in to keep from making a sound, but that does nothing to hide my grin.

"Do I amuse you, little one?" His dark tone is serious, and it shakes the laughter from my body. His hands capture my feet, yanking me toward him. Mine fly out, gripping at the comforter before my ass slides right off the end of the bed, but I stop right before then. My feet rest on his shoulders, knees thrown wide.

Once again, I'm on full display for this man. He's a master of switching from hot to cold. His domineering need for control wakes something deep within me and I give over to it.

"No." I wait, to gauge his reaction. "Sir."

His eyes light with the Devil's flame, ready to play. The sting of the snapping fabric reverberates before I hear the tear of my last bit of modesty. When the wet warmth of his tongue runs along my slick folds, ecstasy dances through my veins. My head hits the mattress and my body arches, pushing my pussy down on his tongue.

The man has skills. He's working my body over like a prodigy on the ivories. His tongue fucks in and out of me and my feet slip from his shoulders, my thighs tightening in on his head. His tongue dips lower still, coaxing the tight ring of my muscle below. I hardly register the novel sensation of his fingers coming into play when he presses them deep inside my cunt, curving upwards and rubbing against the sensitive spot that makes me quiver.

Each stroke of his tongue, mixed with the fullness of his fingers, builds my body higher. I'm so close to falling over the edge when he pulls away.

The whisper of his words blows against my heated skin. I catch my breath and look down at him, my juices glistening on the scruff across his chin. His tongue grazing slowly along his lips, enjoying every last drop. "Tell me sweetness, has anyone ever had you here?"

His finger grazes my ass, but I don't stiffen, instead I relax against his wandering hand.

"Does myself count?" I give him a wicked grin and he bites my inner thigh. Soothing the sting away with a quick kiss.

"You're going to be trouble for me, aren't you?" he asks.

But he doesn't give me the time to answer before I'm lifted from the bed, my shoulders the only point of contact. He's feasting again. His mouth is a wicked thing, never lingering long enough in one place to let me come.

His hands run along my back, ghosting against my skin, until he's got both hands full of my ass, pushing my pussy harder against his mouth, so hard I'm not even sure he can breathe.

"Oh, God. Fucking hell." I'm almost there when a loud, annoying buzz comes from the living room. My hand shoots off the bed, gripping his head. I tighten my legs, dangling over his shoulders and his mouth loses suction.

"Don't you dare fucking stop, Harkin," I demand.

His devilish grin comes right before a harsh slap to my clit.

The sting heightens my need to come, pulling a desperate moan from my throat.

The buzzing sounds again and again, but neither of us moves. This stare down is now a battle of wills, and for once, I think I may have met my match. Thankfully, today, I've won this battle because his mouth is back on me, and it only takes a few seconds before he flings me over the edge and my whole body feels like it's floating. My heels dig into his back until the bliss of my orgasm fades.

He drops my legs to the bed slowly and climbs up my body, gripping my chin. His pupils are blown when he stares down at me, and his fingers tighten. "You call my name when you come from now on. There's no room in this bed for anyone else but us; even God can't have you here, little one."

Then he's gone from the room, his stride a whirl of darkness as my eyes try to regain focus. The ceiling fan rotates overhead. I pull in a deep breath, feeling my chest expand and tighten. I hold it in, seconds pass, but I hold it until it burns. Slowly, I push it out between my lips, steadying my heart rate.

A slam from far off startles me, then footsteps sound in the hall coming back in this direction. I quickly realize there's more than one person barging loudly past his bedroom. The door to the hallway is across the room. It's cracked slightly open, and the hall light illuminates their forms, but they bustle by before I can tell who the other person is. Another door down the hall slams shut. I hope his neighbors don't mind.

Inching off the mattress, I tiptoe across the chilly floor to his closet, pulling a black button-down off the hanger. I slide it over my arms and do up the tiny red buttons. Just like his tee shirt earlier, I'm swimming in it.

Sneaking into the hall, I tread softly, but the raised voices make my efforts futile. I lean forward, pressing my ear to the door. Their conversation is muffled, and I can't make anything out.

It's maddening.

Whoever's in there interrupted our time together.

The handle twists seconds before the door pulls open slightly. My body sways forward, ready to fall with its support gone. I find my balance and turn, ready to scurry back to cover before I'm found eavesdropping. But with it cracked, their conversation is no longer hindered, and I can hear them clearly.

"Are you going to tell her?" the unknown male voice asks.

A sigh answers and then the deep timber of Harkin's voice fills the silence. "No, why would I? It's not hurting anything, and I'm not ready to have her scrambling for the hills trying to get away from me."

The other guy laughs. "You're playing with fire."

"Don't I fucking know it. But she's different, James, she's nothing like Alina."

I suck in a breath, pressing my hand to my mouth to smother the sound. This guy knew my sister, or at least knows of her. And they don't even sound like they're fighting. There's a familiarity in their banter.

"You don't even know her, kid. You've gone on what a couple of dates if you can even call them that. When I was your age, we actually had to ask a girl out, not just show up where they're eating pizza."

Oh my god, they're talking about me.

That little shit; I knew he was watching. I'd never seen him in Luigi's before, but twice after our run in when I'd been waiting for my food, he'd come in. I knew it wasn't a coincidence. I'm too caught up in my thoughts to register the door opening the rest of the way before it's too late.

Two sets of eyes bore into me, Harkin, and my driver. I'm confused.

They know each other?

I back away slowly. This time I turn and run for it. I only make it a couple steps before hands wrap around my waist, twisting me quickly before I'm flung over his shoulder.

I yelp at the hard smack landing on my bare ass. "Fuck!"

"I don't think so sweetness. Bad girls don't get rewarded."

A chuckle behind us grabs my attention, and I fling my eyes up. My driver is still standing in the doorway, a smile tugging on his lips, his eyes on me.

"Put me down." I thrash against Harkin, but he just tightens his hold around my thighs.

"You should go, James, and try not to interrupt again," Harkin says lightheartedly.

"You got it, sir." James skirts around us, laughing the entire way to the front door.

"Harkin, I'm serious. Put me down right now!" I pound against his back, my fury building. I don't know what's going on here and it's not fair.

"Tsk. Tsk. Little one, don't you know it's rude to spy on people and listen in on conversations that aren't for your ears?" he chastises.

He flings me forward and my ass hits the couch, the height of the fall causing me to lose balance and bounce to the floor. I shuffle up off the ground and try to rise off the seat, but Harkin's arms box my body in. I look up into those soulful, dead eyes. He doesn't show any anger but looks amused.

"I'm leaving." I push at his arms, but they don't budge.

If he thinks he's got me, he's got another thing coming.

I pull my legs out and arch over the back of the couch, sticking the landing and running for the front door.

Yanking it open and stepping into the hall, I quickly look up for the exit sign glowing overhead, and run toward it. Harkin's yelling at me from behind, but I don't stop. I'm pissed, and if he thinks he can just keep secrets and bully me into submission, he'd be wrong.

My breathing is labored when I finally hit the last step and reach the building's front door. I mentally add cardio to my to-do-list as I swing the glass open and run right into James.

For fuck's sake.

His eyes scan my body and widen with surprise. I follow his gaze, realizing then that I'm barefoot and don't have my purse. I don't even know what time it is, but when I look across the street Luigi's is open, and that's my opportunity. I'm not thrilled about having to walk across the street without shoes, but I refuse to go back upstairs and get my things.

James sees the decision in my stance and steps in front of me.

"Keira, wait," he implores, but I shove past him. The pressure behind me changes, and I know Harkin is there. I jolt forward, looking both ways and making a run for the other side of the street. My name's being yelled over car horns and the bustle of people on the sidewalks, but I don't stop. I push open the front door to Luigi's and slam the door behind me.

Great, now I'm slamming doors.

"Keira." The slimy accented way he says my name makes my body freeze. I don't have to look up to know Marco's working today. The door thuds against my body. I push against it, not wanting to let Harkin in.

Marco's attention moves past me to the guy banging on the front door and his eye cast back to me, back to my disheveled appearance, my barely there clothing, and my uncovered feet.

He rips me away from the door, swinging it open to an infuriated Harkin.

Here we go.

Marco's yelling in Italian, so I have no clue what he's saying, but the way he's saying it rivals Harkin's fury.

This was not how I imagined today playing out.

My anger at Harkin wanes as I watch the screaming match in front of me play out. Hands are waving through the air. They look seconds away from throwing punches. I step between them quelling the scene for a moment.

"Enough!" I yell at them. Marco has no business getting involved. I assumed Sal would be the only one in the pizza shop. "I just need my spare key." My eyes drift to the register as I nod in that direction, hoping Marco will get the hint. But he's too busy staring between me and Harkin.

I roll my eyes and march toward the counter, ready to get the key myself, but Harkin pulls me back and over to the side door to the apartment entrance. His other hand holds up my small crossbody and shoes. That's why it took him so long to catch up to me.

I want to snatch my belongings away from him, but the look he gives me knocks the wind from my lungs. He might not be yelling anymore, but the tick in his jaw lets me know he's still fuming under his quiet demeanor.

His fingers interlace with mine tightly. I try to pull free, but we're stuck together, and he refuses to lessen his hold. I could fight him, but what would that get me? A bigger scene in front of Marco, giving him more of a reason to try to intervene. That's the last thing I want, instead I let him pull me through the side door. He heads up the stairs, dragging me along back to my place. But then we're standing in front of my apartment, and I have no intention of letting him come in. After all the theatrics and commotion downstairs, I need time to decompress.

Too bad for me, he doesn't agree. Once the door's unlocked, he shoves his way past and walks in like he owns the damn place. He doesn't even stop to wait for me to close and re-lock the door, he just makes his way down the hall into my living room. He drops the rest of my stuff on the kitchen counter and turns to stare me down. His fists clench at his sides.

I slowly tread in his direction, stopping a few feet away. "What do you think you're doing?" I'm so overwhelmed by his unwarranted behavior I'm getting whip lash. He was playful on the couch, but my temper got the best of me, and I did what I do best—run.

His playfulness disappeared completely downstairs. I've never seen him act like that and it's just another reminder of how little I know about this man in front of me, even after years of watching his life through a screen. Now I'm standing before him, that anger still courses through his veins, and I'm not sure if I'm going to get the playful Harkin from earlier or that madman from downstairs.

SEVENTEEN
HARKIN

Silhouette Pushloop Remix – Leon Switch, Truth, Lelijveld, Pushloop

W*hat am I doing?* What the hell did she think *she* was doing, running from my apartment in nothing but my shirt? No shoes, no purse, no panties. I fume at the realization. How far did she think she'd get? Seeing her throwing all reason out the window and run like her life depended on it, left me no choice but to take chase.

"Who is he?" The only thing I really need answers to at this point.

"Who?" Her voice is small, drawn in.

"The man downstairs who seems to think he has some sort of claim on you."

Like anyone else could have you but me.

Her eyes fall to the ground, but she doesn't answer me.

Instead, she walks toward the couch and plops down, throwing an arm over her eyes as she lays back and props her feet over the arm.

"Just go Harkin, I'm done." She sounds like it, too. I'm quickly distracted from her plea by the smooth skin of her upper thighs now exposed from my shirt riding up. I'm not going anywhere.

Her face tilts in my direction, an eye peeking out behind her arm, checking the status of my departure. "Fine, suit yourself," she snaps at me, ever the feisty temptress, before she rolls into the couch back and tucks her legs toward her body.

I use her dismissal to my advantage and take in her apartment now that I'm not sneaking through it. It's small and old. You can tell she does her best to keep it looking nice— well, as nice as possible with the dingy wallpaper and yellowed laminate counters. It all sticks out because there's not much to her space. No girly throw pillows or pictures with unnecessary phrases like—*LIVE.LAUGH.LOVE* on the walls.

I drop onto the couch beside her and reach up to pull a strand of hair behind her ear. Her eyes are closed, but my gentle movement makes her grin.

"Just tell me," I try again.

Her whole body heaves an exaggerated sigh. She doesn't shift in my direction or turn to look at me. "Why does it matter? He's no one, Harkin."

A no one wouldn't have reacted the way he did downstairs, like they have some sort of history built up between them. "He was ready to knock my lights out. He's either a scorned ex-lover or a brother of sorts. Just tell me which, so I know how to handle him."

"God, you're so annoying," she whispers under her breath before her body pushes upward. She quickly tucks her feet under herself so she's kneeling on the couch next to me. I lean back, adjusting into a more comfortable position, and wait for her explanation.

"He's literally nobody to me. He's my landlord's son. The landlord also owns the pizza place downstairs, hence him always being around. He picks up my rent and drops off packages occasionally. I try to keep him out of my apartment." She pauses and picks at her nails. I stiffen. I'll go down there right now and finish what we almost started.

Her hand falls to my knee and she squeezes. "Nothing's happened." Her eyes soften when she looks up at me. "He's just handsy if he gets the chance. I've shot him down more times than I can count, but I need this apartment. It's cheaper than anything I can afford in this area of the city, even with multiple roommates."

Her clarification does little to snuff out my outrage, but I'll push it down and save it for another time when I can deal with her *little problem* myself. She must see the shift in my attitude because she climbs onto me, straddling my lap. Her hands clasp the sides of my face, ensuring my focus.

"Don't do anything." Her tone is serious. It's cute. I smirk at her, about to agree, knowing full well I have no intention of heeding her warnings.

"Harkin, I'm serious. You don't know."

What the hell does that mean? "Don't know what, little one?"

Her hands drop to my shoulders, but her eyes wander to a spot behind me.

"Keira?"

"Who owns this building. You just shouldn't intervene; I can handle him. Trust me, I've been doing it for months."

"Fine, I'll drop it," I promise her and drop a kiss to her

nose. My phone vibrates against my thigh, and I check the time on my watch, realizing how late I am. I tighten my hold under her knees and stand, bringing her with me.

"I have to go, sweetness." She leans forward, fusing her lips to mine. A deep groan builds in my throat, but I pull away and slide her body down from my hold. I've had this meeting set up for weeks, otherwise I'd blow it off in a heartbeat to stay here with her. I pull her with me to the front door.

"Lock it behind me."

Her eyes roll at my request. "I've lived by myself for a long time, Harkin. I think I've got it covered."

"Humor me." I drop one last quick kiss to her lips and head down the hall.

THE AFTERNOON SUN shuts out of the room completely as soon as the door swings closed. The dark wooden oval meeting table takes up the entire small room. Two men I've never met before sit at one end, a mound of paperwork spread in front of them. Their whispered conversation halts when my hands press against the smooth wood table.

"Gentlemen, I'm here. How can I help you?"

The older man on the right clears his throat and sifts through the papers until he finds the one he's looking for. He slides it down in my direction. I scan it quickly and look back up at the pair of them.

The younger man, probably a couple years older than me, pulls a pack of smokes from his jacket. He's watching me, waiting for something while he packs the nicotine unnecessarily before pulling one free and lighting up.

"What do you want me to do with these?" I ask.

The paper has rows and rows of what looked like bank account numbers.

"I'm not an accountant. I'm not sure where you got my card, but that's not the type of work I do." Dropping the paper to the table, I swing around to leave, coming face-to-face with a man who looks like he might've had a former career in the W.W.E. The slide of a gun cocking sounds behind me.

"Sit, Mr. Greyson." The thick Italian accent rolls over my name and the hairs on the back of my neck prick. The giant in front of me nods back to the table, reaching around me to pull out the chair before shoving me back down.

"You must have me confused with someone else." I hope he takes the bait, there's something about them that screams don't take the job. It's probably the Corleone vibes they're throwing off.

"Well, that's not exactly all you can do now, is it, Harkin?" The younger man asks. The gun sits on the table in front of him, his finger resting precariously on the trigger.

"Look at that paper in front of you again. Those numbers are accounts—which I'm assuming from your hasty retreat you've realized."

"Are they your accounts?" I don't know why the ignorant question comes fumbling from my mouth.

"That's not important. What is, however, is that we need you to locate them?" That's all he gives me. His dead eyes stare at me across the table as he flicks ash from his cigarette to the floor.

"That's all? You just want me to locate them?"

"Get the bank information. We need them in three days." They both rise from the table and disappear into the wall, a hidden door popping open and swinging close. I snag the paper from the table and head for the opposite exit. Their bodyguard is no longer behind me.

Shielding my eyes from the sun as I prop the door open, I spot the black SUV and James in the driver's seat.

That's the last time I take an anonymous meeting.

I'm not sure what exactly I just got myself into, but I have a sneaking suspicion that there's no way out of. I hop in the front seat and slam the paper on the center console.

"Bad meeting?" He looks down at the paper and then up at me.

"I've got some work to do. Drop me back at my place. Where is she?"

He shifts the car into drive and takes off toward my apartment. "She's still at home. All's quiet. But..." He pauses, looking at the clock on the radio.

"But, what!" I snap.

"Nothing about her. She's good. But Marco, I did a background check after your brief run-in this afternoon. You won't like who his father is."

"James, I swear to God, if you don't spit it out right now," I snipe through clenched teeth.

"Angelo Dentico is Marco's father." He waits for me to understand, but the name isn't ringing any bells.

"And who's, Angelo Dentico."

His eyes shoot to me, a stunned expression crossing his face.

"You mean to tell me you moved into this neighborhood and didn't realize whose neighborhood you were moving into? I thought you were smarter than that."

His huff of impatience is wearing mine thin. I'd heard whispering around the block, but I never put any stock in it. It's the 21st century, not the 1920's.

"He's got ties to the Italian mob. He's not high up, but I'd bet money that pizza shop's a place to clean money."

I slam my hand against the dash over and over. This day is just one piece of bad news after the other. It's complete shit.

"Is she roped in with them?"

"I don't know, Boss. There wasn't a lot of time. I got lucky with Marco because the idiot's got an arrest record the length of a CVS receipt."

"Send it to me."

"Already waiting for ya." The car pulls up in front of the building and I hop out, pausing before I make my way inside.

"Hey, James?"

"Yeah."

"Keep your cell just in case she calls you for a ride."

His nod is all the agreement I need before I make my way up to my apartment.

ONCE I HIT ENTER, the program fills the screen. The search parameters scanning through hundreds of websites at a time. Pushing away from my desk, I retreat to the kitchen for another cup of coffee. It's going to be a long night if I want to understand Marco's connection. James gave me a starting point, but I need to know her connection to them. I should have caught this before, but all my concentration was focused on *her*. Not the people who owned the damn building.

Maybe she's only a tenant, but the way he reacted this afternoon, there's not a bone in my body that isn't telling me something is up—at least with him.

On top of that, now I have to deal with this lot of account numbers. But I won't hand them over without all the information. They want the locations. I plan on finding out who they belong to first. That meeting was shady as hell.

Thinking back on it causes a memory to filter through my mind.

Men in expensively tailored suits gathered in my father's office. Thick Italian accents and raised voices. One of the men turned in the direction of the cracked door I thought I was hiding behind, out of sight. But even with the hallway dark and deserted for the night, he still saw me.

I didn't have time to turn and run before the door swung open. I expected it to be my dad standing over me pissed at my curiosity, but it wasn't him. This man was shorter and rounder, a lot rounder than my father. His jet-black hair slicked back and his eyes, his eyes haunted me for months afterward.

I'd never seen eyes as dark as this, not even on the blackest of nights when the stars refused to light up the sky or when I'd played hide and seek with my nanny's son and hid in the back of my parent's closet. No, this was the definition of the absence of color, no light reflected. They were the color of death.

He leaned down to me, dropping his voice so no one behind him could hear. "You know what happens to little boys who put their noses where they don't belong?" He asked in his broken English. My body trembled, but my head shook just an inch in answer. "They never see their families again." And then he grinned, stepped back, and slammed the door in my face.

I shake the memory from my thoughts when the coffee pot timer goes off. Filling my mug, I take in a gulp to bring myself back to the right headspace.

My apartment's dimmed down for the night. The amber glow from the lamps lining the street illuminates the night outside. But a sudden brightness snags my attention.

Glimpsing the slightest movement, I'm pulled to the window to observe.

Her curtain is open, which she never does at night. I can see as clearly as if I was looking through a telephoto lens. Her dingy orange chair sits facing the window next to the coffee table. We'd been entangled on the couch only hours earlier, but now its seats look empty without our bodies.

Everything is still. The curtain doesn't sway; the tv doesn't play. She's gone from the picture. And then it changes in slow motion. She drops into the ugly chair; she looks different relaxed, comfortable. It's then I notice she still has my shirt on. Her legs pull up and tuck under her body. She leans over and grabs a wine glass filled to the brim with red liquid. I don't know how she can drink after the night she had yesterday. You'd think blacking-out would be enough to vanquish any desire to drink.

Her lips part on the glass, she doesn't tip it back; the glass is too full for that. Instead, her throat bobs as she slowly sucks the liquid down. Her other hand tucks down beside her body and pulls out a book. She flips through the pages, resting it on her lap until she finds her spot. It's at that moment when her head snaps up, her eyes cast in my direction, and her hand with the wine glass raises in salute.

Her acknowledgement makes me want to forget about the projects I have and march over to her apartment, fling the door open, and finish what we started. But my curiosity wins out as I spin on my heels and sulk back to my office.

Dropping into my chair, I skim through the files online. The list related to the bank accounts is long. Cross-referencing is going to be a pain in the ass, but I refuse to give them information on bank accounts for anyone that doesn't deserve whatever's coming to them. Although, I have a feeling these guys expect all or nothing when it comes to reporting back. If I had any information on them other than the place where we set the meeting, I'd dig into them too.

The night is long. I couldn't stop piecing together the situation. Every new hit that came in built a clearer picture, and it's not a good one. I got up no less than eight times to check on her, even though by the third her curtain was closed, and the lights were off. It didn't stop my incessant need to walk to the window and check, in case she couldn't sleep.

Standing in front of the cork board, I analyze the pages filling every inch of space. James was right; Marco's father works for the Mob but he's no one of importance. He makes enough money, and he's smart enough to funnel it into a legitimate business. As legitimate a business can be, when it's washing cash for the biggest Italian crime family in New York.

Other than the familial connection, there was nothing specific in my search about Marco. His arrest record, on the other hand, was quite enlightening, enough so that I woke James up in the middle of the night to order a full surveillance system install for her apartment while she's at work today.

If I could force her out of that dilapidated apartment and into mine, I would—in a heartbeat. But other than kidnapping her and tying her up in the gym, I don't see that going over well. However, if that low life, piece of shit does anything to lay a finger on her, our little screaming match will be the least of his worries.

EIGHTEEN
KEIRA

Do It For Me - Rosenfield

T he last bag slams against the conveyer belt and my body shoves to the right. Tripping over my feet, I look over and see Stacey with the biggest smile on her face. "Let's go out tonight!" she basically begs.

"Girl, it's a Wednesday night. Where do you think is worth going out to?" I'm genuinely curious. We could go out for a couple of drinks anywhere, but the glint in her eyes tells me mischief is afoot.

"Red is open every night. Tonight's members only, but I still have that guy's number from that night you left early." Stacey reminds me.

Lovely, she wants to go to the that club.

"Do we really have to go there? If it's members only, is it only going to be upstairs?"

She drops me a knowing smile.

Fuck my life. "Fine. Swing by my place on your way over."

STARING INTO THE HALL MIRROR, I fix my lipstick. A knock on the door kills any free time I have left to work on my look, so I pull the door open for Stace.

"You ready?" I spout while shoving my keys in my bag.

A whistle meets my ears, and my eyes fly up. "Now, where are you going looking like that?" Harkin asks, leaning against the door frame.

"I'm going out with a friend. She should be here any minute. I assumed you were her, or I would have checked before I opened."

He stiffens.

"You always check. You understand me." His tone is severe. Dropping my eyes to the floor, I nod in understanding.

"Keirrraaaaa!" I hear my name being screeched down the hall before Stace comes into view.

"You ready to go?" Her eyes roam over Harkin's body. When her eyes finally draw away from him and find my expectant gaze, she mouths: *who's this*?

"Harkin, Stace. Stace, Harkin."

"We've met." He deadpans at her.

"Okay, well, officially introduced then. And as you can see, we're just on our way out. Maybe text next time."

His eyebrows raise and I know I'm playing with fire.

Stacey leans against the wall. "Well, I mean, the more the merrier, right?" she says innocently.

This girl is trouble.

She knows a little about what's happened between us, but we were so busy at work today that I couldn't share the entire story.

"I'm sure he's got plans, Stace, plus aren't we meeting your friend?"

She looks at me and I know trouble's brewing behind her gaze.

"Yeah, but it won't be a problem. *He* can get us all in." She winks at me.

"Get you in where?" Harkin questions.

Ugh, this is what I was hoping to avoid.

If he knows where we're going, he'll assume Red is the type of place I like to go to.

"We're going to *The Red Door*," Stace pipes up before I can say otherwise.

He immediately looks at me, inspecting my reaction, and shakes his head. "It's fine, I can get you in."

Now it's my turn to gape in surprise. "What do you mean, you can get us in?" I ask.

"I'm a member," he says nonchalantly.

"The fuck you are," I bite out. The statement spills from my lips involuntarily.

His body moves swiftly, engulfing mine. Stace moves up a couple of steps.

"What was that, little one?"

"You're not going with us?" I attempt confidence, but it fades as soon as his piercing blues burrow under my skin.

He leans in, his lips skimming lightly against my cheek. "Over my dead body, will you step inside that club without me, sweetness."

My breath hitches at his dominance, which quickly causes a tightening to spread inside my core. I hate how easily he affects my body. It's a traitor every time he's around. My brain fights to stay strong and not give in. But what's the use? When I know the taste of letting go, he's given me, is what I crave, deep down. Unfortunately, for us it's shoved under my innate need for independence and a hatred for being told what to do.

"Fine." I push away from his proximity. "Let's go then."

He nods and we all turn down the hall and head for the street.

THE CLUB IS JUST as I remember, except this time downstairs is empty of people dancing, and the bass isn't pumping loudly. I guess members only means upstairs activities flow into the open bar downstairs.

I watch as couples pair off to booths and benches above. Tables full of God knows what line the back wall. Pulling Stace in, I whisper in her ear, "What are you getting us into?"

She just chuckles at my concern and heads toward a tall man halfway up the stairs.

Harkin, on the other hand, hasn't dropped his hand from my waist. He tightens his hold as I move to follow Stace.

"No, we're staying down here. Let me buy you a drink." He pulls me toward the bar. "Whiskey, neat. And a club soda with a twist."

I glare in his direction but take the drink from the bartender, anyway.

I lean in close to him and ask, "Why are we staying down here?" As I nip his earlobe in the process.

"Because if I take you upstairs, in that, someone else might get ideas." His eyes find mine and there's no playfulness inside them. "I don't share."

I wrap myself against his body, draining my glass before slamming it down on the bar. Reaching up to grip his chin, I ask, "And what makes you think I care?" Ripping my body away, I make for the stairs, on a mission to find Stace and piss Harkin off. He won when it came to coming, but this one's mine. I have no plans to let anyone else have me, but the fact that he thinks he can just mark his claim because of the other night and keep me from having any fun, doesn't sit right with me.

He's hot on my heels, but I sprint up the stairs—hoping to hell I don't twist an ankle—halting at the top where a bouncer stands. It's the same guy Stace knew for us to get in the first time. He ignores me and looks over my shoulder, his chin nodding in recognition.

"You're going to regret this, little one." Harkin's clipped tone fills my head as his firm hand finds my lower back. He pushes me forward to the left and back, past the occupied booths. I swallow down the nervous energy pulsing through my veins.

Each section we pass plays like a different erotic film. The further back we go, the more obscure it gets. I drop my eyes in shock when we come across a man dressed only in tiny leather shorts. A tall woman adorned from neck to toe, in a tight leather body suit, stands behind him, donning a short leash.

The pressure to keep moving falls from my back and Harkin slips beside me to take a seat in a high backed leather chair. If they'd carved it from wood or stone, I'd say it was a throne. I don't know what I'm supposed to do now. The plan was to find Stace. I didn't think Harkin would whisk me away on my own.

"Come here, little one," Harkin purrs from across the small alcove, his foot propped up against the opposite knee. He's leaned back, relaxed, and I take the opportunity to ogle him. His black slacks wrap delectably around his toned thighs. He's rolled the sleeves of the dark claret dress shirt, freeing the swirling black ink that dances across his skin.

He's dangerously beautiful. The red-shaded ambiance of the space intensifies his kingly stature. When he snaps his fingers, I shake out of my trance and strut toward him, ready to take a seat. But just as I'm about to sit, he points to the space on the ground in front of him.

"Kneel." His command leaves little room for hesitation, but I do. His eyebrows are quick to draw up in question.

I've gotten myself into a lose-lose situation. If I give in, he wins. If I don't and walk away, I lose. I sit with that for a moment, contemplating the options in my head. It dawns on me that playing into his hand could end up being in my favor, but I'll have to surrender to find out.

I shrug off my stubbornness, and do as he asked, kneeling before him. The ground is ice-cold against my knees, and the heels of my stilettos dig into my ass. His dark gaze is piercing from this angle, but he doesn't move. A shuffle behind me pulls his attention. I make to get up, but his hand falls to my shoulder to cease my movement.

"Can I get you anything, sir?" Her whinny voice is as irritating as a fruit fly buzzing about.

"Macallan, neat and a vodka soda with a twist."

"And will your booth be open tonight, sir?" she asks.

Open? What the hell does that mean?

Harkin looks back down at me and runs the pad of his thumb across my bottom lip. My tongue juts out to meet it. His breath hitches as he pulls away and clenches his fist.

"Yes, but only for observation."

"Very well. I'll put you on the board." Her heels clack against the floor as she retreats.

I sway back to stand; my knees are going to have bruises if I'm down here any longer, and my toes are falling asleep.

"Stay," he commands

There's that tone again.

If he didn't absolutely disarm me, I'd be ready to throw hands at his demeaning demands, but I'm curious to see what comes next. I wait what feels like minutes before he finally looks back at me.

"You know, I would've thought you learned from your mistakes. Although, I guess it's partially my fault. I should have punished you the first time it happened. Instead of letting it slide."

"Punish me? I—" I don't understand what he means by that.

"Ahh now, little one. You've already got one coming to you. Do you really want to add another for interrupting me?"

Who is this man before me?

He's alluring and infuriating all in one breath. His commands fill me with fury, while his actions smother out the flames before the inferno can grow. I'm fighting a constant battle of wills within myself to push his boundaries one moment while wanting to surrender completely the next.

A round tray infiltrates my peripheral as a hand places two glasses on the small table in the corner.

"Thank you, Cass," Harkin says.

"You're welcome, sir."

Could she try to sound any more seductive?

You're welcome, sir. I mock in my head, irritated by the continued interruptions from this girl.

A sly smile pulls at Harkin's lips, and he tips back his glass. "You're absolutely green with envy, sweetness. Now tell me why that is?"

As I bite my lip, I debate on denying his claim. "Have you been here with her?" I'm disappointed by the neediness that seeps through my tone.

His glass clanks against the table before he leans forward, his face mere centimeters from where I'm kneeling. "And if I have?"

My head shakes of its own accord, just a tweak so small it could have been a muscle twitch, but it wasn't, and he knows it.

He studies me, his eyes drifting across my face. I set it in stone, willing my features to fall and harden.

"You, my little dark one, are the only person I've been here with."

His confession stills my erratic heart until his lips crash against mine so suddenly, I'm thrown back against the force. His hand meets the nape of my neck and holds me steady so he can plunder my mouth. I moan against his assault.

Voices seep into our surroundings, but I push them back, falling deeper into him. A finger traces down the exposed skin of my back, and I shiver at the contradictory sensations. But I'm left feeling empty when Harkin pulls away in a flash.

"Hands off," he snarls.

My brain is in a fog, but my hands are in my lap. I'm confused by his outburst.

"Sorry, didn't think it would hurt." My eyes widen at the third party I was unaware had joined us.

"Our booth is for observation only. If you can't heed that warning, move along." The man says nothing, but he doesn't get up to leave either. Harkin reaches over and grabs our drinks, handing me mine before he throws his back and drains the remaining amber liquid.

I slowly sip mine, but I can't stomach more than a gulp

before I'm handing it back over. Harkin holds his hand out for me. I grab on, and he pulls my body up flush against his where he stands.

"Turn around." The command is more enthralling when he whispers it directly across my skin. I spin and stop, taking in the small crowd that has gathered here with us. Harkin's hand falls across my lower stomach and pulls me in tight to his body.

"This is your last chance to take my hand and go back downstairs," he tells me.

"No." I shake my head in refusal. My need to be obstinate, is stronger than my will for modesty in an unknown setting.

"Have it your way then, little one."

I hear it before I feel it: the rustle of something being pulled free. Then he wrenches my hands backwards, encircling my wrists in a firm hold. My body automatically pulls against the restraints, but there's no freeing them. I stop fighting when I'm shoved forward to bend over the arm of the chair Harkin had been in.

His hand glides up the back of my leg, trailing along the inside of my thigh. A nudge of his foot against mine, pushes them apart. My little black bandeau dress fights against the movement. His fingers grip the hem and shove the dress over my ass. The thin g-string leaves little to the imagination for the crowd.

The exposure cools my heated flesh, but my core tightens in anticipation. The whole of his hand grabs my pussy. "Mmm, so wet for me already, sweetness. Let's see what we can do about that."

I squirm against him, fighting to find an ounce of friction, but he doesn't give me what I need.

"Eyes on me," he demands, and I snap my head to the left, eyes casting over my shoulder awkwardly.

I thought he looked delicious earlier, relaxed in the chair. But now, as he stands behind me, his eyes set ablaze as he takes in my body on display, he's devastatingly intoxicating. The outline of his thick cock is hard to miss and my mouth waters at the thought of taking him in my mouth here and now, audience be damned.

"Do you know what I do to little shadows that listen to conversations not meant for them?" he whispers, his tone dripping with sinful intent.

I'm so enthralled by this switch in his demeanor, that I play right along, shaking my head *no*.

"You, sweetness, were not supposed to be listening to the conversation and hiding behind my office door, but did I get mad?"

Again, my head shakes of its own volition.

"But you did, didn't you? You took off before we could talk it through. You put yourself in potential danger, did you not?"

I pause, playing the situation over in my head. I was so aggravated with him in that moment; I didn't care what I was doing, hence the fleeing sans shoes. A sharp pinch on my inner thigh reminds me to answer.

"Yes."

Another pinch, sharper this time, stings my inner thigh.

"Yes, what?"

"Yes, sir," I squeak out.

"That's not how we handle things between us." He pauses and steps away, walking over to a young guy that's sitting on the couch. He's no longer alone; a cute redhead drapes herself around his side, stroking his cock through his pants.

"You wanted to play. Give me your belt." Harken waits as the guy does what he's asked.

He's in command of all of us.

The thick leather hangs from his hand. He folds it in half and snaps the material together. The echo of the sound fills the room. My body automatically clenches, clueing into what's about to come.

"You ran. You put yourself in harm's way and you caused an unnecessary fight." I want to sass back at the last one. That was all him and his issues, but now's not the time or place.

His callused palm rubs soothingly across my rounded globes, warming the flesh.

"You'll take five as your punishment and count each one for me. You'll stay still, and you will not scream. If you can't handle it at any moment, you will say your safeword, black. Do you understand?"

Am I really going to let him do this to me?

This exhibition is a new line I'm not just tripping over. I'm jumping off a damn cliff, trusting the fall won't kill me. I pull in a deep breath and count back from five.

"Yes, sir."

The anticipation builds as he drags the leather against my skin. My dress is still hiked over my ass, leaving it bare and waiting.

Wack.

The first slap stings my flesh, and I clench against the assault but breathe through it.

"One," I whisper into my shoulder.

"Louder, little one."

Wack. Slap.

"Two. Three." His pacing changes.

With each new blow, the pressure increases, and the bite of

the leather takes a fraction longer to subside. He pauses, his palm smooths the worked skin.

As the pain finally subsides, his hand pulls away. He bends against my back until his lips meet my ear. "You're doing so good for me, sweetness. Two more. Breathe."

I do as he says. As the breath leaves my lungs, the fourth crack breaks the silence. My teeth chomp down on my bottom lip to stifle the scream that wants to break free.

"Four," I groan.

After that, there's no way in hell I want to add to this. He doesn't soothe the space, instead the final spank falls.

"Five."

I don't move. I don't speak. A lone tear traces down my cheek, but I can't reach up to wipe it away. He pulls my dress back down over the battered area. The fabric is hot, tight, and I wish it wasn't against my skin.

I'm yanked from my bent position. The makeshift cuffs release before I'm spun around quickly, and I almost lose my footing. I can't look at him—or maybe I don't want to. Not right now. Not when I know my face is a window to my emotions.

His rough hand cups my cheek, forcing my chin up, but my gaze drops to his shoulder. The pad of his thumb wipes slowly across my face, removing any remnant of wetness. His gentleness seizes my attention, and I wish it hadn't, because the eyes staring back at me are full of concern before it breaks into something that looks an awful lot like pride.

The warmth of his hand encasing mine soothes my damaged ego. Tugging me forward, he squeezes us quickly past rows of onlookers. My face heats under their attention, but I keep pace until we're down the stairs and almost out the front doors.

I stop dead in my tracks. Harkin's momentum wrenches me forward, but I refuse to budge. "I have to find Stacey."

His head shakes, unwavering. Ripping my fingers from his grasp, I cross my arms. I would have stomped my foot too, if I thought it would have gotten me any further.

He stalks toward me, filling the space separating us. "She's fine." He nods up to the next floor, but I can't seem to find the strength to turn around and face it. "Robert's got an eye on her. He knows we're leaving."

He doesn't wait for me to double check his promise. No, his arm snakes around my shoulder as he folds me in next to him before we make our way out of the club and into the night.

NINETEEN
HARKIN

Power Over Me – Dermont Kennedy

There's no way I'd drop her off to be alone after that scene. I knew she wouldn't be happy about it, but I figured she could at least handle it. Technically she did, she didn't move; she didn't scream, and she didn't safeword out. When I released her hands and saw the tear sliding down her face—not one from blissed out pleasure—it took my breath away.

"Harkin, I just want to go home." I don't acknowledge her plea. Instead, I pull her along down the hall toward my apartment, and then into my bedroom. Her heels dig in at the threshold.

"Trust me. You did earlier." Reaching up, I run my fingers through her thick locks and grab the nape of her neck, pulling her forehead to mine. Her eyes are glazed, like she's running on autopilot, but she doesn't resist the rest of the path into the bathroom.

Leaning her against the counter, I toe off my shoes and unbutton my shirt before flinging it into the hamper. I flick on the taps to the tub, drizzling in the lone bottle of scented oil that was here when I moved into the apartment. The vapor from the hot water mixes with the oil, filling the room with scents of vanilla and something fruity.

"Come here." She doesn't move. "Keira!" I say, a little more forcefully, trying to draw her out. Her eyes pop up from the floor, swinging in my direction. Crooking two fingers at her, I motion for her to come instead. She does.

"Arms up." I grip the hem of her dress and slide it up over her body. The quiet hiss of air between her teeth doesn't escape my ears. Grasping her shoulders, I turn her body around to face the opposite wall. The red welts crisscross her chalky skin. Something shifts in her demeanor as her body stiffens at my touch. Her hands tighten into fists.

"It's fine Harkin, just go. I just need some time alone to… regroup." She steps over the lip of the bathtub, sinking down until the water hits her chin.

I drop to the floor on my knees beside her, snagging a washcloth from the basket. The fabric soaks up the steaming water. Reaching for her hand, my fingers interlace with hers, stretching out her arm for me to rub down. Her chin rests against her knee, her eyes trailing my movements.

"Why didn't you stop me?" My words break the silence between us.

"I didn't…" She pauses, swishing her other hand through the water. "It was intense and overwhelming."

"Then why didn't you use your safeword?"

"I didn't want to," she bites out.

I wasn't expecting that answer from her reaction.

"I've never done anything like that before." Her confession stills my heart.

"And you just let me... in front of everyone?" Her shoulders shrug. I told her she'd regret running, but after all this I can't help but feel like the regret is all mine.

Pushing up from the floor, I storm straight into the bedroom, finding the first free object, I chuck it against the opposite wall.

How could I be so fucking stupid?

I should have known. I'm still throwing anything I can get my hands on when wet arms wrap around my middle. Her heated flesh burns my sweat-soaked skin.

"Stop," she sighs into my back. "I'm fine. I promise." Her dewy nakedness slithers around to my front. It's hard not to be distracted by the goddess in front of me. Her soft curves pressed indecently against me. Small hands capture my face and dip my chin, forcing my eyes to focus on her.

"Do I look upset?" I study her face for any semblance of a tell she's lying. But her genuine concern is the only emotion shining through her topaz eyes.

"Never again," I murmur against her palm as I crop a swift kiss, my hands reaching out to rest on her hips. "Do you want me to take you home?" My fingers twitch, wanting to pull her in closer, deny her the option to leave my place.

"Do you want me to go?" Her taunting tone's alluring. If it were up to me, I'd have her on the bed, laid on her back, screaming my name in the next thirty seconds. I rein in my need to be between her thighs and drop a sweet kiss to her forehead before pulling away and walking to the dresser.

"Here, put this on." I fling my arm back, a threadbare tee shirt held out in her direction. She quickly pulls it over her head. It might cover her body, but it does nothing to tame the sensuality she exudes. Her hands pull down on the hem, trying to stretch the material a little longer, but it bounces back as soon as it slips through her fingers.

"Nothing I haven't seen before, sweetness." I smile and shake my head, turning to leave the room.

Her light footsteps pad down the hall, following close behind. I quickly pull out the only ingredients I can find to whip up a late dinner.

"He cooks? I thought it was a fluke last time."

"Man's got to eat." I deadpan.

"Well then, what are you making me?" Her eyes shift around me. "For fourth meal?" Her chuckle fills the room and lightens the mood.

"Please tell me you're not one of those girls who says she's gluten free, even though she's not."

She points to her chest. "Foster kid, remember? I'll eat whatever you serve up."

Good.

"Do me a favor: open that cabinet to my right, and on the top, pull out the bag of pasta."

"Where are your pots?" she asks.

I nudge my foot to my bottom left. While she's digging through to find the container, I finish chopping the onions, garlic, and basil. The can of whole peeled tomatoes sits in a bowl ready for squeezing before they're added in with the aromatics.

"Want to get a little dirty?" I tease over my shoulder.

Her hip bumps against me and I take her in. She's light on her feet, a small content smile gracing her lips. She looks good in my shirt, in my kitchen, barefoot, and playful.

"Tell me what you need, boss," she says.

I shift her in front of me, caging her in with my arms against the counter. Grabbing her hands, I shove them into the bowl of tomatoes, and she rears back against my chest, not expecting it. When I fist my hands around hers, forcing her to squeeze, she shivers.

"Gross, that feels nasty." She laughs, looking up at me over her shoulder. I can't resist and drop a kiss to her nose.

"Make sure you get them all. Then, we'll add them to the pan." Letting go of her hands, I pull mine free of the mess and wash them quickly, checking the water for a boil. Pinching the salt from a small bowl on the counter, I season the water and dump the bag of pasta in, setting a timer for five minutes.

"Done." She perks up.

"Add it in slowly and stir." She does as I ask, stealing a wooden spoon from the jar on the counter.

"Where'd you learn to cook?"

I take in a deep breath. "I'd love to say it was from spending time with my grandmother as she passed down generations of family recipes, but that's not the case. A year ago, I wouldn't have even been able to make you pasta and canned sauced." I let out a sad snicker. "The truth is, after about two months of nothing but take out, even in a city like New York, I was over it. So, I googled the top ten easiest meals to make."

Her eyes swing in my direction, big as saucers. "You're kidding. You taught yourself how to make something that uses…" she picks up the bunch of green herbs from the counter and shakes it in my face, "Whatever this is."

"Basil." I snatch it from her grip. "Not at first, but after a few months, I broadened my horizons. Especially once I found the Saturday farmer's market a couple of blocks over at Westbrook Park."

"Well, aren't you just full of surprises today?" Her cheeks flush a hypnotizing shade of pink, but she shifts quickly, shielding it from me. "And a walking contradiction, to boot."

"What exactly is that supposed to mean?" I question.

She spins quickly on her heels, her hand flying up and down in my direction. "Look at you," she pauses, "you're the poster child for every mother's nightmare. Yet you cook with fresh ingredients from the farmer's market. You obviously have money." Her hand goes flying again as if to make her point. "But you don't seem to work. And..." There's something else on the tip of her tongue, but she stalls.

"And?" I tease.

Her fingers twist in the hem of my shirt—an endearing nervous tick.

"Your hard." She back-peddles. "Stern, I mean. First at the bar and then again tonight at the club. Yet, that falls away and you protect and even care for me." Her eyes lift to mine, and I realize I could easily get lost in their hidden depths, like a dense forest on a foggy day. "I'm not used to it, is all, and I hardly even know you."

I close the mere inches between us and snag her hands free from my shirt, holding them hostage.

"What happened tonight..." Now it's my turn to stop and clarify my thoughts in my head before possibly scaring her off forever. "Shouldn't have happened." Her body stiffens in my hold. "I only mean that I took advantage of the situation. I let my anger and irritation get the better of me. But you have to understand that was me in an uninhibited state. That's what that club offers its members."

"You regret it?" She looks hurt.

"Yes, we should have had a conversation first. Set boundaries. Like you said, we hardly know each other and then I just do that without a plan. It's unacceptable."

Her hands forcefully pull from my grasp. She tries to scooch by me, but I grip her waist to keep her near.

"But," I declare, "at the same time, no, I don't regret what we did. The way you responded to my commands. The way you reacted to my touch. Watching you give in and take it, that's why I'd do it again."

The timer for the pasta defuses the building tension between us and we fade back into the comfortable flow of prepping dinner. The pasta's tossed with the simple sauce and topped with the fresh basil. Instead of dishing it up, I take the fork and drag the serving bowl to the seating side of the island and drop onto the stool. Keira tries to take her own seat, but I haul her into my lap instead.

The first taste on her tongue rips a moan from her lips. The sound goes straight to my cock, hardening it to stone. I shift readjusting but she catches on continuing the theatrics as I continue to feed her bite after bite.

"You're killing me." I groan.

"Hmm?" The cat that ate the canary smirk on her face lets me know she has no intention of holding back.

The fork clatters in the bowl as my last string of patience breaks. She looks over at me, a small spread of sauce on the corner of her mouth. My finger wipes it away, giving me the first taste when I lick it clean.

"Mmm, delicious."

Her eyes lock on my lips, heavy with desire. I know if I don't create some distance, the pasta won't be the only thing consumed tonight. I shift her weight, dropping her feet to the floor as I stand and grab her hand. "Let's get you to bed."

"But I'm not tired."

"You need to rest. You have work tomorrow." Pulling her back down the hall to my room, I lead her to the bed and watch as she so casually crawls in like she owns just as much of it. She immediately tucks herself into the right side, the opposite side I sleep on, and gazes up at me expectantly.

Leaning over the bed, my lips fall to her forehead, and her body relaxes. "Sleep. I'll be back in a bit."

"Wait." She jolts forward. "Where are you going?"

"I have a quick errand to run. I'll be back in an hour or so. Don't worry, I'll set the alarm."

She moves to kick off the blankets and get out, but I stop her. "What are you doing?"

"I'll just go home; I'm not going to stay here if you're leaving."

"Stop, it's the middle of the night. Just stay. I'll be back soon."

"Harkin, it's fine. I live across the street."

"Yeah, and I'll be back soon. When I get back, I want to get into bed and find your warm body waiting for me." My tone leaves little for argument's sake.

"No more than an hour. Stay up and watch TV, but I'd rather you sleep." Her body deflates at my requests.

"Fine." She rips the covers up to her chin before rolling away and settling down onto the mattress.

So much sass in such a little body. I love it.

Smiling to myself, I turn and head for the door, flipping the lights off as I go.

TWENTY
KEIRA

Lilith - Ellise

A nother bag beeps against the scale. 'It's over the limit," I inform the customer.

"No it's not, I weighed it before I got here. Your scale must be off." The excuse I've heard a million times from every type of person.

"I'm going to have to charge you."

"This is ridiculous. I want to talk to your supervisor." Her manicured nails clack against the laminated counter tops.

"Sure thing, ma'am. Give me just a moment to call them over." I step away, speaking into the walkie-talkie.

"Sandra, we've got another one." Her irritated sigh makes me smile. It happens every shift. Some travelers on their way to an expensive vacation over packs and thinks it's our fault. What they don't know is we set the scales two pounds in their favor to ensure we really don't go over max weight.

Sandra's dragged footsteps pull up behind me. "What can I help you with?" Her fake customer service voice penetrates the air.

"She's saying my bag is over, and I know it's not. I just weighed it before we came."

Sandra pulls the bag off the scale, hits the tare button, and waits for it to zero out before slapping the suitcase back down. The scale waivers back and forth between fifty and fifty-one pounds before finally settling on the latter.

"Ma'am, our weight limit is thirty pounds. We can check it no problem, but it will incur the excess fee. Are you a member?" Sandra breaks the news sweetly, never dropping her winning smile.

"What's a member?" the annoyed woman asks.

"It means you either have a credit card or a frequent flyer card with us."

The woman pauses, pushing around in her purse before whipping out her wallet. She slams it down on the counter and it takes all my control not to roll my eyes at her theatrics. Her delicate fingers with the biggest rock I've ever seen pluck a card from the depths. "Like this?" Her snide attitude doesn't hide her expectation as she drops it to the counter.

Sandra pulls the card up and looks over the information, giving the look that tells me I'm going to have to let this one go. Just another rich person on their way to another extravagant vacation I'd never be able to afford, refusing to pay the extra thirty dollars for the bag.

"Well, look at that." Sandra's friendly tone smooths the tension. "You've got just what I was looking for more, Mrs. Carrington."

The line continues until it dwindles down and again, and I'm left staring at an empty check-in line until the next session of flyers come by. My eyes drop to the clock on the computer screen. Midnight. Still six more hours to go until I can hit that button and clock out. I'm ready to head home and sleep before a night of takeout and bad reality tv. The night drags on. Two more flights make it through before my watch vibrates, alerting me to the hour.

"Hey girl!" Stace's bright and chipper demeanor at six a.m. is not what I need.

"Goodnight," I grunt, typing in my passcode to the computer to clock out. I don't hang around waiting for her to talk my ear off.

THE SUBWAY HALTS at my stop, and I gather up my bags and exit, ready to drop into bed. I'm dead on my feet, shuffling along the sidewalk until the building comes into view. The flights of stairs are an extra hindrance to my energy. Lids heavy with exhaustion, my door comes into view but it's not bare like I expect. Instead, a white piece of printer paper lies against the wood.

Ripping it down, I close the door behind me and drop my bags to the floor. Slinking across to the kitchen and flipping on the lights, I finally scan the paper in my hands.

"Rent Late. 30 days to comply before eviction." I slap the paper down on the counter, pissed because I know for a fact, I sent in my rent check before the beginning of the month.

Drawing out my phone, I type in Marco's number before hitting send. The phone rings and rings before I get his voice mail. I don't even say who it is before my anger takes over.

"Marco, you know I sent in my rent check. I've never been

late a month in my year here. You better make this right before I find your father and let him know, what a..." The message clicks off mid rant.

Okay, maybe that wasn't the best way to go about it, but what the hell? If they didn't get the check, that would be one thing, but I checked my account and the money cleared. Which means someone cashed my check.

I collapse to the floor, drawing my knees to my chest when the tears fall. I could check my bank account, but I know the number in there is nothing to cover an extra month worth of rent right after I just paid it.

My phone pings in my hand: a new text.

> Hey. Want to get dinner?

HARKIN'S TEXT SITS UNANSWERED. Minutes pass before I finally push the tears from my cheeks and stand from the cold floor. I flop down on the couch; the exhaustion takes over and soon the life-changing note no longer clouds my thoughts.

Only darkness consumes.

Thud... pound... pound... pound.

Sharp noises draw me into a haze as sleep clings to my consciousness. The sounds don't stop until I push up from the couch, gaining some semblance of realization of what's going on around me.

The door. Someone's pounding on the door.

I figure it must be Harkin coming to check on me after I left him on read, but when I pull the door free, Marco stands before me. He sways in the hall, bouncing from one side of the door frame to the other. The stench of cheap beer wafts off him in waves. He stumbles forward into my apartment, and I back away quickly to keep a distance between us.

"Marco, what are you doing?"

"You called me." His predatory smile sends shivers down my spine.

"You should leave. Come back when you can coherently talk about why I called."

His hand grips my wrist, pulling me into his body. My exhaustion weighs heavily against my limbs, but I push him as hard as I can muster. He stumbles backwards, falling against the counter, shoving my mail to the floor as he grasps for stabilization.

"But you called me baby, and I came." He doesn't take the hint coming at me again. I swerve in the opposite direction.

Calling over my shoulder, I say, "Just give me a second. Have a seat."

Rifling through my nightstand in the dark of my room, my hand skims against the cool feel of my blades. I shove them into their normal spots, wishing I had my holsters strapped to me. A ring filters in from the other room, and I make a run for it, slapping my hand against the counter and bringing it to my ear before it's knocked away from me, clattering against the floor.

"What do you think you're doing?" Marco stalks toward me before my back hits the side of the fridge.

"Marco, just leave. Come back tomorrow when you can think clearly," I plead, but his eyes scan my body, paying little attention to my words.

"I'm going to take what you owe. What you've owed for months." His sneer twists the once playful look into something nightmares are made of; something I've seen many times before as I've battled the prey of this world.

His nose traces my face, the wet warmth of his tongue following suit. I cringe at the contact. My hand slips behind my back, clutching the handle in my palm.

"You need to leave." My voice is firm.

But he doesn't pull away. I take a deep breath, pulling my knee up in a quick sweep, but he shifts, and instead of hitting my target, his inner thigh takes the brunt of my attempt. A grunt mixes with my quickened breath, but his body doesn't budge.

My face snaps to the right before I can process his movement. The sting of his backhand across my cheeks brings tears to my eyes for the second time tonight.

"You bitch." His fingers grip my hair, yanking my head back, my neck exposed when he bites down a chunk of flesh between his teeth, no doubt drawing blood from the pain that bursts behind my eyes. I cry out.

"You prance around the shop. Making eyes at everyone but me. I treat you right. Feed you. Give you this place to live in at half the price." His words slur in his attempt to make a point. My body shifts at his accusation, desperate for space, but it's no use. He's got me pinned.

I take a deep breath, steadying my mind, knowing the only way I'm about to get out of here is with more brains than brawn. When I flip the switch, my body relaxes against him.

"You never asked." I look up through my eyelashes, praying to any deity that he'll take the bait. He stills against me, feather light touches draw up my arm, leaving goosebumps in their wake.

His eyes are quizzical; probably the last fraction of his rational mind fighting against the drunk idiot that's taken over control. And something switches in a second. His chapped lips crush mine with a bruising force. He shoves his tongue against my cemented lips.

I could gag against the stench radiating upwards from his hungry mouth, but I swallow it down. Stale beer mixed with the reek of cigarette smoke invades my nose. His tongue finally wins the fight and my lips part just as my hand sneaks from his shoulder to behind my back.

This time I don't hesitate. Pulling the blade free from its hiding place, I sneak it between our bodies right to his throat and push. The sting must take a second to register because he doesn't pull back at first. But his eyes widen in surprise when he finally grasps the gravity of his situation.

Then they slowly shift to furry, and I push down a little harder. "Don't." My command comes out thick and strong.

"You're going to back away and leave. You will not come back here. Do you understand me?" He steps back, away from my blade, and shakes his head instead of nodding. But his body retreats further out of the kitchen and into the hallway, making it to the front door, his grimy grip on the handle.

"That notice you got this morning. You've got a week to get out." He doesn't pause to take in my reaction before slamming the door behind him. I let out a frustrated shriek, throwing the blade after him. It pierces the wood of the front door, exactly where he'd just been. I run to the door, flipping the lock into place, and pulling the chain closed.

My forehead falls against it next to my blade. I kick the door over and over. Of course, this happened to me. My toes find the wood one last time when my ringtone goes off in the other room. Stomping toward the living room, I pluck it from its useless spot on the kitchen floor, mere feet from where Marco just attacked me.

Stubbing out the ignore button, the noise stops and the room quiets. I take in a deep breath. The ringing starts up again. I hold down the power button and slam it to the counter. Maybe that will get my point across.

I'm not shaken up over what just happened. I'm fucking livid. Attacked and evicted in five-minutes flat; a new world record.

I blow out a frustrated sigh and throw myself down on my bed, pounding my fists against the mattress, simultaneously screaming every curse that comes to mind.

"Why is there a knife in your front door?" The voice jolts me from my temper tantrum as I fly to a standing position.

"What the hell, Harkin!"

"Nu-uh." He dismisses my question, stalking toward where I'm standing, chest heaving from his mysterious appearance. His fingers grip my chin, moving it to the side.

"He did this to you?" he growls, his fingers gripping tighter.

I'd forgotten about the slap, but I'm sure my pale skin showcases the assault nicely. His eyes drop to my neck, growing darker with fury.

Too bad for him.

Because I've had just about enough manhandling for today. I shove his hand away and crawl back into bed.

Lying back against the pillows, I throw my arm over my eyes, blocking out the bright light and any chance of taking in his trembling form hovering over me.

"Are you just going to continue ignoring me?" The mattress dips and my body rolls slightly toward the additional weight.

I still don't answer.

"Why are you here?" I huff out from under my shield. "No,

wait, how are you here?"

I know for a fact I double locked my front door.

"Your light was on; I saw that asshole storming out of your building and you sent me to voicemail twice."

"And?" I wait for him to come clean on the second part of my questioning.

He doesn't answer. Time passes slowly before he says, "I have a key." Like it's no big deal.

I throw myself upward and almost collide with his shoulder. "You what?"

His gaze is piercing, ignoring my exuberant outburst. "It doesn't matter. Now tell me why there's a knife embedded in your front door, or I swear to God Keira, I'm going to fucking lose it."

My eyes roll of their own accord, knowing I'm not getting an accurate account of why he has a key to my place.

"Don't worry about it," I huff.

His hands shoot out, gripping my waist before hauling me into his lap. I've never wished for more weight and a bigger frame, more than I am today. Maybe then it wouldn't be so easy for these abrasive men to get their way.

I try my best to shove away and onto my feet, but his grip is lethal, and I don't move an inch from where he's holding me to him.

"That's the thing, sweetness, I am worrying about it. So, why don't you tell me before I make you?"

I bristle at his crassness, my mind warring with my body's wanton need to push him until he makes good on his promise. I shake away the dirty images filtering through my mind.

"If I tell you, it won't change what happened, so why does it matter?" I deflate against him, relaxing into his warmth that settles my hyperawareness from earlier.

His fingers brush faintly across my chin before he pushes a lock of hair behind my ear. "It matters to me." His tone is stern, quiet, direct.

I sigh, knowing once again I'm going to give in to his request. This man has a magical ability to convince me to do exactly as he asks, my body, mind, and soul useless against his requests.

"Marco, was here."

He stiffens under me and not in the way I like.

"I had a notice on my door when I came home. Eviction," I explain.

His chest heaves.

"I called him when I got in here and left a not so nice voice mail," I continue.

His head shakes in disapproval.

"Before I knew it, he was at my door. I thought it might be you since you'd just texted me." I look up into his striking eyes. "But it wasn't. He came on to me. I handle it. He left, and now I have a week to pack and leave before my apartment gets repossessed."

His grip on my hips loosens and I finally find the leverage to break free, falling backwards to my feet and stepping away to gain some space between us.

"He can't do that," he says.

"Well, he did. So, now, if you'll excuse me, I'd like to wallow in my shitty situation before I have to pull a miracle out of my ass tomorrow and find somewhere new to live without having rent or a deposit."

He stands, walking over to my dresser, ignoring my attitude toward his invasion, pulling out my clothes and setting them all on the bed. One neat little pile next to another when his head turns in my direction. "Got a bag?"

"Harkin, what the hell are you doing?"

"Solving your problem. And mine," he whispers under his breath without me missing it.

Grabbing on to his arm, I pull it away from the last drawer, stopping him in his tracks, "Harkin, stop it! I'm not going anywhere yet," I implore him.

"Yes, you are."

It's then that his intent registers in my mind. "Hell no. I hardly even know you. Are you crazy?"

He doesn't stop, collecting my belongings from one place and moving them to the center of my bed.

Slapping the pile on the floor doesn't deter him from his mission. He disappears into my closet, returning seconds later with my large duffle bag from the back of my closet from my foster kid days.

"Damnit, Harkin. Listen to me." Pulling against his arms, I'm desperate to stop his craziness. "I'll figure this out. I just need some time."

He finally stops, jolting in my direction, eyes meeting mine. "Absolutely not. You can stay in the guest room. But you're leaving this place. Tonight." He shoves everything into the bag before hauling it over his shoulder and heading out of my room.

I watch after him, he doesn't pause, heading right for the front door. "For fuck's sake, wait, would you?" I shove my feet into a pair of shoes, before barging into the bathroom for my toiletries.

When I stride into the living room he's leaning casually against the wall, waiting patiently for me to unplug my phone charger and snag up my laptop. I shove past him and into the hall, heading straight for the stairs.

This man will be the death of me, I swear it.

TWENTY-ONE
HARKIN

Middle Of The Night – Elley Duhe

Her shoulder checks me roughly, stealing the bag from mine as she stomps in from the open front door, down the hall, and into the spare room across from mine. The door slams, solidifying her feelings on the situation. It's fine. Her outburst will only give me time to dig further into the situation she's facing.

Marco had no right to hit her with an eviction notice. I know for a fact that money made it into one of the many accounts he and his father holds.

The angry noises from my spare room quiet as the minutes pull forward, drawing us into the darkness of night.

The more I learn about this asshole, the more my fingers itch to tap the keyboard and sock him where it really hurts. Where he won't know what hit him in the first place, but will take everything away in a matter of seconds.

His accounts sit balanced for the time being. He doesn't know who he's fucking with by upsetting her. She might not have told me the whole truth, holding back on their encounter, but that doesn't matter. I got all the information I needed when I walked in the door and saw her gleaming blade tucked into the flesh of the front door. The recording from the security cameras James installed weeks ago only confirmed my suspicions.

My strong, sassy girl doesn't need me to fight her battles, but that doesn't mean I won't be there to back her up the second shit goes sideways. She might not realize that this is more than a random hook up and a trip to *The Red Door*, but I do. She's not going anywhere, *ever*.

I head for my office, needing to scan through the final reports on those bank accounts before I hand off the information tomorrow. I was relieved to find that every single person on the list they handed me had dirty dealings.

None of them deserved the millions stacked in their offshore accounts. I couldn't care less what the dodgy suits decide to do with the information. Sending the document to print, I wait for the papers before tucking them into the folder for tomorrow's meeting. I pause, listening to my surroundings, waiting to hear anything from her room, but everything is stock still.

The floorboards creek under my weight, the last depiction of age from the building. Twisting the knob, I push open her door, and the silence calms my nerves. Her curves contour the comforter on the bed, nothing but shadows in the darkness. The rise and fall of her chest a subtle comfort.

I move to close the door, respecting her demand for solace when I hear it, faint whispers coming from inside the room. I step closer, the murmurs intelligible. She's captivating, drawing me in. The closer I get, the clearer it becomes. She's fighting with an imaginative being.

"No. Yes. Stop. Please." Her body fights against the blanket, calming only when my hand drops to her side. The mattress dips with my weight as I climb in behind her, hauling her limp form against mine. She automatically calms as I settle in beside her. Her breathing deepens as the little whimpers passing from her lips stop.

"I've got you, little one," I whisper against her ear before dropping a kiss to her temple and tightening my hold against her body, pulling her into the hollow of my chest.

MY CHEST HEAVES to suck in a single breath. The fire tickles against my skin but I can't feel it as my focus pulls in every direction. I scan the wreckage to the left and a body lays limp in my arms, unmoving. I shake her, trying to draw anything to the surface, but she doesn't move. Keira's eyes remain closed as I jerk her with every fiber of my being, but she doesn't budge. Panic sets in as realization dawns that her chest doesn't inflate. "No. No. No, not again," I call out to her.

"Harkin! Harkin, wake up." Her unexpected voice brings me back into a dark room. A forceful grip on my shoulder shakes my body back and forth. My eyes snap open directly into the worried focus of hers.

"I'm sorry… sorry." I try to brush it off before settling against the headboard. Her body crawls up mine, never once breaking contact.

"What was that?" Her concern is palpable between us.

"Nothing, just a nightmare. Sorry I woke you." She ignores my excuses, wrapping her warmth against my rapidly beating heart.

"No way, you don't get to do that. Don't pull away from

me now." Her strong condemnation brings a smile to my lips until she notices and matches me with a frown.

"Seriously Harkin, I opened up to you. Can't you trust me enough to tell me what the hell was going on? I thought you were going to break my rib cage. I've never seen someone try to give CPR in their sleep."

That shocks me. I had no clue I did that to her. The worry must showcase on my face because she softens.

"I'm fine. Just worried about you. You need to talk about it." She's prodding again.

I sigh, pulling in a lung full of air, my mind settling on telling her the truth—well, most of it. "Okay, you remember how we met?" Her small smile gives me her answer. "I was on my way to California. That was the first time I'd been back." She shifts in my lap, settling in for the story.

"My family lives there. Well, it's just my parents. I don't have any siblings." She doesn't miss this new piece of information I've allowed.

"I left for a reason, and I wasn't looking forward to being back there, but my parents insisted. I know you're curious about how I can afford this place for someone who doesn't seem to leave his house. I do work, but I work from home. What I do isn't exactly a conventional 9-to-5." Her eyes narrow down at me, and I chuckle. I know what she thinks.

"I'm a hacker sweetness. So, get those thoughts out of your head right now. I make good money, but you're right, this place isn't technically mine. My parents own it, along with employing James for security needs, although his loyalty is to me after all these years. He's like an older brother or a really young uncle."

"You're stalling," she points out.

"Okay, fine. About a year ago, I killed my girlfriend."

Her body jerks from my lap, landing beside me on the mattress.

"Ahh, there it is. The reaction I get from people back home. You see, it didn't matter that I ended up in the hospital with injuries bad enough that I couldn't remember the accident that took her from me. It didn't matter that the drug and the blood alcohol test all came back clean. It didn't matter that every person in our town knew how slick that mountain road was when a storm blew in. They all blamed me for an accident that wasn't my fault, but a freak occurrence." Her eyes bore into me, taking in the story. She's shifted closer, her hands back on my body.

"I couldn't take it anymore. I knew I'd never have a normal life if I stayed there. So, I decided one day to pack up everything I needed and caught a red eye to New York. I used a spare key my parents had in the house for this apartment, and I hadn't been back." She's back in my lap and I pull her body closer. The warmth of her skin calming my nerves.

"She died because I waited too long to pull her drunk ass from a party."

"Wait, what do you mean?" she asks, hanging on every word of my hapless history.

"Keira, it doesn't matter. Just drop it."

She huffs, shoulders rising in frustration. Her hands clasp my cheeks.

"You matter to me. So, in turn, this matters." There's nothing in her gaze that tells me she's lying.

"My ex, Alina, she was... eccentric. She grew up a typical California rich kid, going to parties by the time she was thirteen. Alcohol loses its excitement quickly when it's so easily obtainable. So, you move on to the next thing that will give your mind a high. Most kids start with weed and quickly move on to blow or pills, depending on what they're looking for. For Alina, it was coke and when she mixed it with alcohol, there was no reasoning with her."

"That night she'd been drinking before I even picked her up. She stumbled into the party on my arm and rushed off to talk with her friends. When I found her again, it was obvious she'd found someone to buy from since I told her not to bring it with her from home." I clamp my eyes shut, running a hand down my face in frustration at having to live through this again.

"By the time I'd ripped her away from some random guy she was making out with to leave, she could barely walk on her own. But she sure could snap at me when she was in that state. We were fighting on our way out to my car and passed plenty of people that were willing to tell the police that after the accident. But in the end, they couldn't find any proof that I'd caused the accident on purpose, therefore causing Alina's death." I pause, waiting for the last tidbit of information to soak in.

"It was just a horrible turn of events that night and it changed my life. Forever."

The silence in the room sits heavily around us. Her eyes search my face, but I'm stone cold, nothing but indifference hovering between us.

"It wasn't your fault, Harkin."

"I know," I whisper. "I couldn't stay there any longer. But that's what the nightmare was all about. I still don't know what happened that night after the car crashed. I think sometimes my brain shows me in bite-sized flashbacks when I'm dreaming, because it always feels so real."

She doesn't pry any further as we sit in a companionable silence. After a while, her lips are gentle as they explore across my chest before her teeth graze my nipple. My cock twitches against her thigh and she doesn't miss my reaction to the bite of pain.

"So, it isn't just giving." Her eyes twinkle with mischief when her hand sneaks out of nowhere and pinches the other side. "I'll take that as a yes."

"You want to play, little one?" I growl, relieved for shift of her focus.

Her demeanor shifts immediately at my tone and her body moves to fall back on her haunches. The light of excitement in her eyes fills my mind with every dark and depraved scenario I've pictured over the last couple months.

I shift off the bed standing, hand extended in waiting. "I want to try something. Do you trust me?"

She doesn't answer. Instead, the brush of her fingers dropping into mine pulls us from the room and out to my gym. She halts in the door frame, taking in the typical setup, confusion written all over her face.

I leave her there to make her assumptions while I trail across the darkened room, hitting a switch for the recessed, rope lighting along the top of the wall. The lights trickle on, brightening the space just enough to see the shadows of workout equipment.

"Do you have a gym fantasy or something?"

"Or something." I chuckle.

Reaching under the table that holds an assortment of drinks, towels, and the Bluetooth speaker, I hit the button. Within seconds, the wall opens displaying my collection of knives. A surprised gasp of air sounds behind me.

"Or something," she whispers.

"Still trust me?"

Her gentle footfalls lessen our distance until she's standing in front of me, gazing up, running her delicate finger along my favorite blade. I smile at her choice when she pulls it off the wall and turns toward me.

"For me?" That sassy smile is back. It's tempting to let her take the reins, if only to see how she handles them. My hand jolts out, twisting the blade free from her grasp before whipping her into my chest, her back against my front, the blade resting flat against her collarbone. Her chest heaves at the unexpected change, but I can see that her pupils have blown wide in excitement through the gym mirror.

My nose grazes along her neck under her hair, inhaling the scent that's all her. A mix of coconut, vanilla, and her own essence. She shivers against me.

"You weren't wrong," I whisper against her skin. "I don't mind a bite of pain when it's given by the sultry vixen in my arms."

Her ass presses back against me.

"But that's not what I have in mind for tonight." My blade sweeps under the collar of her shirt, shifting to the left before I slice downward through the fabric, exposing her left breast to the cool air. Her sharp intake of breath heaves out of her chest, displaying her dusky pink nipple, stiffening from exposure.

My free hand leaves her waist, drifting upward. I'm trusting her not to pull away. My other hand slips the blade up her thigh, tracing lightly with the tip, when she twitches against me, pushing it in deeper. A hiss of air pulls in through her teeth, but she stills.

I twirl her, knocking the backs of her knees before shoving her to the ground on her back. Quickly dropping the blade to the floor, I push up her tee shirt, inspecting the small, sliced area on her thigh. Bright red pebbles of blood against her peachy skin call to me. My tongue runs lightly over the area, clearing it away.

"Harkin." My name drops from her lips in the sweetest plea for more.

"Yes, sweetness?" She's propped up on her elbows, looking down at me between her thighs.

"I need you," she mewls for me.

"I know. You smell divine." She shifts backwards, trying to pull away at my comment, but my palms slap against her thighs and squeeze, ceasing her escape.

Leaning forward, I run my nose across her damp panties, inhaling. Fingers tracing up her thighs to the elastic against her hips, I pull hard, ripping the barricade between us. My tongue thrusts out, the taste of her explodes in my mouth. She's wet, wanton, and waiting. When I feel the tug of her fingers in my hair, I back away and wait. A frustrated huff meets my ears.

I push back and hop to my feet, jumping over her body spread out on the gym floor.

"What the..." She doesn't get to finish that sentence before her wrists are in my hand and I'm dragging her across the room, stopping when we hit the squat rack. Stealing a left-over tee shirt that's dangling from the bar, I quickly tie it around her wrist, connecting it with the metal leg of the exercise equipment. She pulls against the restraint, but it doesn't budge.

"Harkin, what are you doing?"

"You wanted to play. So, let's play."

TWENTY-TWO
KEIRA

Mind Games – Sick Kick

His massive body towers above my helpless one. The struggle to free my hands is a feeble attempt. He's too good with a knot and deep down I have zero desire to break free, but it's fun to play the part. I glare at him as he accesses the situation, retreating to pick up the discarded blade before returning with a gleam in his eye.

He handles it with such grace, balancing the tip of the blade on the pad of his finger before flicking it into the air and catching it in the opposite hand. It's mesmerizing to watch, which is why I'm calm when he stalks closer. He squats next to my prone figure, outlining my curves with the silky metal. His eyes are dark and focused on every rise and valley it follows.

I work to keep my breaths even against his wandering touch, but it's the fast as lightening movement when he splits the rest of the shirt from my body that causes my breaths to quicken. Frosty air from the AC breezes across my skin, pulling goosebumps to the surface. It's a slight reprieve from the fire in my veins igniting from his constant exploration.

My legs rub together shamelessly, trying to dull the ache in my pulsing clit. My desire coats my inner thighs, slick with my need for more of his tongue, his fingers, and hopefully, finally, his cock.

"Harkin," I whine unabashedly voicing my craving for him.

"Mmm?" His gaze roams freely, his touch ghosting against my skin.

"You look beautiful like this." His appreciation shines through his tone.

"Please." The plea slips past my lips, but it doesn't hurry his movements.

"You know, I've never had you like this? Sober. Every time you've let me near you, in you, you've been drunk." His eyes are predatory as he walks back and forth around me, still refusing to make a move.

I'm done waiting.

My knees drop out toward the ground, opening me up wide for him to get his fill. My body gyrates against the floor, searching for an ounce of friction to grant me a semblance of relief. The movements do nothing to soothe the ache building inside. My taunting intrigues him, and his eyes darken as they rake down my entire body.

"You're asking for it, little one." His tone's laced with a hint of deviltry.

A sudden blur has him straddled on top of me, his hand wraps around my throat, those striking eyes piercing into my soul. His weight feels delicious. The view of his chest is a welcome distraction, but it's the sweats covered bulge between my thighs that rips a moan from my throat.

Wrapping a leg around his waist, I pull him closer, deeper against my center, grinding my hips in a frenzied hunger to dull a fraction of my need to come. His hand tightens around my throat as he tries to pull away, but my leg only tightens further. The glint of glee in his eyes when he realizes I'm fighting back, only spurs my insolence on.

"If you come, I promise you'll regret it."

My movements cease in an instant, and he knows he's won. The pressure around my throat lessens as my leg drops from around his body and he pulls back. He looks down between us. The wet spot on his pants heats my cheeks in embarrassment.

"Aww, isn't that sweet?" he mocks, tracing my cheeks with his fingertips. "There's no room for that between us. So, get that thought out of your head right now." His touch doesn't linger against my face long before my clit feels a tight pinch and a dark growl leaves his chest.

"If I can't come. Can I make you?" I'm desperate to taste him for the first time. His weight shifts off me as he stands, taking me in. The gray sweats hit the floor and he's gloriously naked. His cock is the epitome of perfect, thick, and hard. The head tinged purple and when he shifts, I get a glimpse of the vein that runs up the side. My mouth waters in anticipation to take him deep and make him just as needy as he's made me.

"Is this what you want?" The rough tug of his cock pulls a drop of pre-cum from the tip. My tongue licks against my lips before I bite down to tamp my eagerness. But my chin nods in answer.

He kneels over my chest, cock proud before me. Tapping his thickness against my lips, my tongue leaps out, searching, licking against the saltiness leaking free. He hisses at the contact, spurring me on. When his hips push forward, his cock shoves deeper, my cheeks hollow, my tongue dances across his velvet skin. But it's when he falls toward the ground and pushes down my throat, I finally get what I want. The moan that leaves his mouth followed by a sharp *'fuck'* taunts me.

His hips piston down into my face, and tears drip from my eyes as drool runs down my cheeks. He fucks my face with abandon, and I'm with him. Taking as much pleasure as I'm giving. My cunt pulses, a desperate need to be filled as his cock jolts against my tongue.

Closing my throat, I push him out and snap my mouth shut. He jerks away at the change. "What the fuck, Keira." His whole demeanor shifts with that name drop and he finally gets what he's put me through.

My satisfied smirk frees the beast hovering over the top of me. His body moves so fast, that before I can register our new position, I feel his cock shove against my entrance. His face settles close to mine. "Touché, little one."

I stretch against his assault. "Oh, God," I moan.

"We've been here before; you know whose name to scream." His fingers grip my chin tightly.

He pushes into the hilt, stretching me wide. He's big, and it's been a minute for me, but the slight burn of pain quickly subsides. The veiny ridges sliding against my walls make my toes curl. This is everything I always imagined and more. My fingers tighten against the tee shirt holding me hostage and at his disposal.

"God, the things I want to do to you."

I'm delirious from the pleasure. "So do them," I egg him on.

His thrusts cease as his eyes meet mine. "You were made

for me." His lips crash against mine, teeth meeting teeth. The sting of a bite against my lip pulls at my core. He consumes the moan that melts from my lips, his thrust resuming, beating into me.

My sweat slicked back glides my body across the floor with every assault of his cock. His fingers grip tighter against my hips, the pressure sure to leave bruises, but I'll take them. A physical reminder that a day I've imagined a thousand times over in my head actually happened.

Just before my head bashes against the metal leg I'm tied to, he flips me over like a rag doll onto my knees. My fingers grip the fabric, wrists twisted, and shoulders straining at the awkward angle. His strong grip fuses with my throat, using it for leverage to pull my body backward to meet his front. The ache in my arms disappears, but the one between my thighs only grows heavier.

This change in position makes him feel even deeper. I breathe through the dull pain as he pounds into me, hitting a new spot that makes my vision swim. I've never been with anyone his size, and it feels like he's tearing me in two.

A guttural groan and a whisper of my name meets my ears. I'd take the sting between my thighs any day just to hear that sound again. His free hand slides between my breasts, pinching a nipple along his descent. My core pulses from the bite of his fingers, but it's dulled when they meet their destination.

Filled with his cock, my orgasm swells. I'm so close, tingles are starting to dance across my skin. My hips jerk back against him, slamming myself down to quicken our pace. He gives as good as I take. Adding his fingers against my swollen clit, I jerk in his hold at the added pleasure.

"Harkin, please." I beg, chest heaving, as he slows his magical fingers and rough thrusts.

"Mmm, say it again," he challenges.

"Please, let me come." My pussy quivers around him. His hips pick up speed, his fingers slide against my clit, pinching cruelly. It's the last straw that pushes me over the edge as euphoria washes over me. My eyes fall shut as I ride the waves of ecstasy, moaning out his name.

That seems to unhinge any sense of control he's held on to as he jerks twice more before emptying himself deep inside me.

"Jesus, fuck," he groans in my ear.

I wait for him to pull out, but he stills against my back, gripping my hips to him, still pulsing. I grind against him, milking every last drop.

Our shared climax runs down my thighs as he finally pulls free. An unexpected pang at the loss of him consumes me. He shifts, hastily freeing my hands from their confines. His thumbs run gently across the redden skin, drawing blood back into circulation.

"You, okay?" His worried eyes raise to mine.

"More than okay." My small smile softens the concerned crease in his forehead.

Thick arms encase me, lifting me from the gym floor. A shriek escapes my lips at the sudden weightlessness. I tighten my hold on his bulging shoulders as the rest of me relaxes against his muscular chest. My head flops to the side, resting in his warmth.

"Where are you taking me?" The question fumbles past my lips as my eyes droop heavily.

His lips brush lightly against my temple as his murmured

answers fill my head in sounds I can't process before my eyes fall close and the blackness takes over.

IT'S SWELTERING, my skin has passed damp and gone straight for soaked. My eyes flicker open to darkness, odd shapes reflect gleams of moonlight sharing their shadows. A heavy arm pins me in place against the furnace at my back and it's clear what has me overheating.

Slinking across the mattress to detangle myself, I shift slowly until I'm free and out of bed. His face is a portrait of serenity, untroubled, as he snores softly into the night. I tread lightly across the floor and out of the bedroom, naked in the dimmed light.

His office at the end of the hall beckons my curiosity. The door stands cracked. He's never shown any concern at my entry. Pushing it open, I'm relieved when it doesn't creak. A small table lamp in the corner illuminates the dark wood and leather, decorated in the same style as the living room.

A floor-to-ceiling bookcase fills an entire wall, lined full of books that are wrapped in leather. A small section devoted to newer fiction, which, if I had to guess, would be Harkin's doing. The rest looks styled by an interior designer. I randomly wonder if any of these hide a hidden switch if pulled, revealing a safe room or secret passage.

My finger glides along the shelf, not a speck of dust sticks to it as it comes away clean. I take in the rest of the room. A live edge desk messy with papers and multiple computer screens fills the tabletop. Two oversized leather chairs sit in front of it, ready and waiting for their next meeting.

I wiggle the mouse and the screen comes to life, lighting up the dim room. Nothing exciting pops up as it's password protected, and I shouldn't have expected anything less from a computer nerd. I plop down in his chair, soaking in his everyday view. The chair leans slightly to the left, formed against his body. A large white board hangs on the opposite wall. Scribbled letters and numbers that make my mind whirl with confusion as I take them in.

He's such a mystery, undoubtedly smart. Everything I learned about him over the years peering into Alina's life through a screen, painted someone completely different. And maybe he was before the accident, but it's this Harkin that's drawn me in so deep I'm drowning. He's illusive, secretive, domineering—to an obnoxious extent.

I thought I knew who he was, but the more time we spend together, it's blatantly obvious that isn't the case. There's only so much one can learn through social media and peering across the street for a year. I never expected the man who shut down my sassy side in front of a crowd. Or the guy who didn't think twice before he packed up my life and forced it to fit into his. For every infuriatingly overbearing move he makes, he unknowingly broadcasts his affection.

The drawers of the desk draw my nosiness as I'm determined to find something to one up his overflowing insights into my life. Pulling one out after the other, they hold nothing but office supplies, work papers, and mail. It's the last drawer I tug that doesn't give against my forceful pull that tells me I've finally found something good.

Pushing back through the last drawer I rifled through, I snag out a couple of paperclips and straighten out the metal. Sticking the two ends into the drawer's lock, I fumbled with the two pieces as they slide against each other in the tight hole. The shift finally happens, and the lock clicks free. The drawer opens fully when I tug at it again, opening it fully.

Files upon files line the cabinet drawer. Each labeled with a business name on the tab. Some I recognize as huge corporations, while others I skim past with no knowledge of. It's the K's that catch my eye and stop my fingers. *Keira Fitz* stands out on a tab in big, bold letters.

I take a deep breath, my emotions warring against the logical side of my brain that scolds me for having any type of reaction. I drop the file on the desk and flip open the first page. It reads like an undercover expose of my life. Every little detail, down to my height and weight.

But all of that is trivial information. It's not until the last few pages that it gets more personal. Daily logs of my comings and goings. Transcripts of my text messages and months worth of my call logs. There's nothing incriminating anywhere in this information, but that isn't what has my curiosity rising.

These go back almost to the day we met. He's been looking into me this entire time. The multiple run-ins are no more a coincidence than a bee finding a flower in a park. A slightly relieved breath leaves my lips that the logs don't date before our first run-in.

If he went back far enough and could connect the dots, his suspicion of me would be valid. Hell, if he saw my web history, it'd be valid. I don't know what to do with this information.

So, he investigated me?

I've had my eyes on him for years, albeit not to this depth, but only for lack of skills and ability. It'd make me a hypocrite to fly off the handle, but being even tempered has never been one of my strong suits.

My skin tingles as the air thickens. I finish the last page, closing the file and pulling it hastily into my lap before my eyes flick to the door. His tall frame leans lazily against the wall, inspecting my movements in his space.

"I... uh. I'm just." I stop, silencing the fumbling explanation.

He pushes from the wall, strolling leisurely toward me, eyes scanning the surface of his desk. When he finds it empty, his eye crinkle in confusion.

"Looking for something?" His tone is flat, and it does nothing to help me gauge his genuine reaction to me invading his space. I shift the chair further under the desk, hoping to hide the evidence on my lap.

Clearing my throat, I swallow down my anxiety. "I couldn't sleep. I figured if you're going to force me to move in here, I should at least know what else is in this place." His gaze doesn't waver as he steps around the corner of the desk looming over me.

"And you decided my office was more interesting than the other rooms? Not much in here." He gestures around the small space that took me all of five minutes to snoop through.

I shrug. "I mean, there's lots of reading material. Could keep a girl entertained for hours."

His foot kicks out, pushing the chair out from my hiding spot. Taken by surprise, the folder spills to the ground, papers scattering everywhere. I hop up, ready to make a break for the door. But his lips tip up in a smile as he takes in the mess at his feet.

"Well, I guess you had to dig a little harder for some interesting reading material." His eyes shift to the bottom drawer, the paperclips still jutting out from the lock I picked.

"Why do you have these?" I pause. "How do you have these?"

He dips sweeping all the papers back into the folder before

dropping it on the desk. "I told you, I'm good with computers. It's easy information to find when you know where to look. The other stuff is reports from James."

"Jesus," I mumble under my breath. "You missed my cycle and birth control type," I taunt him.

He rifles through the file and picks out a paper I must have missed, slapping it on the top. I scan it quickly and am shocked that I'm wrong. He has that too. I know I told myself not to be angry for this earlier, but the longer he stands there mute without an explanation, the more the flame flickers back to life.

My fingers clench around the paper, balling it up in my fist before chucking it at him. Pulling an about face, I stride for the door, shutting it closed behind me. It's a pointless move since the door swings back open almost immediately.

"I thought we were past this." His deep voice booms down the hall as I make it into my guest room, ready to slam yet another door in his face. But his palm slaps against it, holding it wide open. "You're running again, sweetness."

I spin around, crossing my arms over my chest. "Explain." I pop out a hip before tapping my bare foot against the floor.

"It's a habit in my line of work," he says unconcerned, stopping at that like it's explanation enough.

I turn my back on him, hooking my duffle from the floor and dropping it to the bed. I rip his shirt over my head and throw it at his feet. His heat engulfs my bare back. A rough grip at my waist halts my digging through the bag for something to put on.

His chest heaves a deep sigh as his nose nuzzles my neck. It's gentle and throws me off my game. I can't keep up my safety wall, erected from my anger when his gentle side shows.

"What are you doing?" he whispers in my ear, a faint hint of sadness draws through.

"Tell me why."

"Will it really change anything?" he asks.

"Won't know until you tell me."

His fingers dance across my skin in opposite directions, pulling my focus when one traces under my breast, the other skates too close to the apex of my thighs. My ass involuntarily thrusts back into him.

I whip around in his embrace, pushing forcefully against his chest. He staggers back, catching himself against the dresser. "You can't distract me with sex, Harkin."

His head drops and both hands grip the roots of his dark locks, pulling hard showcasing budding dread. Whatever the truth is, he's far from wanting to tell me, but I've pushed too far to let this go now. I realize then, with his heat gone, that I'm still naked, waiting for him to decide.

Quickly pulling on a shirt and shorts, I plop onto the mattress, pulling my legs under me, patiently waiting for him to break. Seconds blur into minutes. My patience is wearing thin when his eyes finally lift to mine.

The pain I see in them stabs at my heart.

I'm screwed.

TWENTY-THREE
HARKIN

Do you really want to hurt me – Nessa Barrett

The scenarios running through my head all end the same: I tell her the truth, she freaks out. What girl wants to be compared to your dead girlfriend? A lie only lends to her sniffing out the truth eventually and delaying the fight.

My hands tighten around my thighs, digging in against the skin, grounding me when my eyes lift and meet her expectant ones. There's no way out of this. She wants an answer.

"This is it Harkin, I'm serious." Her tone means it, too.

"I know." I let out a frustrated groan. Nothing with her has been easy. The sexual tension between us is undeniable. It builds anytime we're in the same room. But the secrets between us have been building, and it's now or never. I can't imagine letting her walk out the door and never seeing her again.

If she thinks those files are bad, pushing me away now, building a wall, and cutting me off from her, will make it so much worse.

I clear my throat. "That first day we ran in to each other outside, I recognized you."

Her eyebrows scrunch in confusion.

"But I'd never met you?" She says hesitantly.

"Or, I, you, but you looked so familiar. I thought it was just a coincidence, but…" I trail off, not sure how to round this corner. "You look just like her. I couldn't wrap my head around it."

"Look like who?" she asks.

"Like Alina." I'm so far in my head. The swift draw of breath she takes pulls me back.

"What?" she whispers.

Her eyes glisten, tears on the brink of falling down her red tinted cheeks. I didn't expect that. Anger—yes, hurt—probable. But sadness? Now that one's throwing me off.

Shuffling closer, I sink on to the mattress beside her and draw her over into my lap. Her eyes refuse to meet my gaze, but that's unacceptable in this situation.

"You asked for this, but I'll stop if you say so."

Her head shakes, but the tightness in her shoulders tells me she still isn't sure if she wants to hear more.

"I told you the other night about her and the accident. But what I left out is you're her damn clone. If I didn't know her family, I'd swear you guys were sisters. Shit, twins even. That's how much you guys look alike."

She pulls against my tightening hold at my candor, wincing at my words.

My hands drift against her cheeks, grasping and directing

her eyes at me. She closes them tightly when she can't turn away.

"I'm sorry." I know this must be hurting her, for all the limited time we've spent together she's wormed her way into my heart and, seeing her react like this, does nothing but stab my favorite knife through it.

I should have hidden her file better. Put it in the safe where she wouldn't have been able to break in so easily.

She sniffles. "Harkin." Her weak plea plunges the knife in a little deeper.

"I'm so sorry." I drop kisses across her face. Meeting every inch tinged with her emotions. I want to wipe them away with my lips. Letting her know it doesn't matter. I'm here with her. It was just a need for more information. My inquisitive mind never resting once a puzzle presents itself.

"Harkin, No!" Her declaration settles me. I drop my hands, lifting her back into her own space next to me on the mattress. Creating distance between us so she can breathe; process. Hanging my head, I sigh in resignation, digging around for the right words to help her understand.

"That only started the curiosity. It was never the reason."

"What the hell is that supposed to mean?"

"Watching you in the cab snapped something back into place for me. It'd been almost a year since I cut myself off from everyone back home, started building a life for myself here. I isolated myself because I didn't deserve any different. Then you came along, and I found a reason again. And maybe that's not fair to you, but how do you ignore the feeling in your chest like the elephant that's been living there for months is finally gone? You don't."

"Yeah, that's great and all, but you could have just come up to me at the pizza shop and continued our conversation. This,

this is just—" Her thought trails off. The silence building between us. I shift uncomfortably.

"Can I ask you something?" Her tone's laced with resentment.

"I think you've earned that right at this point."

"Why use the notes? Why didn't you just step up and step in?"

"The notes." I heave in a deep breath, blowing it out slowly through pursed lips. "It wasn't the right time."

She shoots off the bed, whirling on me from across the room. The anger pooling in her golden eyes radiates off her in waves. She looks ready to throw hands, and can I really blame her?

"At Luigi's? And the club? My Apartment? Oh, my, god." Her hands shoot up, veiling her face, a flustered screech spilling from behind them. The sound ceases. Then she's in front of me. The quick stinging slap slices against my cheek. "You watched me, sent cryptic as hell notes, but it wasn't the right time? What the hell kind of bullshit excuse is that?" Her fists clutch at her sides, her knuckles turning white to staunch her anger.

"Keira please, I can explain." This time, I see the shift in her stance before her hand hurtles toward my face, and her fist is closed. This girl never ceases to amaze me. Blocking her attempt and clutching her wrist, I yank her into me, wrapping my arms around her as she bucks and flails against my hold. Her head catches my chin. I hiss at the pain, but my grip doesn't loosen.

"Calm down, little one." She stiffens at the term. "I know you're pissed but stop fighting me. I won't let you hit me again." Her movements slow, her body gradually relaxing into mine.

"That's it," I whisper against her hair, releasing my grip to rub her back.

Her body disappears from my hold, the emptiness stings. She blurs through the open door, her footsteps pattering against the hardwood. I sink further into the mattress, pissed at myself that I let this situation slip through my fingers.

When I finally locate her, she's shoving her legs through a pair of my running joggers and rolling them at her hips. She's drowning in them, but that doesn't stop her from ripping one of my sweatshirts from a hanger and sliding it on over her crop top.

"Harkin, don't!" Her tone is cold, indifferent. She's pulling away, disappearing into that beautiful head of hers, where I have no chance of reaching.

My feet ache to go to her, wrap her in my arms, calm the temper raging inside, but I can tell she needs space. I stick to the door frame and watch as she searches for her phone and slides on a pair of running shoes.

"Where are you going?" I ask.

"I don't know, but I'll figure it out. I just can't be here right now."

"At least take James. He's out-front waiting." Her eyes swing to mine, there's a war raging within them to disagree with me. Wanting to fight me for another inch when I feel like I'm giving her a whole fucking mile.

She stops next to me and drops her phone in my hand. I cringe. Without this on her, I won't know exactly where she is, and she must know it. She brushes past and within seconds; I hear the front door latch. My legs carry me swiftly to the windows to view the street downstairs. I watch as she exits and turns left, away from the waiting SUV.

I dial James up immediately. "Follow her."

"You got it boss," he replies.

I drop to my knees, my head heavy in my hands. Time passes slowly, my mind plays through the big reveal time and time again.

The street below get busier as the morning stretches on. My watch vibrates as the alarm goes off. I check the time; shit I'm going to be late if I don't get my ass in gear. My body moves but my mind wanders, refusing to part from the thoughts of her regardless of what's on my schedule.

I STEP up to the same dilapidated building, this time the giant guard doesn't wait outside.

My phone pings, a text from James.

> Lost Her

MY WORLD TILTS SIDEWAYS. Schooling my features, I pull open the door and walk inside.

The same men from before sit waiting at a table in the back corner. The file drops with a thud against the surface in front of them. "Everything's there. Check if you must." The younger of the two slides it across to him and flips through the pages and pages of information I gathered for them.

"My transfer?" I ask.

He nods and pulls out his phone, typing something quickly.

"Done."

I nod and turn to go, desperate to get back to my place and figure out what the hell I'm going to do about Keira.

"Sit down, Mr. Greyson." A deep voice, raspy with age comes from behind me.

I spin in his direction not thrilled that he knows my name. "We have another job for you," he states.

"Sorry. I'm all booked. No time for other jobs." I quickly inform him as I make for the door again.

"Hmm, that's too bad. We'll have to let your father know you weren't as helpful as he assured us, you'd be."

What the fuck did he just say?

"My father? What does he have to do with this?"

The twinkle in his eyes tells me there's more going on here than I know.

"Like I said, sit. We have another job for you."

I can't deny I'm curious, that little piece in my head that works in overdrive to solve puzzles is calling. Why can't my brain just let the little things go and not harp on the smallest tidbits of information. Those details are what I crave to find out and put together to see the bigger picture. I drop into the booth in front of them. "Again, what does my father have to do with this?"

"Your father has been an associate of the families for years. He let us know you moved to the city a year ago and to reach out if we had any *jobs* that fit your expertise. This little job," he taps the folder on the table, "was a test." He looks to his accomplice and gets a nod. "And it looks like you've passed."

"Look, I don't know what kind of arrangement you have with my father, but that has nothing to do with me. I don't work for him," I inform them.

"Hmm," he ponders, drawing out the moment with a scratch to his salt and pepper beard, "that's really too bad to hear, especially since we seem to have a more in common than your dear old dad."

My fists thud against the wooden table as I lean closer into his space. "Are you always this damn enigmatic? Spit it out!" I'm playing a dangerous game here.

His head falls back, and a boisterous laugh fills the heavy air around us. "You've got some serious balls, kid. Anyone else would have a bullet between their eyes for that little outburst. But I think it's time for you to go. We'll be in touch when we need you."

TWENTY-FOUR
KEIRA

All The Things She Said— Ponette

I groan into the darkness behind my eyelids while the air around me shifts. Peeling my right eye open slowly, Stace's concerned gaze peers down at me from a mere inch away.

"Okay, enough is enough. You need to tell me what's going on with you," she prods.

"Stace, come on. It's a long story," I sigh.

Her hands grip my shoulders and pull me up from my supine position on her couch. "Nope, you don't get to show up unannounced, dressed in someone else's clothes, without telling me what the hell is going on. Let's start with whose closet you raided."

I dive into the whole situation, recapping everything from the moment I got home to see that stupid paper taped to my front door. To the very end, where I freaked out on Harkin and left without grabbing any of my stuff. I filled her in on the notes I'd received and how my miraculous giveaway winning was him, too.

"So, you know I love you, right? But how is what he did any worse than what you've been keeping from him? Sounds to me like it's a whole lot of the same stuff from a different angle. Hate to be that friend, babe, but you don't really have a leg to stand on in this fight, if you ask me."

"Well, I didn't ask you," I snap, immediately regretting it. My head falls heavy in my hands. "I'm sorry. I know, you're not telling me anything I don't already know. But, what if..." My thought trails off.

"But what if he really cares about you enough to look out for you? What if you just ran because you're scared? What if you finally found the one guy in this city of millions that's exactly what you need to break down those mile-high concrete walls you've surrounded your heart with?" she says.

"You know I came here for a couch to sulk on. For the friend I thought would ease my wounds with a couple shots of tequila. What's gotten into you?"

Her face reddens at the accusation, and I know something's up.

"Spill! I need a distraction."

"Not what, but who," she corrects, raising her eyebrows at the innuendo. "You remember the bouncer from the club? Robert?" she asks, a sly smile creeping across her face.

I nod in confirmation.

"Well, last time we went, after you left, he got off early. I expected him to want to leave and have a drink, but he's a member there too. He's only allowed to enjoy the activities on member only nights though because the crowd is easier to control."

It's all falling into place now. If he's anything like Harkin, no wonder my beautiful, free-spirited friend has quickly become the voice of reason. It's that good dick.

"So, you've finally been tamed, huh?" I tease.

"Bitch please, he wishes. But I really think you should talk this out with Harkin. Does being compared to his dead ex-girlfriend suck? Hell yeah. But you've been caught up on his ass for years. Are you really going to let something like this stop you from finally being with him?"

Rolling my eyes, sick of her logic, I break down and agree. "But can we get drunk first?"

"Of course!" She sing-songs across the apartment to her liquor cart, and says, "Pick your poison."

THE SCREEN ON Stace's phone blurs, but if I squint at just the right angle the images blend back together and I can see what I'm trying to do. I haven't had it for long, but his number sits at the front of my mind as I type it into the contact bar.

I can't replace her.

MY EYES DROOP with heaviness as I wait for a response. A bottle of tequila and a few hours of much needed mind-numbing trashy TV later Stace was ready for bed. Her oversized plush sectional my home for the night. It envelops my body as I sink deeper and deeper into the comfort of my drunken haze. The phone vibrates against my chest over and over. Not a text notification; a call.

Hitting the green button, I automatically put it on speaker. I can't balance the phone against my ear in this state. I say nothing, waiting for him to fill the silence with more than just the deep breaths flowing across the line.

"You we're never a replacement for me, Keira." His tone is so sincere. I can almost see the worry etched in his brows behind my closed eyes.

"I just can't get it out of my head. Harkin, you loved her. You still dream about her, even with me in your bed."

"Shit, those aren't dreams, they're the fucked-up reminders of the worst day of my life." He scoffs, but his words are laced with sadness.

The silence builds again between us. I know it's not fair to blame him for what happens when he's unconscious. But I'm grasping at straws for a reason to stay mad when all I want is to blurt out that it's fine because I have secrets too. Secrets just as bad; if not worse. That would certainly change his mind about me. It's why he can never know about my connection to Alina. And especially why I'll continue to play the victim even though it's eating me alive every time I have to lie right to his face and make him out to be the issue, when I'm equally as guilty.

"Tell me where you are, little one?" His question pulls me from my vortex of self-spun lies.

"In Manhattan, on a very cozy couch—all alone." My words slur.

"Are you drunk?" He doesn't sound too pleased at the possibility, actually he sounds rather irritated. I can't help the giggle bubbling up in my throat.

"Maybe.... I needed a distraction." *From you, from me.*

"Let me come get you."

"Mmm, you're too far away. And I'm too sleepy."

"Then sleep, sweetness. I'll see you in the morning." My languid limbs refuse to move to end the call, so I leave it, he'll hang up eventually or not. It doesn't matter as sleep pulls me under and the world around me fades to black.

My head aches before my eyes peel open. My mouth is sticky, coated in syrupy spit. And my stomach threatens to revolt when I roll on my side. Something solid blocks my efforts to get off the couch. A cool hand brushes loose strands of my messy hair behind my ear, and I sigh in contentedness.

"How are you feeling?" His honeyed tone melts away the discomfort.

But my answer still comes out as a groan.

A glass of icy water meets my lips, the wetness clearing away the lingering nastiness of cotton mouth. When he demands I open for him, he drops little white pills on my tongue, forcing me to swallow them back as his strong hand follows the movement down my throat.

I want to push him away, question why he's here, how he found me, but for once in my life the fight in me that's always at the surface doesn't have the strength. Plus, the gentleness in which he's caressing my face as I find my equilibrium stops my inner sass from shining through.

Pushing myself up to a seated position, I tug the blanket into my lap, covering up my naked legs. Not because I'm feeling shy. No; because one heated look from him as he peruses my skin will trigger a spark and kindle the fire that burns inside me for him. I need my wits about me when he's sitting so close that I can smell his clean, earthy wood-like scent.

I lift my gaze to meet his, but his eyes are already on me, burrowing deep into my soul. His ocean eyes are dark, like a storm brewing in the middle of the sea.

Steeling my emotions, I have to ask, "How'd you find me Harkin? I know it wasn't my phone." He takes that opportunity to drop it in my lap and I thank the Gods above because I don't have the money to replace it. I was in such a state last night, wanting my space from him. I knew I couldn't take it with me. Ditching James was one thing, but I knew to truly disappear, I'd need to leave it behind.

"It's not important." He brushes my question off, standing to pace in front of the couch.

"Like hell it isn't." My irritation rises, and he must hear it in my tone, because he stops dead in front of me, crouching down. His large hands drop to my knees, squeezing, I'm momentarily distracted by the thick veins running up his forearms.

Focus woman.

"Why couldn't you have just stayed, Keira? We could have talked it through. You keep running from me. And I'll tell you now, it doesn't matter. It doesn't matter how many times you do it, or where you go, I'll find you."

What. The. Fuck.

I'm stunned into silence. What's that even supposed to mean? His intensity level just rocketed through the damn roof and I'm not sure how to respond. It's one thing to keep tabs on someone from a distance over the years like I'd done to him—especially when that someone's attached at the hip with your long-lost twin. But this man has known me for two-point-five seconds, and he thinks he has some claim on me.

"Answer my question." I finally pull my spinning thoughts together.

His shoulders droop with a drastic sigh. "You told me you were in Manhattan." He pauses at my eye roll, squeezing against my thighs in a silent warning. I knew it would get to him, but if he won't be honest, why should I show any respect?

"Robert texted me. Stacey mentioned you were here and upset. He had a feeling I might want to know after we left the club together last time," he finishes.

"That fucking club," I whisper under my breath. Stace and I are going to have a serious conversation regarding girl code. What the hell happened to sisters before misters?

"I would have done the same for him," he says with no uncertainty.

"What do you want from me, Harkin? I need to get my stuff and figure out where I'm going to live. I know what you said, but I don't think it's a smart idea. It's obvious we have too much baggage between us—and we're not ever together."

Uttering that statement breaks my heart. I've wanted him for all these years. Yearned to be near him and a part of his life. Now he's offering me my deepest desires and I'm still too scared to trust him fully. I lean back, forgetting how deep Stace's couch is, the tips of my shoulders hit the back pillows and now I'm reclined in an uncompromising position with him between my legs. He takes advantage of the shift crawling on top of me, caging me in but holding his weight off my frame.

"We have enough baggage to fill a 747, but you're sadly mistaken if you think we're not together." His weight drops on to me, trapping me under his hard body. There's no way for me to get free, but when his lips ghost against my chin, drawing up my jawline and to my ear that thought flies out the window.

"James and I moved the rest of your stuff over to my place last night. Come home," he whispers.

My resolve falters at that one word, home.

TWENTY-FIVE
HARKIN

NFWMB - Hoizer

I feel it the moment the word leaves my lips against her sensitive flesh.
Home.
She took to it like a moth to a dancing flame. The fight in her enraptured eyes dissolves between us, her frame going slack beneath me. It's no surprise she'd have a deep-seated need for a place to call home after being bounced around most of her life. As the quiet moment passes, I promise myself to make my place just that. A home for us.

When the small smile creeps upon my lips she follows the tilt with her eyes, her brows pinching tight with a fake pout. "Fine, you win," she huffs, "but first, coffee."

. . .

STROLLING down the street hand-in-hand feels foreign. I'd resigned myself to a life of solitude. To the loneliness that filled my veins after what'd happened to Alina. But the ice-cold sludge that kept me from caring for anyone else has to turned to magma around my little dark one.

Keira's gate slows as we make it back to *our* apartment.

"I put all your stuff in the guest room. We didn't bring over any of the furniture, but if you want it, I can add it to my storage unit."

"None of it is important, let him have it for my missing rent." Her eyes roll at that.

It doesn't matter now that she's under my roof. Marco tried to play big man with some fucked up mind game. He probably thought he could use it to manipulate her into finally giving him an ounce of attention. Well, his plan turned to shit and backfired right in his face.

I still had to make it right for my girl. There was no way, I was going to let him keep the cash. With a few clicks of my keys that money, plus a slight bit of interest for the shit he put her through went right back into her account.

She heads straight for her room. If I didn't know it'd cause another fight between us, I would have moved her straight into my room. But I'd rather have her across the hall, than across the city. It won't take long to draw her in closer. If history has a habit of repeating itself, it only took me a couple weeks to move her from across the street into my place. I give it a couple days before her body warms my sheets at night.

"You good?" I ask as she shuffles around, cataloging her things. We did a thorough sweep of her place. I didn't want her to have any reason to go back. It was a nice little insight into my girl's inner workings. I didn't expect to find a collection of blades to rival mine in count, but no comparison in artisanship. I wonder where her fascination lies with them.

Her knees hit the ground softly before she leans forward to dig through an open box. Her round ass is on full display in those black skinny jeans that cling tightly to her fit frame.

"Yeah, I'll unpack a bit, then probably shower and nap. Since an inconsiderate jerk woke me up way too early." Her head whips in my direction over her shoulder with a saucy smile, but I'm already behind her. Her eyes flick up to mine and I tamper down the groan that rises in the back of my throat at the sight of her on her knees before me.

"Watch it, little one." My fingers tangle in the short hairs at the nape of her neck, turning her chin further to me. "You ran out of here yesterday, leaving me no way to reach you or find you. But when I did as I always will," I say through gritted teeth, my fingers tightening in her hair, her chest rises in quick succession as her breathing picks up, "you call me the inconsiderate one."

Stepping around her shrinking form, I drop to a squat in front of her, meeting her blackened gaze. "You shouldn't be able to sit for a week." Her eyes drop to the floor, in shame or surrender, I'm not sure. I grip her chin and bring it back to me, "But I promised myself after our last scene together, we'd talk out everything before I doled out another punishment. Regardless, of how much you might deserve it."

Standing abruptly, I stride for the door pausing as I step into the hall. "You're the only thing I take into consideration these days," I throw over my shoulder before escaping to my office and away from the maddening woman.

Leaving the office door open to keep an ear out, I stride to my desk and pull up short. A white envelope with no markings lies across my keyboard. Whipping out my phone, I hit two and send. It rings twice before James's raspy voice cracks through the speaker.

"Yeah, boss?"

"Did you leave this envelope on my desk?"

"No, sir, I haven't been in the apartment since we finished moving things over."

I don't respond, picking up a pencil and pushing the heavy envelope off the keys, the contents shift and peek from the opening.

"Harkin?" James calls over the phone. "Need me to come up and check it out?"

Tilting the envelope, the rest of the way, photos spill out onto the desktop and my heart stills.

"No, I've got it. Thanks, James," I tell him, before hanging up.

Black and white photos of Keira litter my desk. One of her working at the airport counter, another of her at the cemetery, a grainy pixilated rare moment through her apartment window when she left the curtains open. My fists clench as the realization hits that I'm not the only one who's had my eyes on her.

Signing into my computer, I pull up the security system for the apartment. Access shouldn't have been possible without a notification directly to my phone. There was only a brief window of time from when I left to Keira and I getting back that someone could have been in here. I scroll back to the beginning of that time frame and start the recordings. Nothing on the internal camera, so I switch to the hidden external ones I have positioned at the building's entrance and facing the sidewalk in front of the building.

No one stands out. The only people to come in or out are Ms. Jensen and her yappy little dog and a food delivery person. The hairs on the back of my neck rise as I pause on the figure; a cap pulled down to cover their face, a brown paper bag with no descriptive emblem to determine where they work. Their frame is slight, and it doesn't help that the oversized clothing shields me from any further evidence. Could be nothing, but it's the unnecessary backpack slung over their shoulder that tells me not to let it go.

I shift the photo to the opposite screen and toggle back to my internal camera blowing up the six different feeds that run simultaneously all day.

I should probably tell Keira about them.

The thought pops into my head, but that's not what's important right now. That's when I see it. All six cameras go black, their backup batteries kicking in a few seconds later. Then an almost undetectable glitch that loops the footage first at the front door and then through the rest that cover every angle of my apartment.

This shouldn't be possible; I built my program from the ground up. It's a closed-circuit system, programmed to work with the app I made and have sole access to. Its encrypted password protection should have kept anyone from gaining entrance, but apparently that's not the case.

My anger heats, building from earlier. I'm so focused on digging through my code to find where they found entry. I don't hear her footsteps approach, but the firm grip of her fingers on my shoulder pulls my focus from the screen. She lowers the most incriminating photo into my view, the two of us amidst our display at the club. That one I hadn't noticed; it must have been at the bottom of the stack.

"So much for the member's confidentiality clause at *The Red Door.*" She drops the photo in my lap and moves to pull away, but my grip flies up tightening around her delicate wrist. Swiveling my chair in her directions, I move the photo from my lap in exchange for pulling her taut ass into it. My thumb rubs against the detailed line work covering the raised scars running vertically up her inner arm.

"Mhm, yes. I'd have to agree with you on that one, little one." I whisper into her ear, trying to keep the malice from my tone.

Her head snaps in my direction. "What's that supposed to mean? You're the one who broke it. Who even took these photos, anyway?"

"Well, that would be the million-dollar question." The look of confusion coating her eyes tells me she still hasn't clued into the situation. But that slowly slips away as the light bulb goes off and concern replaces it.

"It wasn't you?" The whispered squeak passes through her dusty rose lips.

"No. But I'll figure it out." Her stare leaves mine scanning the photos again and taking in the computer screens. While one runs through the security system code, the other still displays the camera system. *I knew I should have told her.*

"You have cameras in the apartment?"

"And outside." I confirm. Her finger trails across the screen, mentally tallying their locations.

"Don't waste your time, I'm going to have to change their hiding spots now anyway."

"Wait, what? Why?"

I take a deep breath, finding the resolve to be open about the situation instead of keeping it from her. We saw how well that worked the last time. "I didn't take the photos. And James didn't leave them for me. Which means—" Before I can finish my thoughts, her hands tighten on my thighs, her eyes cast away, staring off into the hall.

"Someone else left them. Someone was in the apartment." She finally puts two-and-two together.

I sigh. "Yeah, exactly." My anger peaks. "Which they shouldn't have been able to do with my system in place. And if they saw the camera feed it's safe to say they're smart enough to calculate where the cameras are located."

"Call the company who installed it. They should have footage of whomever it was."

The laugh tumbles from my lips, jostling her in my lap. "I am the company, sweetness. It's my design, my program, my build. It should have been impenetrable." My fist slams next to us against the solid desk. The unexpected outburst has her pushing from my lap and creating an unwanted space between us. She backs away slowly, turning to the built-in bookshelf. Her hands rest against the ledge of the counter, head hanging between her shoulders.

I follow her retreat slowly, swiping her raven locks to one side before I press in close. Her frame stiffens, but as the heat grows between us, each and every muscle relaxes as my lips meet the sensitive skin just below her right ear. The shiver it extracts causes my lips to tug with a smug smile. She might have pulled away when things unraveled before her eyes, but at least she didn't run this time. We're making progress.

"You're safe with me, little one."

Her huff of disagreement irks me.

"You literally just told me someone broke in because they made it past your homemade security system. That doesn't exactly instill much confidence for me."

"Mhm," I press out, exhaling as I trace my fingers up and down her arms, pushing in harder against her back. "And if they'd tried while we were home, we'd be having a very different conversation, little one."

TWENTY-SIX
KEIRA

Dirty Mind – Boy Epic

My life has always been a mess, filled with a plethora of trauma, so much so that this situation doesn't even rank top three. But it has me intrigued. Why would someone care what I was doing enough to watch me from a distance? Besides Harkin, that is. Recording the ins and outs of my life and then dropping them off for the guy I'm...seeing? Fucking? Dating?

Shit, I don't even know what we are, but Harkin has this intense, all-consuming need to be near me. As much as I've fought to keep the independence I'm so keen on, I can't deny how nice it is to have someone in my corner for once. Regardless of how our relationship started.

But I have no need for him to keep me safe; I've been doing that on my own since I was eight. Turning in his arms, I look up, taking in his haggard features. Between yesterday's commotion, our quick reprieve, and this new discovery, I can see it all weighing on him.

Tracing my fingers lightly against the crease between his thick, dark brows.

"I can take care of myself, Harkin," I remind him.

His lips graze against my palm, warming the skin with the lingering pressure. "I have no doubt about that, sweetness. I packed up your small armory. Tell me, do you use them?"

"A time or two. But only when absolutely necessary."

"Mhm." His tone hints at a note of approval.

I break against his caging embrace, moving back toward his desk and the catalog of surveillance photos scattered about. Picking up the least intrusive photo, I turn it over.

Friday, JFK, Night Shift. It reads across the empty space.

I drop it back down onto the table, picking up the next photo. It's the same thing.

Wednesday, *The Red Door*, Member's Guest, Not alone.

I flip through the rest of the photos. Each one follows the same pattern: day, place, small description.

Not only was I being spied on, whoever it was also took stock of my schedule. How long had this been going on around me without me noticing? Picking up the envelope they arrived in, I shake it, making sure nothing's stuck inside, but flipping it over leaves me more confused.

Your next job

"What the hell does this mean?" I shove it in Harkin's direction. He takes it in, while I watch his expression, his eyes go wide, before he quickly schools his features back into place.

"You know something, don't you?"

"Fuck," he whispers under his breath, running fingers through his already tousled hair.

"Harkin!"

"I have an idea."

"Would you like to enlighten the class?" My annoyance drips from the question.

"So, I did this job for—well, I don't actually know who it was for—but let's just say they weren't on the up-and-up."

Interrupting before he can continue, I ask, "When you say, *did a job...*" My universal sign for whacking a person, making my question pretty damn clear.

His vociferous laughter eases my original concern. "Sweetness, I told you what my job is. Do you think I moonlight as a hitman or something?" His face lights with amusement.

I shake my head at my ridiculousness, but the thought had filtered through.

"I mean a mysterious envelope full of surveillance photos. A creepy note. It seems kind of cut and dry."

His arms pull me in against his chest, crushing my cheek against his rigid muscles. "Look, I know how it seems. But I have no clue what they expect from me. The last thing I did had to do with locating information. Maybe that's the case here, too. They obviously know we know each other." He pulls back, looking down into my eyes. "Whatever it is, I'd never do anything to put you in harm's way, little one. And I'll stop anyone who tries."

My eyes cast down at his intense declaration. His fingers dig into my chin, pulling my gaze back up to meet his. "Do you understand?"

My head nods in agreement.

"Will you tell me what they want?" He doesn't answer me, weighing his answer behind closed eyes and a drawn in breath.

"Yes."

DAYS GO by as I settle into my new warped reality. I'd spent years obsessively watching his life through a screen as an unknown bystander. Then, almost a year across the street, soaking in every glimpse of him I could manage before that fateful day we ran into each other. Now, we're sharing a space, and I don't know what to do with myself. You'd think I'd take advantage, but I can't help feeling awkward.

I've never lived with a man, let alone one that sets my skin on fire with need. All it takes is a mere innocent look across the kitchen counter and I'm booking it back to my bed for a date with my battery-operated-boyfriend.

He's kept his distance ever since those photos showed up for some infuriating reason. Before I moved in, it seemed like he couldn't keep his hands off me every time we were in the same room. It's been days, and he hasn't so much as grazed a wandering hand across my ass.

Did I get friend zoned without me noticing?

Enough, is fucking enough. For the past week we've been dancing around each other, and I can't take it anymore.

I pull my door open just a crack, peeking out into the hall. It's clear both ways and I can't hear anything from the living room. With my laptop tucked under my arm and my headphones already in, I slink down the hall. The sky darkens outside, the slightest sliver of grey lines my old apartment building across the street. The room's empty—as I suspected—and I blow out a relieved breath.

Setting my computer on the coffee table in front of my favorite high-backed leather chair, I make a beeline to the liquor cabinet and Harkin's extensive collection of top shelf alcohol. Guilt fills me the moment I blend a mixer with the amber liquor, when I'm pretty sure they're meant to be sipped and savored. But my palate can't tell the difference between a bottle of Jack or Johnnie; it burns all the same and leaves my limbs feeling warm and heavy.

Finishing up my concoction with a generous pour of grenadine and a maraschino cherry, I'm ready to settle in. I prop my feet up on the solid wood table, my fuzzy socks dancing to the music filling my ears. The fire flickers beside me in the grate, the ambiance shockingly cozy for how minimal and clean it is. I stare out the windows, watching the lights from the buildings across the skyline twinkle, New York's equivalent of a starry sky.

My fingers find their familiar pattern to search the same pages I've looked at repeatedly. But it's been months since I've peeked. I'm not surprised to find it's still frozen in time, the last entry from over a year ago, way before I stumbled upon him in my neighborhood.

Pressure falls to my shoulders and a loud shriek leaves my lips. My body jolts in the chair, my laptop nearly crashing to the floor but my cat like reflexes snatch it just before it plunges down. I whip around to Harkin's mischievous smile, taking a deep breath to calm the racing rhythm of my heart.

"Really, with everything going on, you thought sneaking up on me was the right move?"

His lips suck in trying to avoid the expanding smile on his face.

"What were you looking for, little one?" he asks, reaching over my body in the chair and pulling the screen back in our direction. I sink into the furniture, avoiding eye contact, with his questioning glances.

He takes in the screen, making a small noise of understanding. His fingers move like lightning across the keys and a website I haven't thought about in years fills the screen. I never would have thought to check Tumblr since he'd given up on posting to Facebook long ago. But even if I had, I'd never been able to put two-and-two together to realize this page belonged to him.

He walks around the chair, plucking me and the laptop up before he steals my spot, settling me on his lap. His chin nods in the computer's direction as his hands drop, resting on my exposed thighs. His fingers run up and down my warmed skin, tracing small shapes, and diverting my attention.

It's been days since I've felt his skin on my mine. That friend zone I thought he punted me into is possibly a figment of my imagination.

"Look." His deep command stills my wandering thoughts, and my eyes roam back to the screen.

Scrolling quickly without taking them in there's tens—if not hundreds—of black and white photos, silhouettes mostly. I slow my scrolling, only to realize the silhouettes look an awful lot like me. That night in front of the window, my body cast in a red hue, when all there was between us was a chance meeting and a couple of white cards. Me sleeping in Harkin's bed after that night I still can't remember from the bar. There are other random things thrown in, but my eyes keep homing in on the ones of myself.

"In case you needed more proof that I didn't take the photos on my desk. I'd say I have a more artistic eye, wouldn't you?"

My breath catches at his confession. "You little sneak."

I can't be upset with his intrusion. They're beautiful, intriguing, haunted even. My eyes cast above the fireplace to the oversized canvas and a knowing smile tugs at his lips. Nodding my chin in its direction, my non-verbal question asked.

"It's you." He nuzzles into my neck, and a small sigh escapes my lips. I slip the computer off my lap and turn to face him, straddling his lap.

The oversized hoodie that usually hangs low on my thighs, rides up, almost exposing the black-lace, boy-short panties hidden beneath. His heated stare drops between us, sending tingles of pent-up excitement through my limbs.

"You've been avoiding me, sweetness."

I smile at his observation. "It's not like you couldn't come find me."

"Mmm, is that what you wanted me to do?"

Was it?

Was I waiting for him to make the first move again after everything that had come up between us? Probably. But how long could I keep shoving my need for him aside? One taste isn't enough. My body craves him with an intensity that only grows the longer I go on tip toeing around the apartment.

I've played coy long enough. The whole reason I dragged myself out of hiding and made myself comfortable in the middle of the living room was to draw his attention away from the computer screens that have had him occupied the last couple of days.

I have a sinking suspicion one of his special security cameras has a hiding spot in my room. If I'm right, he's gotten a shit ton of very explicit, free content I could have easily charged hundreds of dollars for online.

I want his dominant side to come back out and play. To take my choice away and make me give in. I'd never been submissive in bed. I always went after what I wanted, knew what I needed to get off, and took it. But with Harkin it's different. He's shown me he could play my body without guidance. I'd never had that with a guy before. They're usually clueless in bed.

"I can hear the gears churning in there." He taps my temple before returning his hands to my thighs. The black-inked rose on his right hand, and the moth on the other, contrasts against the colorful mirage of florals that skate up my legs.

His thick fingers slide higher, disappearing under the hoodie finding the lacy edges of my panties. My pussy tightens in anticipation when his thumbs brush under the hem, teasing my sensitive skin, making me quiver with the smallest movements.

I squirm in his lap, trying to get his fingers closer to the needy bitch between my legs, but he refuses to grant me my wish.

"Talk to me, little one, tell me what you want."

I whine a sigh of irritation, desperate for him to take control, shaking my head in response because I'm curious to see how this will play out.

His full lips pull into a smile. "You don't want to tell me? But I bet those dirty little words out of that filthy mouth would sound fucking delicious." His hand pulls free from its torturously slow assault against the side of my pussy to grip my chin. His thumb pushes down on my bottom lip and those ocean eyes darken like a raging sea.

I capture his thumb between my teeth, dragging them sharply to the tip before running my tongue around it slowly. He watches my measured movements with intensity, pushing in deeper when I close my lips around it, giving a harsh suck. A deep growl pulls from his chest as I moan, my own pleasure rising from teasing him. He pushes the drenched lace coating my pussy to the side as his other hand finally contacts my core.

"That mouth has better uses then words, I see." He teases, but his tone is full of desperation.

His lips crash against mine ferociously gaining entrance and commanding my participation at the same time two fingers push deep inside my wet heat. My hips rock back and forth, pushing his fingers deeper inside as we work together to find the perfect rhythm.

His free hand falls to my hip, stalling my movements and the race for the orgasm building deep inside my core.

"Look at you, so desperate to take what's rightfully mine to give. Careful, little one, or you'll have to wait even longer."

My body stills completely.

There he is.

TWENTY-SEVEN
HARKIN

Gimme Love - Rosenfeld

She was so close, chasing her high on my fingers. Looking like a goddamn goddess in my lap, every care thrown away. She doesn't move once the threat leaves my lips. Is she ready to be my good girl tonight or is she just that desperate after the days we've spent going out of our way to miss each other in the halls?

That doesn't mean I haven't had my eyes on her this entire time. Her nightly performances have had my dick in my hand more than when I was fifteen, raging with new hormones. But I know they were just for me and that made my need for her spike.

"She listens," I tease and her eyes fill with flames. I know it doesn't come easy, and that makes it all the sweeter.

"Harkin." My name off her lips is my favorite sound.

"Yes, sweetness?"

"Take me to bed." There's no question in her tone, it's a demand without the stern admission. She's being careful.

My hands grip the back of her thighs tightly, lifting us from the chair and heading down the hallway. I stop in front of the gym, tempted by my collection of blades, but continue for my room. Throwing her onto the soft mattress, she bounces and pushes away from me until her back meets the headboard. I follow, slowly crawling up her body.

"Lose the hoodie," I order, and she quickly pulls it from her gorgeous body, tits on full display through the sheer, black-lace that matches those wicked little panties.

"Arms above your head."

She waits a beat before slowly moving. The little tease traces her finger up her sides, stopping to grope her breasts with a tight squeeze before continuing upward through her dark locks, finally getting to the smooth edge of the headboard. "Don't move." I fight the desire to run and grab my camera to capture this moment and add another print to my collection. But I can't pull my gaze from her—let alone leave the room. They'll have to wait for another time.

The leather of my belt whooshes against the fabric of my jeans, popping free from the loops. Those warm amber eyes watch me with precision and interest.

"Yes or no, sweetness?" I ask, holding the belt tightly in my grasp.

Her chest heaves, approval coming with a quick nod.

Threading the tail back through the buckle, my fingers race through the intricate steps to get her cuffs ready, but my patience snaps when her thighs rubs together. The shift grazes her thighs ever so slightly against the rough material of my jeans.

Fuck, this is taking too long.

I should have just grabbed the cuffs from the closet. Her small needy whimper breaks the little concentration I have left. Flinging the belt across the room, my eyes swing back to the vixen in my bed.

My hand shoots out across the intimate space between us, grasping her lowering wrists and shoving them back above her head, pinning them tightly to the headboard.

"Stay," I growl into her neck, biting down carelessly before coating it with a with a warm lick to ease the sting. A hiss of pain pushes through her lips as her body trembles under me. My cock strains painfully against the zipper of my jeans, more than ready to slide between her slick folds. But that'll have to wait; I don't think she's suffered enough for her teasing.

I'd never been jealous of an inanimate object before. That fucking pink vibrator she keeps buried in her nightstand almost went missing after the first time I caught her on camera with it. But the way she writhed against it with her hand between her thighs and the other tweaking her pierced nipples... I couldn't steal it. The visual was better than any porn I could find on the internet.

"Are you going to be a good girl and listen, little one?" I ask, my voice laced with craving. Though something deep in the recesses of my mind hopes she says no.

Her fingers tighten against the lip of the headboard, turning white at the knuckles.

I don't wait for an answer. Quickly dropping to the mattress between her legs, I shove them wider. The scent of her arousal washes over me and I drive forward, the tip of my tongue running against the drenched fabric concealing her cunt. We moan in unison. If the day ever comes when I'm offered my last meal, I'd request Keira on a silver platter.

Rolling to the side, my fingers make quick work of sliding

her panties off before pocketing them in my jeans. A small noise of protest comes from deep in her throat, but no words accompany it.

"Mmm, so wet for me, sweetness. Do you drip like this for your plastic toys?" I ask before giving a quick nip to her clit. A mousey squeak escapes her lips, followed by a quick shake of her head.

I didn't think so.

I run the flat of my tongue from the tight ring of muscle we've yet to explore back to her swollen bud. Her hips jerk up and recede, warring between seeking more pleasure and running from it when it becomes too intense. I drop a heavy hand to her lower stomach and press two fingers against her weeping entrance.

Her groans of pleasure spur my fingers on as they work her cunt faster and deeper. My tongue doesn't let up and I can feel her pussy gripping me, that orgasm she was so desperate for earlier climbing again. I shove my hips into the mattress, my cock hard as steel. My balls tighten but there's no way I'm going to come in my pants like I'm tasting pussy for the first time.

Casting my eyes slowly up her naked body, I stop at those hands again, not where they're supposed to be. I tsk at my sweet girl and pull away quickly, leaving her teetering the edge. Her eyes fly open, meeting mine with heated furry.

"What am I going to do with you, little one. You said you could listen and follow directions, but here we are again."

Her nostrils flare with indignation, but that gleam in her eyes softens when she comes to terms with the fact I'm right.

"I'm sorry, it just—I just felt so good," she pleads.

"I know baby and you were doing so well." My hands brush softly up her calves to the back of her knees. I pull roughly, her light weight sliding down the mattress with ease until her center meets the bulge in my jeans. The little minx grinds against my shaft, and I swallow down the moan her heat easily pulls from me.

Our eyes lock and the corner of her mouth tugs slightly, she knows she's playing with fire, but my girl isn't a natural born submissive. She's obstinate at every turn, but I can't say I don't like the challenge.

My lips descend, closing the space between us Her neck falls back like I knew it would, granting me better access. "But you see, little one, only good girls get to come on my tongue. Bad girls who don't listen, get stuffed full of my cock, and fucked hard for my pleasure and my pleasure only."

She mewls at my threat.

She was seconds away from falling off that cliff and if I fuck her as rough and fast as I need right now, she won't be able to stop herself from coming all over my dick. And she's far from deserving that right now.

I reach between our bodies popping the button of my jeans and her eyes zone in on my fingers. Dropping the zipper slowly, allows my throbbing cock reprieve from its tight confines. Our bodies are so close my knuckle glides against her slick slit, the deep intake of air she just sucked in confirming how sensitive her pussy is.

"Take it," I demand.

Her eyes fly back to mine confusion setting in.

"Put those pretty little hands on my cock, sweetness, and make me come all over that needy pussy."

She doesn't hesitate, using one hand to stroke me. The other disappears lower, finding my heavy sack.

"Harder," I growl, and this time she listens. Taking a quick beat to gather her juices on her own fingers before coating my shaft and doubling her efforts.

Fuck me.

Working my own cock will never do now that I know what it's like to have her delicate fingers wrapped around me instead. But I didn't start this with the intention of only getting a hand job.

No, that pussy is *mine* and for the life of me in this moment, as my balls tightens and the base of my spine tingles, I can't remember why I'm not buried to the hilt inside my girl.

Fuck it.

Shoving her hands aside, I grip her wrists and pull them above her head, holding them tightly in one hand. I guide my cock to her entrance, teasing her with an inch, but her greedy cunt tightens around me pulling me in deeper against my will. The goddess underneath me must be borrowing a silent siren's song to fulfill her desire, and I'm just another poor sailor with no chance of breaking free.

I pull out completely, my body cursing my decisions with a throbbing cock in hand.

Slapping her sensitive clit with it, pulls a hiss from her swollen, seductive lips.

"Harkin," she says, pleading through a lustful haze in her eyes.

"Whose pussy is this, sweetness?"

Her thighs are wet, her pale skin flushed pink from her cheeks down to her heavy tits. Those dark orbs staring up at me are half lidded, but still a cheeky little smile breaks through.

Don't do it.

"Mine." Her bright smile lights her face, like the cat that got the cream.

What a fucking brat.

This time a sharp slap from my hand hits her cunt and that smile fades quickly

"Want to try that again," I ask. When my knuckles push roughly through her folds, stopping at her engorged pearl, the threat lays between us. The standoff between us builds, my knuckles applying pressure that falls just short of the painful pinch she'll be getting here in a second if the next words off her tongue aren't what I want to hear.

"Yours," she agrees, but fire dances in those golden eyes.

It's like staring at a bonfire for hours, under the stars, on the beach. Mesmerizing, but deadly if you fall in. And my dumbass is ready to dive in headfirst, third-degree burns be damned.

I squeeze hard anyway.

"Ahh," her breathy voice shouts into the still room. Let that be a lesson to her continued insolence.

I don't give her a second to adjust from the pain before I slam home deep inside her. A cacophony of our ragged moans dances around the room, the slap of skin mixing in to create our own sensual melody. I should split the audio from the camera recording in the corner. How salacious it would be to create a soundtrack I can keep on as background music throughout the house.

I wonder how long it would take her to catch on.

My wandering mind comes back into focus when the daggers she calls fingernails skate down my back, no doubt pulling droplets of blood to the skin. The sting only spurs me on. Each thrust against her core shoves her body further up the bed until her head hits the headboard.

Pulling out of her warm heat, my cock coated in her juices, my hand drops from her wrists to her flared hips.

"Flip over for me, little one; ass up."

She scrambles over quickly. The view of her pale skin swirled through with colorful ink makes me want to leave my marks in the empty spaces. Add my art to her canvas.

"Harkin, come on," she mewls, shoving her ass back against my raging hard on. The slickness glides it through her ass cheeks. A groan drags from my chest. Gripping her hips, my fingers dig deep against her hipbones.

"Mmm, baby, one of these days you're going to give this up to me." Dragging my thumb through her wetness, I rim her tight hole, giving her just enough pressure to feel me. She shifts her hips back, taking me inside. Her loud moans fill the room as she fucks her ass on my finger.

Fuck.

"My greedy girl. You want me to fill both your holes, don't you?" I ask, barely above a whisper. Grasping my cock, I sink back into her tight pussy. Gathering saliva at the tip of my tongue, I let it fall, pulling my thumb free and adding more lube for her pleasure. My hips pound forward, balls slapping that delicious spot that causes her to spew an incoherent plea for more.

She's close to falling over the edge. It's in the way she pulses around me. But there's something holding her back. Her rhythm falls erratic as the pleasure builds and courses through us both. Our moans paint the room in a glorious harmony.

My balls ache with the need to fill her full of cum and watch it drip down her creamy thighs. But I hold back, determined to let her lead the way to our joint ecstasy.

It'd be easy enough to shove her over with the right stroke of my fingers against her clit but that would mean taking my thumb out of her ass. Selfishly refusing to do so, as that thin wall between my cock and thumb causes my cock to harden to an almost painful fullness with each stroke.

"Touch yourself, little one," I order.

But she doesn't move, her hands grip tighter into the plush comforter. My hand cracks hard against her tight backside, eliciting a drawn-out muffled moan from her lips. But no doubt the sting got her attention since those fingers slowly dip below her body.

I rub the red patch of skin staring up at me, before a lighter smack hits the same area. The third time my hand meets her sensitive flesh, the dam of euphoria breaks, washing through her as her body quakes against me. Her core drenches my cock, inciting my last violent thrust forward. A deep groan tears free from my diaphragm, rivaling any beasts roar, as I empty down into her heavenly depths.

Our bodies crumble into a heap on the mattress, limbs tangled, bodies satiated from the carnal hunger burning between us—for now.

Rolling to her side, I pull her into my chest. Her cheeks flush a deep-rosy, red, those dark thick lashes fighting to keep my gaze, as sleep tries to steal her away. Brushing an unruly lock of hair behind her ear I whisper, "Baby, you need to get up and use the bathroom. We didn't use protection."

She stirs under my soft words but comes to when my lips caress hers gently.

"Do I need to carry you, or do you think can you make it?"

Her lips quirk quickly to the side at my offer. When she doesn't make to move, I take that as my queue and slide from the bed, pulling her relaxed form into a bridal carry. Her limp arms hang heavy around my neck as her head thuds against my shoulder. She nuzzles into me; a contented sigh blows the baby hairs at the nape of my neck, sending a chill through me, and I tighten my hold.

Dropping her feet to the warmed tile floors in the bathroom, she sways before finally opening her eyes and steadying herself upright.

"Thank you." Her hoarse gratitude sticks in my chest. A tightness physically constricting the muscles around my heart at the look in her uninhibited eyes. Every exposed piece of her drags me in. The need to be with her, protect her, consume her whole hasn't lessened a modicum in the week she's been here. If anything, it's intensified at her closeness.

My fingers wrap around her naked waist, tugging her flush against my front before I drop a quick kiss to her forehead. I turn back for the bed; the door clicking shut behind me. Falling flat across the mattress, my body sings as I breathe in the sweet muskiness clinging to the sheets.

I'll never be able to let her go.

Not that I planned to. I just hope my grip's strong enough to hold on through the storm heading straight for us.

TWENTY-EIGHT
KEIRA

Scars – Boy Epic

The frigid winter weather bites against the tips of my ears as I pull the door shut behind me. Settling into the warmed leather seats, I lean forward toward the vents blowing out toasty air. A sigh of relief brushes passed my lips, and an amused chuckle fills the cab of the SUV. My neck snaps to the left, in the driver's direction–where I assumed James would be, as he always is. But Harkin sits there instead.

"What are you doing here?" I ask.

"I thought we could get some coffee and breakfast," he says casually, but there's an air of unease surrounding him.

"Can we just go home? I've been on my feet for the last eight hours and I'm tired." Silence falls around us when he doesn't answer my question. I have no energy to deal with the silent treatment right now.

"Harkin." His name comes out clipped, demanding the answer I'm owed.

"No."

My eyes shoot daggers into his profile, but he ignores me, pulling into the traffic exiting from the airport.

"Excuse me? What do you mean, no?"

He cranks his neck left and right, popping the joints, a long deep breath accompanies the dramatic display.

"I'll explain at breakfast. But for now, can you just cooperate with me?" he implores.

Crossing my arms over my chest, I grant him a huff of irritation before turning away to face the passenger window.

Am I pouting like a damn child? Sure. But I can't stand the cryptic as hell answer he just gave me. Why not just explain now while we drive? What could be so important that we need to go sit in a public place to have the conversation.

My body freezes as a thought creeps into my mind.

What if he knows?

But how could he know?

I haven't mentioned Alina at all. The computer I use now is squeaky clean when it comes to her.

What about the thumb drive? my subconscious taunts.

But that's hidden, deep in a ring box, in a makeup bag, in a backpack, inside my duffle bag that I shoved to the back of the closet. Was it overkill? I thought so at the time, but maybe I was wrong.

The car slows to a crawl, waiting for the only open parking spot on the street. For a native Californian, Harkin has no issues guiding the oversized SUV into the tight opening. Parking spots in New York are few and far between in this area. The city has a sick sense of humor with how tiny they made them.

He reaches behind me into the back seat, poking around for a few seconds before his hands pull a beanie over my head, covering my ears.

"It's just around the corner, but you were obviously cold on the walk to the car."

I should thank him for his thoughtfulness, but my blood's heated from this unexpected journey. My ass had planned to be back in bed by now, after a hot soak in the grand freestanding tub my ensuite has.

Instead, I jump out of the car and slam the door behind me. Apparently, my penchant for door slamming is not limited to inside. But Harkin doesn't seem to notice, he's too preoccupied by whatever thoughts are clouding his mind. He wraps an arm around my waist, pulling me into his side and starts guiding us to wherever he's taking me for breakfast.

As soon as we step around the corner, the building comes into sight and there's no missing it. My vision swims and my blood turns to ice. I dig my feet into the pavement and refuse to go any further.

The suppressed memories from my childhood come rushing back. Pixilated at first, like when you'd turn on an old TV and the screen took time to warm before the channel came through clear. But when they do my stomach turns at the blood pooling around her lifeless body. The screeching tires make it to my ears, even after the deafening shots ring out around us. My hands cup my ears even now as my body drops into a crouch on the sidewalk.

My head pounds from the onslaught of unwanted images. I just want them to stop. My vision grows blurry as I blink away tears, only for them to fill to the brim again and run down my face. His rough fingers grip tightly to my lowered chin, dragging my watery gaze up to meet his hallowed eyes.

His lips move against the air, but I don't catch what he's saying. My subconscious refuses to release its claws from my reality, pulling me deeper and deeper into a past I try my damnedest to forget.

"Fight it." Mumbled whispers slowly pierce the world I'm drowning in, resurfacing me inch by struggling inch.

"Keira, focus on me, baby."

And I do; I take in his handsome face, jaw clenched tight, eyes filled with concern. His thumbs run soothingly against my cheeks as he holds them tightly to keep me from peering around his body.

My chest still heaves as I struggle to pull oxygen into my lungs. If I had it in me, I'd use the pranayama breathing my therapist recommend I use in times like these. But who was she kidding? Instead, my eyes lock on the small scar parallel to Harkin's hairline, using it as an anchor until the gasping subsides.

Before I can utter a word of explanation, I'm hoisted into Harkin's arms and carried back the fifty feet we'd made it to the SUV. Instead of depositing me into the passenger seat like I'd assumed, he pushes me across the bench seat in the middle and climbs in after me.

"What are you doing?" I question his weird choice of seating arrangements.

"Are you okay?" he asks.

His eyebrows tilt down, the crease between them deep. I reach my finger up without thinking and run it down the spot of concern, smoothing it away. Taking in the first deep breath my body will allow and letting it out slowly, I nod sharply to answer him. I know he'll want an explanation, but I'm worried doing so with throw me back into a tailspin.

"This place—why'd you bring me here?" My tone slides

close to accusing, but he doesn't know the whole scope of what happened that day. Especially not the specifics of where it went down. What was he supposed to do avoid every diner from here to New Jersey, just in case?

"I didn't know. Fuck Keira, I'm so sorry. They must have torn down the original building and changed the name. I never would have brought you here if I'd known. I only picked it because it's close to where we need to go after this." He looks down at his watch, swearing quietly to himself.

"And now I have no time to explain things the way I wanted to."

"Harkin, slow down! I don't care where we need to go, tell me what's going on." The change in topic has taken my mind off what just happened, and I need to keep it that way.

"I set a meeting with the people who sent those surveillance photos."

"And you're taking me?" I push away from him, scrambling to turn quickly and find the handle, looking for escape. I know he said he'd protect me, but why would he be taking me in to meet whoever this person is. My foot doesn't make it out of the SUV before an arm is snatching me back and closing the door again.

"What are you doing?" he asks in my ear, a trace of hilarity in his tone.

I turn slowly to meet his eyes, letting my annoyance show. I should have known better.

When has running from this man ever gotten me what I wanted?

"You're not making me meet with these people who have been watching me, Harkin. What if they have some sinister motive? What if you're leading me to my slaughter? Come on, use your fucking head!" I bite out.

I thought this man was supposed to be smart.

His body slinks back against the other door, taking me in as my temper gets the best of me—as it usually does.

"Are you done?" he asks with a smirk. "What did I tell you?" He pauses, waiting for my answer that doesn't come.

Shaking his head he says, "Over my dead body would I ever put you in a situation for something to happen. I don't trust these people. But I need you to be close. If it's something inconsequential you come in, we figure it out and move on. No more worries of these men following you."

"And if it's not?" I ask worriedly.

"Well, then I know where you are. I get all the information out of them and then we figure out our next move."

"Seems to me like I could have just gone home, and you could have monitored me with that fancy hidden camera you refuse to remove from my room," I sass.

He looks unimpressed by my suggestion.

"It's too late now. I have to be there in ten minutes. These aren't the kind of men you keep waiting." He hurries into the driver's seat, starting the car and blasting the heat.

I don't make to move up front. The fool interrupted my sleep schedule. Stretching my legs out across the bench seat, I slip down, cozying into my puffy parka.

Harkin looks back at me and smiles.

THE SUV PULLS UP to a nondescript brick building at the edge of town. Vast windows face the parking lot. The ones that aren't busted out look coated in grime and years of dust, blocking a view of the inside. Empty pallets and other discarded items line the edges. The building looks deserted, the perfect place for a sketchy meet up.

"Okay, stay here. Don't get out of the car and don't leave.

The windows on this SUV are tinted so dark, that even with a nose pressed to the glass they won't be able to see in. They won't know you're here unless you show yourself. Got it?" he asks, staring at me through the rearview mirror.

I huff at his insulting directions.

Again, could have just let me go home and we wouldn't have to worry about them finding me, sitting a hundred feet from the building.

Harkin whips around in his seat when I don't answer. "Keira."

That one word's laced with seriousness, but it's the air of concern around him that finally makes me fold.

"Yeah, I got it."

He nods, trusting me enough to listen to him this time.

Although, history shows I'm not one to follow directions. He leans over popping the glove box open, pulling out a gun and two mags, checking to make sure they're loaded. Quickly loading one into place, he turns back to me handing the two pieces over.

"Do you know how to use this?"

I wrap my hand around the cold metal, cocking it to load a bullet into the chamber and checking the side to make sure the safety is in place. I slide the extra mag in my pocket.

"You know Glock makes a better concealed carry 9mm, right?"

"I'll take that as a yes, then." He laughs.

"What about you?" I ask, wondering if he should take this with him instead.

"Don't worry about me, little one. I much prefer my blades to bullets, but even I know when not to bring a knife to a gunfight." He smirks. "Stay here. Don't open the doors for anyone. I'll be back."

His long strides cross the wet pavement quickly. When he approaches the building, he doesn't slow, disappearing through an open passage where a door once hung.

The minutes tick by and nothing seems to happen. I haven't seen anyone else enter and there are no other cars in the parking lot.

Something doesn't feel right.

TWENTY-NINE

HARKIN

Bad Moon Rising – Mourning Ritual feat. Peter Dreimanis

The warehouse is eerily quiet. My boots slap against the soaked concrete, echoing through the building and announcing my arrival. I take in the open space. Dulled whisperings pull my attention to the back. A small closed in space looks like it once housed an office of sorts.

Before I make it to the door, two men in suits walk out, the hulking bodyguard from before trailing behind taking in our surrounding with an eagle's eye.

"Ahh, Mr. Greyson, we meet again." The older of the two clasps his hands in front of him jovially, like this is a meeting of old friends.

"You broke into my apartment. I find it hard to ignore such disrespectful displays of opportunity," I bite out.

Junior, on his right, stifles a snort, and my eyes swing to him. Staring him up and down does nothing to dull the heated animosity stirring between us. I'm not sure what this guy's problem is, but I school my features, tampering down my irritation.

"Mhm, my apologizes. My associate is fond of theatrics if you will."

"So, what's this all about, anyway? I get pictures of some random girl left on my desk. I'm not sure how I can help you with that."

His body stiffens at my dismissal of the situation. "Mr. Greyson, let's not pretend you don't know who she is. She's a striking resemblance to Alina, is she not?"

Everything in me wants to shout out the questions rushing through my head.

How does he know Alina?

Why was he following me into *The Red Door*? How did he get in and take photos?

But I know better than to voice them. Men like him don't answer questions, unless the answer's already mutually known.

"Hence, why she drew my attention. But, playing with one random girl at a member's only club hardly classifies as knowing her. There's *usually* a tight grasp on the entrance list. Why not ask the manager?" I ask, playing off my interest as nonchalantly as possible.

An electric pause hangs in the air between the three of us. But I'm not about to throw my cards on the table until I know what they want with her.

Wrinkled hands, rub against his gray beard as the older man waits out the building silence. Finally, clearing his throat he says, "You know, I had higher hopes for this relationship. Your father was always willing to cooperate with us. He expected the same from you."

"What can I say, I'm not my old man," I tell him.

I swear I see a spark of understanding in his eyes. I don't know if that's a good thing for me or not. "Like I said, if you can't tell me anything else about this girl, I don't know how I can help you."

He nods to his partner who removes another folded paper from his inside jacket pocket. Goliath walks it over to me and drops it into my outstretched hand. Quickly scanning the paper, it's obvious it's a rental agreement. Before I even flip to the back page, I know I'll see Keira's signature at the bottom.

"Keira Fitzpatrick, that's her name?" I ask, like the girl hasn't been invading every thought running through my mind over the last month or so.

"Exactly. Now you've got a name, and you've got a face. I assume, that's enough for you to go on," the young, Scarface wanna be taunts.

"Enough for what exactly. You've given me information but nothing to work toward or a reason for it. I don't care what my father promised you. I decide what jobs I take. So, if you want me on this one, you're going to need to give me a little more than a file folder full of PI quality photos and a rental agreement." I need to know what they have in store for Keira before I make my move.

Then it happens, youngster drops his chin in a signal to the man guarding my six. He wrenches my hands behind me roughly, making quick work of securing them together. The sharp sting of hard plastic tells me he used zip ties, rookie mistake. I play along as if I won't be able to get out of these the second their backs are turned.

"Really, gentleman. I thought we had an understanding. I don't think what I'm asking for is exorbitant."

"It seems we're at an impasse, Mr. Greyson. Maybe some

time with my associates here will show you the answers to your incessant questions are unnecessary for you to do the job," he informs me before slapping my cheek in a patronizing flourish and taking his exit.

"Well, then this should be fun," my upcoming opponent tuts as he paces back and forth in front of me.

"You know, you sure show a lot of interest in a girl you seem to know nothing about," he taunts, trying to goad me into revealing some insightful secret he seems to think I'm hiding.

"Just trying to figure out what it is exactly you want me to do. I'm still waiting on that tidbit of information." I pause, thinking it over.

"I mean, it can't be that you want me to find her. Those photos are evidence enough that your man had no problem following her around at one point. So, what would you need me for?" I'm dying to see if he'll give away a sign that confirms my suspicion. But it seems the family business raised him. I'm sure they teach blank stare 101, in elementary. His teacher would be so proud because he's acing it right now.

"If it's not that you want me to find her, what else could it be? More information on her?" I probe again, at this point I must be annoying the shit out of him. I take immense joy in the possibility.

His eye twitches at my continued questions, no doubt on the edge of reaction.

"Or is that it? You've lost her and can't find her again." The laughter builds and escapes, echoing out into the open space. Of course, they have. Last night was the first day in a week I let her out of my sights. Her fight to go to work and not let me keep her safe at home was one she had to work hard to sell me on. Our compromise, she put in for an emergency leave starting today. We tried our luck on the possibility that someone was still watching.

The punch comes from my right, landing square against my jaw. My head whips to the side, the metallic tang of blood filling my mouth quickly.

A wicked smile creeps onto my face. I expected him to dole out some pain once his handler left. The problem is, pain doesn't shut me down. No it only livens the dark entity that hides in my depraved depths. His pleased smirk riles me further. But when I spit the excess moisture in my mouth at his feet, he snaps.

His fists batter against my body, but it's the punch to the gut that gives me the opportunity to transfer my weight forward. Lifting my arms up quickly, when they're released momentarily at the weight shift, I pull them down with the force needed to snap the plastic cuffs freeing my wrist and giving me the advantage, they sought to remove.

A calm washes over me as my body dances through the movements I've trained it to over the last year. Dropping to a knee, I slide the blades I promised myself I wouldn't need to resort to free. But they're my only option since the brick wall patted me down, and felt my piece tucked behind my back. relieving me of it. Idiot only did a half-assed job, not searching the inside of my boots.

"I wouldn't if I were you." The cold metal of my own gun presses against my temple.

I still my hands, blades still clutched tightly in my grasps. A tut from up above and a shove of the barrel, makes me fight against every instinct I have to keep them with me. Instead, I do the opposite letting them clang to the cement.

"He still has some sense in there after all," he says, tapping the gun against my head.

"You know, I'm sure we can easily find someone else to replace you. You don't seem worth the hassle. Tyson, get the tarp," he barks to his quiet bodyguard.

"Look, I don't think—" A shooting pain radiates against the back of my head. My vision swims with little white spots while bile climbs the back of my throat.

"You're right, you don't think. Now, shut up."

I watch as the thin translucent plastic's rolled out directly in front of me. A hard shove throws me forward onto my hands.

"Crawl." The order's thrown out without care.

My mind whirls, quickly computing distinct possibilities for this scenario. Trying to find a reasonable way out of this.

Before I work out my great escape, a crash sounds from across the warehouse. Everyone's gaze swings to the offender. It's the distraction I need to slide back to my discarded blades. Shaking free the last of the disorientation in my head.

The damned stubborn woman refuses to listen, but in this case, I'm relieved. The other two men move quickly in her direction. She doesn't falter. I watch as she strides nearer without hesitation, quickly subduing Tyson with two quick rounds, one to the chest, the other straight to the head. My interest piques between her comment in the car and her action before me. There are certainly more secrets hiding in that pretty little head of hers.

Blood splatters onto the lone obstacle between us. He pulls up short when his human shield thumps to the ground in front of him. Stalling his advancement in her direction. I watch as his hands shake to keep his gun pointed in her direction. We're closing in on him, he knows he has nothing to lose. Which only makes him more dangerous for my girl.

Keira, however, doesn't bat an eye at the gun pointed in her direction. She's completely collected with her pistol trained to echo the previous shot. But the words pull from my throat before she can. "Keira, don't." I call out to her.

His head pivots in my direction, a look of knowing in his eyes, and I know there's no other choice now. I stride forward, quickly closing the distance between us.

Keira fires again, distracting him for the moment I need to step behind his tense frame, blade at the ready. I bring it to meet his throat.

"You should have just answered my questions," I state coolly into his ear, before slicing the sharp blade across his throat in one quick motion. Blood spills quickly as I push his body away from me. He panics, gripping at the gaping wound there's no chance of staunching.

Keira steps up to me, carefully avoiding the blood pooling at my feet, eyes trained on the body count we now share.

"Once again you didn't listen, little one," I taunt, brushing a wild curl of hair behind her ear. Her lazy smirk holds an immense amount of proud unvoiced sass.

THIRTY
KEIRA

Him & I – G-Easy, Halsey

The ride back to the apartment is quiet. Harkin hasn't moved his hand from my body since we climbed into the SUV. When I saw the man in the expensive suit exit the building on his own and the minutes ticked by without Harkin following, my anxiety peaked. As soon as the blacked-out town car pulled out of the lot, I grabbed the pistol he'd left me with and sprinted across the pavement into the building.

Seeing him on his hands and knees, a gun pointed to the back of his head didn't leave me with much of an option but to shake off the metaphorical dust on my shooting skills. It wasn't the first time I'd watched the light in someone's eyes dull at my hands. But it was the first time I'd had someone bear witness to the crime.

That ceased to matter when Harkin sliced through his

second captor's throat spraying blood across the floor. Any sane person would have lost their mind at the quick succession of events. My brain, however, didn't care.

What's another dead body for my psyche to gloss over?

It was Harkin or him, then me or him. We made our choices, and they'll leave us with a toxic bond for the rest of our lives.

Harkin pulls up in front of the building, where James is standing at the ready. He quickly opens the driver side, whispering what I can only assume is what just happened. James jumps into the driver's seat, and the moment we're both out of the car, he takes off.

"Let's go," he says, pulling me into the building firmly, heading straight for the elevators.

The apartment door latches and locks behind us, then he's on me. A rough hand tightens around my throat, the momentum behind it shoving me back against the wall in the entryway. My head connects from the impact.

"Who the fuck are you?" he barks, his grip tightening against my flesh.

I can't breathe, let alone answer. So, I stand there stoically, sucking in a minuscule amount of air through my nose. I watch as his eyes grow black. A terrifying calmness settles between us. I don't fight him off. I wait until he realizes his mistake.

"Fuck," he yells into the empty apartment, dropping his hand from around my throat and leaning his forehead against mine. His right fist comes out of left field crashing into the wall just millimeters from my ear. This Dr. Jekyll and Mr. Hyde insanity is giving me whiplash.

Shoving against his shoulders, I take back my space before pushing past into the living room. My feet don't need instructions. We need something to dull the rising panic as the realization of what's happened starts unravelling.

What about the bodies? Who were those men? Someone will know they're missing and come after us, what then?

My fingers fumble with the crystal stopper, trying to free the clear liquid my body so desperately craves. Finally pulling it open, I empty two fingers in one tumbler before filling a second. I down my glass, wincing at the fire like substance warming my veins. I refill it swiftly before taking both back over to where Harkin still leans against the wall that separates the kitchen from the entryway.

"Drink this," I demand.

His icy fingers grip the glass, shooting it back without pulling his gaze from the darkened windows. His whole body shutters once the liquid coats his insides.

"Vodka?" He grimaces in disgust.

Not a vodka guy; noted.

I shrug, pulling him deeper into the living room. "We should talk," I coax.

He must still be reeling. I'm almost certain that's the first time Harkin has ever taken a life. Alina's profile flutters into my mind, but I bat it away. He didn't take her life, and I refuse to be one of those people that puts the burden of their accident on his shoulders.

His eyes focus as they drift slowly from the windows in my direction. "Yeah, we should." His throat clears the frog stuck there.

His frame collapses against the leather and all I want to do is crawl into his lap and stay there, ignore the mess we've made. Instead, I sit across on the hard coffee table, allowing its sturdiness to support my body and mind.

"What did you find out?" I ask as he huffs out an irritated sigh.

"That good, huh?"

"Not even that. They didn't give me anything. Only your name. They had your apartment's rental agreement. When I played off that I didn't know who you were, the big guy left me with his friends in there. I'm assuming, they knew where you lived and followed you from there. After the incident with Marco," his hands tighten into fists at his sides, "they lost your location."

"Speaking of his friends." I raise an eyebrow in question.

"James is handling it." That fact releases some of the pressure on my shoulders.

"That's great and all, but Harkin, we killed two people. Two people who will not go unnoticed when they don't show up back where they're supposed to in a couple of hours. What are we going to do about that?"

"I'll figure it out. But first, I want to know what the hell you were thinking walking in there like that?"

I scoff. "In case you hadn't noticed, I can handle myself just fine. I'm not sure where you got this idea that I need to be handled with kid gloves and protected. But I promise you, it's unnecessary."

His body swells toward mine, his bloodied hands encase my knees. As morbid as it might be, the droplets and smears look artistically beautiful against his black ink.

"Oh, trust me, I noticed the moment you walked in the room, looking like a winterized Lara Croft. Want to tell me where you learned to shoot like that?"

A small smile tugs at my lips as my memories of Stan flicker into my head. "You really want to do this now? With everything going on?"

He doesn't answer, just waits for me to continue.

"Fine. So, you know about my mom and the girls group home after that. Well, I didn't last there long. Things happened, and I'd had enough. One night, I packed what little I had with me and left. Snuck out through the back door and never looked back." His body relaxes against the couch as my story continues.

"I don't know how long I walked for, or where I was going. I was nine by that time. A scrawny little thing—if you can imagine." I say sarcastically. "By the time nightfall had come, my feet were tired and covered in blisters. I knew I needed to get off the street. It was the tail end of summer, so while the days were still nice, the nights were getting colder. I found an old greenhouse to bunker down in for the night. Not knowing who it belonged to, but I didn't have any other choice." I take a deep breath, realizing this is the first time I've ever told this story to anyone. "I woke in the morning to a screeching scream. An older woman, Rita, prodding me with the edge of her gardening shoe. When I finally came to, rolling in her direction, her wailing stopped but not before her husband, Stan, had come out with a shotgun." I laugh at the memory. The look on her face had been utter disbelief. I'd found out she'd only come out to the greenhouse to grab herbs for breakfast, she never expected to find me.

I continue, "Stan and Rita, we're in their late seventies. They'd never had children, though Rita desperately wanted them. But the war left Stan with an injury that kept them from getting pregnant. So, when I essentially ended up on their doorstep, little orphan Annie, Rita finally got what she wanted, only fifty years later."

"They took you in?" Harkin asks quietly.

"Yeah, they never once made me think they were going to

turn me back over to child services. Though, I think that had more to do with my nightmares then them wanting the responsibility of raising a child in their later years. They told everyone in the neighborhood, I was a long-lost relative's surviving kin that needed a home after a terrible accident. That was only a partial lie for me. Because I didn't have any paperwork, no social security card, medical records, nothing, Rita home schooled me."

"Do you still see them?"

I quiet at his question, my heart pinching at the truth. "No, they passed when I was fifteen." The melancholy quickly swallows me whole as I remember the few good years, I had with them. From nine to fifteen, I had a safe place to lay my head at night. A warm meal to eat. The equivalent of what I always imagined it'd be like to have loving grandparents.

"Anyway." I clear my throat of the emotions clawing their way out from the depths.

"Is that how you learned to shoot?" Harkin asks again.

"Oh, right! Yeah, Stan had been in the Army and unlike a lot of the men in his generation, when he got back, he didn't become a peace trailblazer. He stuck to what he knew, which meant he had quite the collection of firearms. When it looked like I'd be staying with them, he made sure I knew how to keep myself safe from them. But on my thirteenth birthday, he'd decided I was old enough to learn how to handle them. He spent the next two years, until he got sick, teaching me everything I needed to know about them. Once they were gone, I smuggled a couple out before their extended family could get their grimy hands on them and left. It wasn't as hard as you'd think to get ammo on the streets. Money talks when you know where to look."

I've just dumped so much information on him. He sits in

front of me; stunned. And then, I realize I've shared more with Harkin in the last month then I've ever shared with anyone. He disarms me; easily pulling bricks free from my self-erected barrier. Razing it to the ground.

I shake my head, clearing the walk down memory lane and focusing on our current situation. We still don't know what these men want from me. Why they want to find me so badly. And now we've ruined our only in by killing off two people within their network. If they were desperate to find me before, they'll be gunning for both of us now.

"We should get out of town for a while." Harkin finally breaks the silence.

"What? I can't just leave the city. I know you've planted me into your little bubble of fancy apartments and everything, but I'm not about to become some kept woman to a man I don't even know what to call."

His eyebrow quirks in confusion, "What do you mean? Don't know what to call."

"Harkin, what the hell are we. We haven't even known each other two months, yet we live together. Are we roommates?" His face sours at my question. His hand quickly wrapping around my waist and tugging me across the space between us, before settling me to straddle his body.

"Now, where would you get the idea that we're just roommates?" His eyes dance with mischief, the air thickening around us with tension from the day. But that's not it. With our bodies so close, I automatically heat toward him. The flame sparked the moment his skin grazed mine in the most innocent way. I don't answer his question because I'm so lost in what to label this thing between us.

"I thought I'd made it pretty damn clear. You. Are. Mine. You can call us whatever you need to but know we're together, and anyone, including you, that puts that in jeopardy, will be sorry."

My breath hitches at his declaration. There was no hesitation as he claimed me with his words; the way only his body has done before. That fact alone, has my pussy weeping and clenching with need. His hand tightens against my throat as my core brushes shamelessly against his crotch.

"Why don't we get cleaned up?" he asks but doesn't wait for an answer, before he's hoisting me into his arms and heading straight down the hall for the master bathroom.

THIRTY-ONE
HARKIN

Nails – Call Me Karizma

What are we?

Her question runs through my head as I storm down the hall into my bathroom. This woman, I swear. If she has questions about what we are after I'm done with her tonight, then she wasn't meant to be mine. But that doesn't mean I'll let her go either.

Her lips move slowly down my neck to the little patch of skin peeking through at my shoulder. When her teeth sink in deep, my cock twitches against the zipper of my jeans, and a growl pulls deep from my chest. Her ass wiggles in my hands as she tries to find the friction, she was so desperate for on the couch. But I pull her body back, denying her the relief before I drop her feet to the floor.

"Strip," I command. And for once in all our time together, she listens without a snide comment to match. I knew she had it in her. It's plain as day how desperately she wants to relinquish control, but she fights it every time. It goes against every fiber of her being, but after all we went through today, there's an extra layer of trust between us. Whether we anticipated it or not.

Clothing falls to the floor, piece by piece, revealing the pale tattooed goddess beneath. Small speckles of blood blend in on her chest and hands with the freckles that are scattered across her body. Her skin's not marred with blood the way mine is after running the knife across his throat. But the sight of that minimal discoloration does something to my body.

Can your blood boil with rage and turn your cock to steel at the same time?

Her nimble fingers work quickly to unbutton my shirt, pausing when she notices I haven't made a move to join her nudity. The movement pulls me out of my head and back into the moment with her.

"What are you doing, sweetness?" I ask as she works my belt free, shocking me when she places it in my hand instead of dropping it to the floor with the rest of our discarded clothing. She doesn't explain, instead making quick work of what's left on my body.

She steps back, inspecting my nakedness. I smile as her eyes drift slowly across my skin, lighting me up without a touch. I wait for her to get her fill, those delicate fingers tracing across my back. Following what I can only assume is the line work of the ink spread across my shoulders.

"Like what you see?" I inquire, desperate to hear her opinion.

A rumbling purr is my only answer and my dick twitches at her appreciation.

"And what do you want me to do with this?" I ask holding

out the belt she purposefully had me hold on to. Her eyes sparkle, mischief swirling between her amber eyes.

"I ignored your instructions today." Her sentence cuts off as if she's still processing what she wants to share. "Sir."

My breath hitches at that one word. I know what she wants. What we've avoided after how she reacted at the club.

"You're sure?" I whisper, stepping into her while my free hand traces up her skin. The quick chin dip is enough to reassure me she can handle it this time. That she wants it. Needs it even.

"Do you remember your safeword?"

Another quick nod.

"Words, little one. I want you to say it."

"Yes, sir."

I cup her cheek, and she nuzzles in like a cat does to their master.

"I will not accept you pushing through this time. Do you understand me. We are going to take this slow. I want you to tell me when it feels good with green. If you're getting close to your limit, you will let me know by saying yellow. If you reach a point that you can't take it anymore you will say, black. That is your safeword." I snag her chin, drilling my gaze into hers.

"If you can't communicate with me while we do this Keira, I can't trust you to do it again." When I drop her name, her body stiffens, but it gets my point across. This trust thing goes both ways. I have to trust she'll tell me if it gets to be too much, and she has to put her trust in me to stop when that time comes.

"I understand, sir. I'll use my safeword if it gets to be too much; I promise."

"Good girl. Go to the sink. Hands on the mirror."

I watch as her luscious ass sways across the floor. Hurrying to the shower, I turn both faucets on to the hottest setting. The water falls from above and the room quickly fills with steam. Instant hot water is a first-world luxury I can't live without.

When I step up behind her, she's already in position. Her feet slightly parted, delicate hands with her sharp black nails splayed wide against the fogging mirror. Her back arches to accommodate the edge of the vanity. She looks absolutely stunning on full display. I haven't even touched her skin, but I can see the evidence of her arousal glistening against her inner thighs.

"You're right," I whisper, pressing flat against her backside. My hard cock sliding against her wet heat. Her body shivers at the contact and it quickly becomes my goal to make her do it over and over, until she's crumbling into my arms.

"You didn't listen today. You disobeyed me and broke your promise. Not only that," I rub my palm over her supple perky ass, "you put yourself in danger."

Her body shifts, her eyes looking back over her shoulder, the words at the tip of her tongue to argue with me. Because she obviously wasn't in any danger when she walked into the warehouse locked and loaded. But that's beside the point. She should never have put herself in a position to need to protect herself.

That's what I'm here for.

I wait, my eyes zoned in on her pouty lips when she decides against speaking out. I drop a searing kiss to acknowledge her strength and she shifts back to her original position.

"However, even though you did that I'm in awe of your talent, little one. You've been holding back on me." I nip at her ear and the little mewl that breaks free makes my cock throb with anticipation.

Trust me, I want her too, buddy.

"I need you to put yourself first in those type of situations, do you understand me?"

"Yes, sir."

"Just to make sure you really understand, I'm going to redden this gorgeous flesh." I smack her ass once to warm the skin. "One for each offense and one for each bullet that you fired. How many is that, little one?""

She pauses, calculating her punishment.

"Five, sir."

"Five it is, then."

Her skin comes to life under the leather kiss of my belt. The first strike, pulls an excited whimper from her lips and her back arches into the second lick of pain.

"How are you doing, little one?"

"Green, sir."

My hand caresses the reddened skin, no doubt seconds away from welting over. When my fingers glide south against her drenched cunt, they find their way home into her heat. I moan when her hips buck backwards sinking deeper onto me.

"Fuck sweetness, is this all for me?" I ask pulling my fingers free.

"Suck," I demand. Her wet tongue slides around my fingers licking them clean.

"See how fucking delicious that sweet nectar is? Do you like the way you taste?" When I don't get an answer, my hand wraps around her ponytail cranking her neck back so she has no other option but to meet my eyes.

"Well?"

"It's okay, sir. But I like the way you taste more," she says with a saucy smile.

My lips crash against hers, muting her devilish ways. She's always finding a way to one up me even from the bottom. She battles for dominance in our kiss. Directing the deepening pull as she sucks me into her mouth. But it's the quick sting of her teeth biting into my bottom lip that makes me pull free. A quick, severe smack meets her backside, and she stills.

"Hands back on the mirror. If you can't appreciate your intoxicating flavor, I will."

Dropping to my knees, I palm her ass, spreading her cheeks and exposing the last of her modesty. My tongue laps against her glistening folds, devouring her like she's my last meal on death row. The noises she's making spurs me on harder. I could live here. On my knees, worshipping at her alter.

When I find the strength to pull away, an angry growl pierces our lust filled haze. I move just far enough to whip the belt against her upper thighs, one to each leg. It's her lengthy moan that assures me she's good.

She looks beautiful, folding under my hand, desperate for more. My fingers fuck into her, gathering her wetness at the same time my tongue meets the tight ring of her ass, pushing in.

"More," she begs with a barely audible plea.

"More what, little one?" Her hips push back into my face shoving my face deep between her cheeks. I know what she wants. Fuck I've been dying for this day. My teeth sink into her ass cheek hard, drawing pin pricks of blood to the surface.

"Words, baby. I need your words."

"I want you to fuck my ass."

"Your wish is my command." I stand taking her in head to toe.

"Get in the shower. I'll be back in a second."

My cock pulses, ready to join in the fun. I quickly grab the lube from the vanity drawer, the silicone butt plug an unexpected offering, I grab it too. The room billows with thick steam, thick moisture hangs in the air as she stands waiting under the falling water. The droplets run over her sinful curves, brightening the ink across her skin. She's every man's wet dream, literally.

"Turn around, little one, let me see that marked up ass. Should I soothe them with my cum?" She quickly follows the instruction, reaching for the conveniently placed shelf in front of her.

"Bend over, stick that ass out for me, sweetness."

The click of the plastic cap opening fills the glass enclosure, grabbing her attention and pulling her eyes back to me. "Eyes on the wall, baby, just feel what I'm going to do to you. Remember, you asked for this."

I coat my fingers, rubbing the excess around the toy being careful to keep it out of the stream of the steaming water.

"Play with that clit for me, love. But don't you dare make yourself come." Her right-hand slides down the tiles, disappearing in front of her. But I know the moment she rubs the sensitive nub between her folds, and my finger pushes through the tight ring of muscles not used to the intrusion.

"Breathe and relax for me," I coax in her ear, slipping in fully. When her body moves against me, I add another digit, stretching her further and dropping more lube against her hole. When it no longer feels like a fight, I pull free from her body. A sharp hiss meets my ears. But the toy replaces my fingers quickly, and she mewls at the introduction.

"How does that feel, little one."

"So good, Sir."

"That's only the beginning. I'll have you seeing the galaxy before the water turns cold."

I grab my rock-hard cock, lining it up to her perfectly

displayed entrance and drive home. Stopping to adjust to her vice-like heated grip on my dick.

"Fuck, Harkin," she yells, her sentiment echoing off the glass.

"I'll let that one slip, baby, but just this one because you feel like the most euphoric drug running through my veins."

I reach between our bodies, finding the toy and hit the button hiding at the base. The toy comes to life vibrating against the thin wall between us inside her. Her whimpers come immediately, spurring my body back into motion.

"Color." I grunt.

"Green. Fucking, green, sir."

My hand cracks against her ass but she's so lost in the pleasure I doubt she has any clue what's spewing from those pouty lips. My hips retreat pounding into her body, her ass meeting me thrust for thrust. When her pussy tightens against me, quivering against my assault, I know she's close.

"Do you think you deserve to come, sweetness?" I roar the question, seconds from doing exactly that.

"Please, I need to come. I can't..." But her words cut off as her breath quickens and she spasms around me throwing her head back in ecstasy. The damn goddess pulls me off the cliff into the abyss with her.

I pull out, spilling onto her ass, smearing the cum quickly into her marked skin, staining her further, claiming every last inch of her body as mine before the water can wash it away. My chest heaves, fighting to pull in a decent breath in the humid bathroom.

Her body sways, and I quickly move forward, flipping the shower off, gently pulling the still vibrating toy from her body. Her soft whine at the shift in pressure has my satiated cock twitching for another round. Ignoring it, I hoist her limp form into my chest and walk out of the shower.

"You did so good, baby. Such a good girl for me."

She doesn't respond, but a small smile pulls at her lips. She's everything I've ever wanted, no, needed in a partner. The vixen might drive me fucking insane, but the way she melts for me is nothing compared to what that smile just did to my insides. The cold stone around my heart fractures, another piece chipping away and she worms her way further inside.

THIRTY-TWO
KEIRA

Wicked as They Come – CRMNL

A floorboard creaks, pulling me from my fitful sleep. My body is deliciously sore, but when the soft cotton sheets glide against my bare ass, I hiss at the contact. Harkin had coated the marks in a cream last night after he dropped me in bed, brought me water, and a couple Advil. My brain replays the scene from the shower in a half conscious, half dream-like state I'm still wrapped up in tightly.

Then that sound comes again, but this time it's closer. I can sense I'm in bed alone. Because Harkin's hard, muscled body isn't attached to my side. When I crack open one sleep-filled eye, a figure looms in the shadows of the hallway just standing there.

My body instantly pebbles in goosebumps. I can't tell if it's real or a figment of my imagination. My sleep demon summoned by a terrible dream that was probably based in the reality of my life. I lie still, not sure if it's because I'm stuck in sleep paralysis, or because I'm simply too freaked out to move.

I should call out; see if it's Harkin. Figure out if I'm getting myself worked up for nothing. But something deep down tells me that's not the right call and I've spent my entire life listening to that gut feeling to keep myself safe.

Fuck, it better be him and not some psychopath off the streets. The blackened form stalks toward the bed, but I will my body not to move for two reasons. If it's him, this could all be a game where he wants me unknowing and afraid, and I love to play our games. If it's not, the smooth hilt my fingers are tightly gripping from behind the headboard won't have a problem freeing me from the situation.

I close my eyes and relax my body, stilling my breathing to listen to the changes in the room. The form's taking its time moving closer. The air electrifies, heating with the change in body count when he makes it to the edge of the mattress. My fingers work smoothly to the pull knife from its clip making sure that the rest of my arm seems only to be offering my head extra support under my pillow.

And then it happens at whirlwind speed. The intruder pulls my feet off the bed, my body following close behind. I hit with an ungraceful thud, right on my sore ass cheeks. I'm exposed completely, the sheet abandoning my naked body.

I screech in protest. Even if this is Harkin, I'm not giving in without a fight. My legs kick, contacting the figure's legs and chest, but all I get back in response is a grunt at the impact. When my hand comes up with the blade at the ready, he doesn't stop. It's not Harkin. I quickly swipe it across his forearm, hoping to break skin and his concentration as he tries to wrangle my legs together with a zip tie. But I feel as the metal grates across something hard.

I huff in irritation and get in a second thrust between our bodies before the knife pulls free spewing blood across my skin. The hands release from my legs, and he falls back against the floor. I struggle up using the blood coated blade to free myself from the half tightened plastic ties around my ankles.

"Fucking bitch." The deep voice pulls my attention as he starts toward me again, hand holding the gash on his side as his feet limp in my direction. I widen my stance, naked as the day I was born, coated only in his life's blood, and armed with my new favorite christened blade.

"You're going to pay for that." His thick accent tips me off that this is payback for yesterday. I don't know where Harkin is, but if he hasn't heard the scuffle by now, he's either in the soundproof gym or out god only knows where. I'm in this alone, but that's okay. Life's never been any different. Why should that change now?

"I highly doubt it," I stupidly taunt the man twice my size.

In typical brute fashion his body rushes mine, but the perk of being tiny and naked is the ability to shift out of the way quickly. His large form crashes into the mattress exposing his back. I don't hesitate, thrusting the blade deep into his lower back, hoping to God it finds my intended target and leaves him bleeding out.

Before I can drive it home a hand grips my hair, snatching me backward and killing my momentum. My scalp burns as the follicles pop free, I ignore the pain, throwing my head back but it meets air not connecting like I'd hoped.

His chuckle fills my ear. "You deserve far worse than this," he spews, anger lacing each syllable. That's when I feel the quick prick, followed by a cold flow of fluid into my neck. My hand springs up, covering the area, but it's no use. The effects take hold almost immediately.

But it doesn't happen like you see in the movies. My body doesn't drop to the floor, automatically pulling me away from reality. My eyes grow bleary, my limbs heavy. I stumble away from my attackers, heading for what I think looks like the bathroom. The garbled argument of the men in the room gives my brain something else to focus on, when I need it to pay attention to getting out of this situation. We're rivals at the moment, not teammates, and that's what fucks us over. Something hard hits the back of my skull and it all fades to black.

MY EYES FIGHT to open and take in my surroundings, but the moment one's able to, I screw them shut again. The bright light gleams through my closed lids, which only sets off the horrendous pounding in my head. The searing pain causes a wave of nausea to rise in my gut. I fling myself off to the side, gagging until the contents of my stomach release ahead of me.

I take a deep breath, slowly pushing it out, trying to settle the queasiness. I gradually come back to, my body's still heavy, weighed down by whatever drug they'd dosed me with. My hands and feet are bound, but I'm lying on my side on something cushioned.

I'm finally able to peek through the blinding haze filling the room. I'm alone, in what looks to be a pristine office, not much different from Harkin's at the apartment. The worn leather couch I'm lying on sits across from a large wooden desk. It's oddly comfortable and sleep threatens to pull me back under, but the stench of my sickness helps me shove into a seated position.

My brain is still foggy, but I remember what happened at

the apartment. I recall fighting a grown man in the nude. It's ridiculous now that I'm thinking about it. Someone must have dressed me because a light-white cotton dress and sandals cover my skin. They're not from my closet. I own nothing that looks like this.

My arms and legs are tight and uncomfortable from holding the same position. There's a bandage wrapped around my elbow; a small cotton ball taped to the center.

Did they take my blood? Holy fuck, they're going to sell my organs on the black market. I'm screwed.

I scan the desktop, searching for a pair of scissors or a letter opener, but the tidy space only holds a couple of things. None of which have a sharp edge that might help me get out of these damn plastic cuffs. Rocking forward, I balance my weight on my joined feet. I've only got one chance to get this right or I'll be back on the floor writhing in pain from the fall.

I make my way quickly across the carpeted floor. Thank God my jumps are soft, or I'd be alerting whoever took me to my wakefulness because there's nothing graceful about my movements. Shuffling around the side of the desk, I pull against the drawers, but the only one that opens holds nothing helpful.

"Well, what do we have here?"

I whirl toward the voice, swaying as my momentum threatens to topple me over.

My hands quickly glide through the contents of the open drawer, snagging a pen. Not the best option, but it'll do, especially since it's one of those fancy metal custom made pens and not something you'd pick up at the store while your grocery shopping.

I thrust the object up between us, quickly shuffling my feet awkwardly in the other direction away from the intimidating man. I take in his looming form across the room, but he doesn't overtake me. His gaze is watchful and calm. And it's eerie as hell.

"Who are you? What do you want?" I ask him. My ass rams into something hard stalling my progress.

He doesn't answer, but his eyes slowly take me in, scanning every inch of me. It doesn't feel hateful or full of rage like the men from the apartment and it's not like every other male off the street, taking their fill for later. No, it seems like curiosity and wonder. Like someone examining a painting in real life that they've only seen in textbooks.

He hurries to the desk, reaching for a drawer I hadn't made it to yet. When he stands back up, the scissors I was looking for are in his grasp. "Why don't we get you out of those things and a little more comfortable?" He nods toward my wrist.

I don't answer, but I know I have a better chance of protecting myself with my limbs free, so I hold them out as far away from my body as possible. He makes swift work cutting me free. I rub at the raw skin; I don't know how long I was out for or where I am. For all I know I could be in another state or shit another country.

Fuck.

"Take a seat." His hand sweeps out, back to the couch I woke up on. When his eyes take in the mess I made on his carpet, they darken. I wait for the explosion of anger toward me for it and shy away, but he stomps from the room.

He returns with a man who could have easily been the guy that grabbed me and a small, timid woman with an arm full of cleaning supplies. The well-dressed man snaps toward the sofa and she rushes over, dropping to her knees to clean the mess I've left. A gnawing twinge of guilt forms in my gut while watching her clean up my mess, but then I remember I was fucking drugged and kidnapped.

We all stand in silence, waiting for her to finish her task. When she stands, tucking the soiled rags back into her little bucket, it's the starting gun pulling us back into the situation at hand. The extras leave as quickly as they joined us and once again, I'm alone with this man that exudes importance.

"Please, sit." He motions again. This time I follow his suggestion. I perch at the edge of the couch ready to bound up if the need arises. Could I take this man? It's possible, weirder things have happened.

Yeah, like being kidnapped and held hostage.

He looks older than me but still young enough to be handsome. His dark hair looks thick, peppered with gray at his temples, only distinguishing his sharp features. He sits against the front of his desk, legs outstretched in finely tailored suit pants. He crosses his feet at the ankles, the shiny leather loafers laying neatly on top of each other.

If this situation wasn't completely fucked up and my heart didn't already beat for another, I could see myself trying to flirt my way out of this. But his haunted eyes make me nervous enough to keep those thoughts locked down.

"Can I get you something to drink?" he asks, finally breaking the silence.

I shake my head. I'm not interested in hydrating at the moment. But he pushes away from the desk walking over to the drink cart in the corner. He quickly fills two glasses bring one over to me and dropping it into my hand. I take a drink, anyway, sucking down its contents quickly. The water clears my throat of the grime, removing that nasty bile taste coating my tongue. I keep hold of the bottom-heavy glass, if nothing else, it's a decent weapon. A hard hit to the side of the temple should have someone crumpling to the floor.

"You've been a hard woman to track down, Keira." He finally speaks, pausing on my name. Almost as if he's savoring it on his lips.

"Why were you looking for me? Who are you? Why am I here?"

"Well, that's a long and interesting story, *mio cuore*."

THIRTY-THREE

HARKIN

Find You – The Phantoms

The elevator numbers light up red as the floors pass by. I check my watch again, three o'clock in the fucking morning. We'd only been asleep a couple of hours, exhausted from a night of worshipping Kiera before my phone started buzzing nonstop on the nightstand. I'd angrily swiped it, about to give whoever was waking me a little lesson is common decency when I read the texts.

> Harkin wake up
>
> I'm in town. We need to meet.
>
> Harkin. Now not later!
>
> Answer the damn phone

They went on and on, mixing with the three missed calls I had from him. Pulling my exhausted body from the warm bed with a serene and snoring Keira was physically painful. Anyone else would have been silenced and discarded. But here I am, because apparently when you get a cryptic as hell message from your father in the early hours of the morning you drive across the city to meet him at his hotel.

The elevator dings and a yawn rips from sleep deprived body as I walk the hall to his suite. I knock quietly, not wanting to be the asshole that wakes anyone else unnecessarily at this hour. He quickly pulls the door open, ushering me inside, before peeking his head out the door and peering down the hall left and right.

"I came alone," I say, taking in his disheveled appearance.

A rare occurrence for him.

"I was making sure you weren't followed," he tells me.

"I wasn't followed either," I assure him, knowing it's true. My body might be half dead on its feet, but my brain was alert the moment I stepped out of the door, after locking up and setting the alarm. I'd texted James to head over and watch the place, but I didn't have the time to wait the fifteen minutes it would take him to get there.

"Coffee?" he asks, stepping into the full-scale kitchen that looks like you'd find it in a condo, not a hotel room.

"Please. So, are you going to tell me why you're here in New York?" He doesn't pause as he bustles around the kitchen quickly getting the coffee machine up and running.

"I think it's best we have a seat for this conversation."

I huff a sigh of irritation. I just want to get this over with, head back home and climb into bed before Keira realizes I ever left. He hands me the cup of espresso and we move into the small seating area.

"I'm here for work, nothing exciting. But I received a call from a business associate here in the city that I've worked with for a long time. Well, his family, at least. He asked if I knew where you were."

I suck in a deep breath.

Jesus Christ.

"I'm assuming by your reaction you know exactly who I'm talking about." He tilts his head in that way dads do when they already know the answer to the questions they've asked.

"Jesus, what have you gotten yourself into," he whispers to himself before draining the small mug and placing it on the table in front of us.

"What did I get myself into? You mean what did you drag me into! What did you tell him?" I ask, keeping my composer and trying not to show the anxiety spiking in my chest.

"The truth. That I wasn't sure where you were since we haven't spoken in weeks. But he knows where the apartment in Brooklyn is, so I figured I'd call you as soon as possible and get you out of there. I was already in the city, so it made sense to draw you here."

"Fuck." I jump to my feet, dumping the small mug on the glass coffee table before heading for the door.

"Harkin, wait. Where are you going?" he calls after me.

"I have to get back to the apartment. I left her alone." That's not entirely true. James should be there by now, but I'm not. And if I'm not there to protect her, every promise I vowed last night is about to be broken.

"You need to tell him where she is." His comment stops me cold in my tracks, fingers laced around the handle seconds from pulling the door free. I turn slowly to face him, taking in his worried eyes.

"What do you know?" I ask, leaving no room for falsities between us.

"He wants her. There's more to the story than you know, Harkin. Just tell him, he won't hurt her, but he needs her."

My blood boils. *He needs* her? Too bad; she's mine. There's more to the story. Shit, there's more to the story than he knows from my point of view, too. But I'd hand her over, no sooner than hell freezing over.

"That's never going to happen. I have to go. Thanks for the warning, I guess. But don't be surprised if you don't hear from me for a while," I tell him before walking out the door, with one thing on my mind.

Her.

My feet pound against the cement steps, too on edge to wait for the elevators. I peel out of the parking garage, nearly missing a jogger on their morning run when I careen around the corner to get onto the road. It only takes fifteen minutes to get from the hotel back to the apartment, but it might as well be hours for how long it feels.

I dial James' cell, but he doesn't answer. It's after the third ring with nothing more than his voicemail on the other end that has my skin itching as nerves crawl up the back of my neck.

I'm pissed at my father for his incessant vague texts. But also, at myself for not just calling and demanding he tell me what was going on. Now, I know nothing more than they're coming after us if they haven't already. I slam my fist against the steering wheel, letting the frustration build instead of wean from the outburst.

The apartment isn't safe; it doesn't matter if I reworked the security system. If they got in once, I'm sure they can make it happen again. Though this time after what we did, I don't think they'd bother being stealthy.

I slam into my parking spot and jam the SUV into park. When my feet finally make it to the third floor, I slow, quieting my pace. But then I see it. The front door is open just a crack. "Fuck," I hiss under my breath, pulling the gun from the holster at my back. The cold metal in my grasp is another reminder of how fucked up this whole situation is.

I creep into the entryway, praying to God she's still here. Sweeping the kitchen and living room, I notice nothing's amiss. Pushing open her old room, I find it's dark, no movement from within. Stopping outside my room where she was sleeping earlier, I pull in a deep breath calming my nerves before pushing into the room.

No one's in here. Her compact form doesn't take up the right side of my bed. Her beautiful dark hair doesn't fan across the white bedding. A brick forms in the pit of my stomach when I step around the end of the bed and see the floor coated in thick red blood. A cold sweat beads across my forehead at the sight. That's too much blood, and if it's hers, I can't wait to make whoever thought they could come into our home and steal away my girl pay.

"Keira!" I call out, not expecting her to answer but quiet just in case she's hiding somewhere now, waiting for me. When the only sound I hear is my ragged breathing I drop to my knees, head bowing in devastation.

A white piece of paper snags my attention from this angle. I reach forward under the bed and unfold the one clue they left.

I hope she was worth what's coming to you. But she's mine now.

RAGE IGNITES IN MY CHEST, filling my limbs with a need to move. I've never felt a predatory need to destroy someone, but it's the only thing filling my head now. The world will parish around me before I give up on finding and freeing her. Even if it's the last thing I do.

I'm coming for you, little one. Hold on.

I STOMP THROUGH THE APARTMENT, heading to my office, phone tucked against my shoulder trying to reach James again for the millionth time. The front door slams open, and I stall my pacing across my office floor. Quickly ducking behind the door, I freeze, gun at the ready for whoever is running down the hall toward me.

"Kiera!" the deep voice calls out. I recognize it instantly and meet him in the hall. His gun points at my chest, but he quickly drops it when he sees it's me.

"She's gone," I state, any emotion I'd felt earlier locked down deep as I shifted into problem-solving mode.

I take him in, he's got one hell of a shiner and a cut above his left eye.

"What happened to you?"

"Someone jumped me as I was coming in from the garage after you texted. Stuffed me in the corner. I just came to and came straight up here. Fuck, I'm sorry, man." I dismiss his apology. I unintentionally dragged him into some serious shit over the last couple of days that he didn't sign up for when he took this gig. He's got the training, but I know he wanted something relaxing after being shot at most of his life in a war zone.

We head back into the office.

"Do you have any clue where they could have taken her?" I ask him. He's been digging into these guys since the photos showed up. I had a strong suspicion they were behind them.

"A couple. The place where you guys had your first meeting. I've been tracking two men from there. They frequent some local businesses, but it's the compound I'm more interested in."

"A compound?" I ask with an air of intrigue.

"Yeah. You're involved with the mafia, man. I don't know how you got here, but it's about to get messy."

"About to? Did you not see the state of that warehouse? Shit got real the moment they tried to kill me. The big kicker is, my dad's involved with them. I don't know how deep, but he's the reason I wasn't here this morning. He pulled me away to warn me. Real fucking helpful that was." My fist goes flying into the wall, rage boiling inside as I worry about my girl and what she's going through.

"My dad said the man who has her wanted her. No, that he *needed* her. But he didn't have the decency to tell me who *he* is."

"I've had some luck identifying some of the guys, but they're all muscle. No one of importance, at least not after the guy you two took out at the warehouse. The word on the street is, the family did a little rearranging a couple years ago. The

Don was taken out by his own nephew. Now the crew takes orders from him."

I take in all the information, squirreling it away for when it might lead me to an answer that will help.

"So, where's the compound?"

If I can find it and get close enough, maybe I can hack into their security system, get eyes on my girl, or cut it off the list of places we need to search to find her. I'd rather not go in guns blazing to the mafia's fucking headquarters. Because I don't see us coming out of there alive.

"A few hours outside the city; in the middle of the woods. There's a couple of hiking trails out that way we can use to get close without being obvious. We can ditch the rig at the trailhead and close in." Nodding in agreement with his assessment. I trust him for this shit. His background will get us further than mine will to find her.

Who knew my life would go from black sheep rich kid to some mafia action movie all because I couldn't let a girl slip through my fingers.

This is insane.

THIRTY-FOUR
KEIRA

Can You Keep a Secret - Ellise

I wait anxiously for this stranger to explain why I've had my privacy stripped, been attacked, and kidnapped, and then treated like an invited guest in his home. The longer I look at him, the more I notice his subtle traits, like his dark cinnamon eyes that crinkle around the edges with age or his humped, uneven nose that looks like it's been broken a few times too many.

We sit in an extended silence, and my hands tremble in my lap while my knees bounce trying to exude the nervousness building. I need to get out of here and back to Harkin. Has he found the apartment quiet? The blood on the floor next to the empty bed where he left me?

My body runs cold, with the possibility that he still hasn't come home, or worse yet, something horrific has already happened to him and he's not coming after me. And if he's not coming, that means nobody is. No one will notice I'm missing. We sold Stacey a fabricated story of what's been going on. She knows I'm lying low. She'll probably just think Harkin's got me stowed away at the apartment for safe keeping.

If I want out of here, it's up to me.

The man clears his throat. His penetrating inspection hasn't stopped consuming every detail of me as I sit across from him. "I knew your mother." His statement snatches the air from my lungs. I've never met anyone who knew my mother. A wave of emotion crashes over me as I absorb his admission.

"Your father too."

That one piques my interest, pulling me from my dive into melancholy.

"What? How?" I whisper.

"We grew up together. Went to the same Catholic school. The one place where you'd find a truce between the families," he says with a tight-lipped smile.

I don't know what he means. I know nothing about my parents. The fading memories I have of my mom are wrapped in things we did together, not her past. Since she refused to tell me anything about my father when she was alive, and there was nothing in the apartment after she passed, I had nowhere to look. Even if I'd had wanted to.

I move forward to the edge of the couch, waiting for a breadcrumb of more information from him. I have a million questions; I want to know everything. It quickly blurs my reality and I no longer care about my current circumstances.

"I was sorry to hear about your mother's passing. I know it was a long time ago, but it was an immense shock to me." My jaw drops. He talks as if we're old friends sitting down to catch up. I don't know how to respond. My brain is shell-shocked from the realization there's someone else in the world that knew her, knew them. It somehow makes me feel less alone.

"It was terrible," I stutter, not wanting to relive that day again for the second time in as many days.

It finally dawns on me that if he knew my father, he might know if he's still alive. It's likely, given how young my mom had me. But you could say the same thing about her. There's no reason a woman in her thirties shouldn't be alive. Unless something unthinkable happens.

"My father," I watch as his whole body stiffens against the desk, but his chin drops guiding me to continue with my question, "do you still keep in contact with him?" I ask, almost desperately. I'm not sure why, I never had a desire before today to know him. He'd always been this illusive creature. A fairytale I used to tell myself when life got too hard. That maybe one day, he'd come find me while I was walking the streets or staying in sketchy apartments to have a roof over my head. But then the years passed by, and he never came. So, I stopped dreaming. And eventually stopped thinking about him altogether.

"Yes." He stops, gauging the words on his tongue. "We grew up together. Your mother might've been an Irish princess, but your father and I were cut from the same cloth, practically inseparable."

"What does any of that mean?" I pry.

"She didn't tell you anything, did she?" His eyes hold a shred of understanding, but his fingers wrapped around the edge of the desk turn white. "I guess after the trauma she faced that day from handing over your sister, I can't really blame her."

My eyes widen in shock.

He knows about Alina too? Who is this man?

"How do you know about her?"

"I was there the day you both were born. It was a chaotic morning." He stalls, his eyes locking in on something across the room. After enduring the stilted silence, my curiosity gets the best of me. I shift on the couch, turning to find where his attention has disappeared to. A small silver frame sits on a bookshelf, a fuzzy, faded picture of a young girl and a single baby in her arms fills the frame. I gasp in recognition. She's young, but my mother's strong features peek through, even if the bright blonde hair I was used to is dark like mine in the photo. There's no doubt it's her.

"Why do you have that?" I ask accusatorially.

He doesn't answer me but starts off again where he left off, "We'd been in class. Your mom spent eight months hiding her pregnancy. Not only from the staff, but from all our friends and her family, the only person who knew was my uncle. If her father had known, he'd have shipped her off to live with his family back in Ireland. I remember the day she found out. She came stomping over from the girl's bathroom, eyes rimmed red, cheeks to match. Her porcelain skin had no way of masking the emotions she was battling. But when she walked up to your father, there was a defiant gleam in her eyes. I saw the same thing when I walked into this room from you. You have her eyes." He pauses, taking me in from head to toe. A sad smile donning his face.

"She stepped up to your father ignoring the busy hall and told him right there. It'd taken a moment for the news to sink in, but he didn't believe her. Claimed she was lying to trap him, but that was a stupid thing to accuse her of. What fifteen-year-old wants to be pregnant, especially one from a family like hers. Not only that, being pregnant with *his* baby would have been the worst part for her father. His little Irish princess, defiled by some Italian scum and not just any Italian prick, no. The heir, being groomed to take over the family business."

This is too much.

My mind whirls as the information slowly processes, forming around the memories I had of her. I knew she was young when she'd had us, but that didn't really sink in until I was older. Then I could grasp why our lives seemed so different when I was little.

"Wait—" *He can't be serious.* "You're telling me my parent's families were involved with the New York crime families?" I stare at him in horror.

This can't be happening.

"Not involved with, *mio cuore*, they we're the heads of the families."

"Why are you telling me this? Who are you?" I ask again for what feels like the hundredth time. This feels like extremely dangerous information to know. The type of information where it doesn't matter if you know because you won't be alive to tell anyone about it.

I jolt to my feet. "Listen, I don't know what you want from me. I don't know anything about my parents or their families." Maybe I'm on the right track. Is he planning to use me to get to them, to use me for ransom? Why would they care? They don't even know me. What's a blood relation when you never knew they existed?

"Sit, Keira," he says calmly, but there's a tone of authority I have a feeling he's used to having obeyed.

"I think I'll stand," I tell him, folding my arms over my chest.

His lips twitch and his mop of dark hair shakes ever so slightly as his head shifts back and forth. "Just like your mother," he whispers under his breath, but I catch it anyway. "Fine, have it your way." A loud buzz fills the room, pulling his attention to the intercom on the wall by the door. He moves swiftly across the room, pushing a small button before speaking.

"Yes."

"Sir, we need to show you something." The speaker crackles loudly into the intimate space.

"Right now?" he asks irritated.

"Yes, sir. Sorry."

"Fine. I'll meet you at security."

He turns, taking me in one last time before heading through the door. The lock clicks into place on the other side, and my body automatically collapses onto the sofa behind me. Self-preservation is an interesting trait. You can sense it take over your body and flip a switch in your brain. It tells you to push through emotions, shove them to the side, lock them down and move forward. To ignore societal decorum and respect, to put yourself first and get yourself to safety. The funny thing is, when you've spent almost your entire life battling your fight-or-flight responses, you become desensitized in genuinely alarming circumstances like this.

I don't know how long he'll be gone for, so I come to my senses and push myself off the couch to look around the room. Heading straight for the frame with my mother and the tiny baby in it. I can't tell if it's me or Alina. How fucked up is that? But the thing that strikes me as odd, there's only one of us.

The picture's taken outside a small brick house as if she's leaving.

Who leaves with only one of their children?

But then again, maybe Alina's adoptive parents took her right away. I'd always wondered why she didn't put us both up for adoption. Why she'd kept one of us when she was already doing the challenging thing and saying goodbye to the other?

I'm so transfixed by the photo, taking in every minor detail of her face, absorbing everything I've missed for the last fifteen years without a photo of her.

"That's you." The deep voice coming from behind scares the shit out of me. The frame almost goes flying from my hands, but I grip tight to keep it safe.

"Why isn't Alina with us?" I ask timidly. He might not know, but all the information he's already shared, it's worth prying.

He heaves a heavy sigh. "They handed her over to her adoptive parents minutes after your mother gave birth."

"Why'd she keep me?" Emotion clogs my throat. I'm desperate to understand what happened on this day twenty something years ago.

"No one knew about you." His words come softly.

I swing around to face him, he's close, but he doesn't move to take a step back.

"What? How did no one know about me? That makes no sense!" My mind can't grasp the concept.

"Your mother hid her pregnancy, remember? She didn't see a doctor throughout the entire thing. Plus, you weren't exactly born in a hospital."

"Were you there?" I ask, watching his chin drop quickly in answer. "And she didn't know she was having twins?"

"No, she didn't. Nor did she have a regular birth either," he says.

"What do you mean?"

"When her water broke, she didn't want to go to the hospital. She knew if she did, they would contact her father. It might not be hospital policy, but that wouldn't stop someone on staff from reaching out to Fitzpatrick. She called frantic not sure what to do, where to go. I finally—" He stops, eyes growing wide.

Mine follow suit. "Why would she call you?" My entire body freezes, the oxygen in my lungs evaporates.

Holy shit. It can't be.

My feet move back of their own accord, my back hits something hard before I collapse onto the floor. This can't be, he can't be.

But what if he is?

"Keira." My name splits the air, a plea so desperate and full of yearning.

"You're—" I can't even say it. The title feels foreign. Even in my head.

"Listen, I didn't mean to tell you this way. Trust me."

"Trust you?" This is a cruel, sick joke. I don't know who this man is, but he can't be my father. What kind of father kidnaps their daughter?

"No." I shake my head refusing to believe what's so blatantly obvious.

"No?" he parrots back to me.

"You can't be. This can't be."

"It is, *mio cuore.*"

His confirmation breaks me. Tears I've been battling since my eyes peeled open in this room fall. I don't know if I'm crying from relief, or emotional pain, maybe it's anger, or for the little girl who always wondered why she was never enough for the man who sired her to stick around.

THIRTY-FIVE
HARKIN

No Rest for the Wicked - Klergy

The SUV glides around a bend in the road, the tires crunch over gravel coming to a jolting halt at a trailhead. The dark looming forest goes on for as far as the eye can see. No light peeks through anywhere, no sign of a compound. My eyes scan the area, trying to grasp what I'm about to get myself into. The car door slamming grabs my attention, and I quickly scramble to follow James to the hatch.

"So where is this place?" I ask, pulling my pack out.

"About five klicks northeast from here just over a ridge. How close do you need to get?"

"That'll depend on their signal strength. Because they're out in the middle of nowhere, I'd assume they have a booster to clear all these trees. If that's the case, I should be able to pick it up as far as a mile out."

"Good, you'll still have coverage there." I nod in understanding.

"How far out is your team?" When James told me about the compound and we agreed it was the best place to look for Keira, he showed me the to-scale diagram he'd made of the compound. It's huge, a one-story modern cement fortress, except for a security tower in the right corner of the property. It must be over five thousand square feet and that's if there's no sub-level he couldn't see. As we studied it to map out the best entry and exit points, we quickly realized this was a suicide mission on our own. That's when he called in a favor.

"They're about five minutes out."

I nod at the update. "When they get here, we'll hike out. Once I'm in position, it shouldn't take me long to locate the signal and get into their system. Then I'll scan their feed for Keira." We're banking on a lot of unknowns here. We're assuming they'll have security throughout the property and praying one of those cameras picks up a feed of my girl. They'd be smart not to have a camera where they're keeping her. Since that's a possibility, I plan on going in regardless of what the cameras show me. James just doesn't know that yet, but if I tell him, he'll hog tie me and leave me in the car.

The whirl of an engine spills through the quiet night. We both freeze and wait for the car to come to a stop next to us. James relaxes once he can see the driver. All four doors push open, revealing a group straight out of Call of Duty, masks included. A weight lifts from my shoulders as I watch them gear up.

Then we're on the move, careful to be quiet on our approach. James was right. This place is enormous and hidden. The six-foot concrete walls that surround the compound are going to be a problem, or so I thought. Until

Axe, the giant of the group, taps the rope curled around his shoulder.

Jesus, these guys come prepared.

I mentally remind myself to give James a raise after all this is over. I snag my laptop from my bag; my fingers quickly fly across the keys locating the system I need. It only takes a few seconds and I'm in. The CCTV like security feed fills my screen. There's more than I expected, and it takes me time to scroll through all the exterior camera feeds to locate the interior points.

The entry way is clear, bedrooms, living room, nothing shows up. There's no one walking around covering the place. Either they feel comfortable enough in this space to relax, or everyone is somewhere I haven't come across yet. As soon as that thought passes, the camera lands on an office and my fingers freeze. My body stills, but the anger builds. James shifts next to me, but he doesn't say a word.

My girl sits curled in a ball on the floor, tears streaming down her beautiful face, while a man I've never seen before looms over her. She doesn't look injured, there's no blood anywhere, but I notice the small bandage wrapped around her arm.

"Well, now we know," James confirms. "Make the call," he tells me.

"We're going after her." Before I can stash my computer back in my bag and sling it over my shoulder, a rustle draws our attention down the small ravine separating us from the property. The group stills, crouching low to the ground as we wait on bated breaths.

Two men walk toward us scouting the area, bickering in hushed Italian. The irritation washes off them in waves. James motions to the team. They're all waiting on his command to strike. Two slink off from the group, while the rest of us wait motionless among the quiet backdrop of the forest. Seconds creep by. My heart hammers in my chest. I've never been involved in something like this. I had no aspirations of joining the military. The closest I've ever come to something like this is playing campaigns of COD in high school.

Then they're there, behind the men, arms wrapped around their necks in a choke hold. They move so fast, there isn't time for a fight. Their bodies thrash against the assault but they're quickly subdued and drop to the dirt floor. The guys take their weapons, heading back in our direction.

"We need to move now," James tells me. "They'll expect them to check in and when they don't, the rest of his security will know something's up. If you want to do this, we have to go now."

"Let's go," I command. I may not be leading the group, but I'm in charge. They're here on a favor from a friend, but James told me it wouldn't come cheap. When I told him money wasn't an issue, he made the call. She's worth every dime.

I'm coming, little one.

Instead of scaling the wall, much to big man's disappointment, we find an iron gate to the east of us and break through. We split into two groups, taking opposite sides of the property. The team's been briefed on the office's location. The plan is to take the property from the outsides in, meeting at the office to retrieve *the asset*. Asset—like she's some piece of property. I didn't object. This team has its way of running and as long as they do their jobs; I couldn't care less what terminology they use.

James leads our trio silently down a cement path that parallels the main building. We dip past every set of windows, even though most of them are black and empty. He halts once he comes up on the kitchen's exterior door. His eyes meet mine at the end of our little train and with a quick nod, he breeches the building.

The dimmed house feels like an ominous warning. We dash through the kitchen and down the hall when we don't run into anyone else in the house. Static from an old radio plays classic Italian music through a closed door to our left. We hurry past and I turn to monitor it before sliding around the next corner.

This is too easy. The hair on the back of my neck stands, and my fingers tighten around the SIG in my hands.

"Gentlemen," a voice calls. All three of us swing our heads in the opposite direction, looking for the offender. When I look to the ceiling, a small red blinking light snags my attention. But I looped the camera feeds. They can't know where we are. I tap the shoulder in front of me and he does the same to James. I signal to keep crawling forward.

We make it a few more feet before the voice comes again. "Your men are waiting with my security. Why don't you meet me in my office," he says, nonchalant, like we didn't just break into his home.

This might not be the worst-case scenario. I figured we'd have to come in here guns blazing, but it has us walking right into the lion's den, any element of surprise down the drain. The last long stretch of hallway meets dark mahogany double doors, the office.

One door pulls open, and a young man in guard gear fills the doorway. The light from the room beyond casts a shadow against his features in the hall.

"Mr. Greyson, he'll see you now."

My team stops in front of me blocking the way. I know James, he won't want me to go in there alone, but it doesn't look like I'll have a choice.

I step up next to him and whisper, "Get your men out of here. Get them paid. I'll take it from here."

He goes to argue but I'm already heading for the office. I can hear her.

I step up to the guard, but he doesn't move to let me through. His meaty hands snatch the gun from me, shoving it in the waistband of his pants. He pats me down roughly, not finding anything else since he refused to bend over all the way. My favorite blades remain strapped to my ankles when he finally lets me through.

The breath knocks from my lungs. She's here, and she doesn't look harmed. No, she's sitting on the couch, legs tucked under her small frame, a blanket draped across her knees and a clear glass of amber liquid in her hand. She looks comfortable, safe even. Like she's catching up with an old friend or cozying in to read one of her favorite horror books.

However, the moment my boots hit the hardwoods alerting her to someone's presence, and her eyes swing to the door and they tell me a different story. They're rimmed red and puffy, haunted by whatever she's been through in the last twenty-four hours. Her skin is pale—more than usual—and that's when I notice the slight tremor in her hand that's gripping the glass, which tips the second our eyes lock.

Her body bounds from the couch and across the floors. She collides into my chest, her arms flinging around my shoulders. Mine automatically wrap around her, pulling her tightly into me, trying to fuse our beings into one, so we never have to face the possibility of being separated again. A small sigh escapes her lips as she clings to me and nuzzles into my chest.

"You came," she whispers, but then her body stiffens, and she pulls back looking up into my heated gaze. "You shouldn't have come." She tries to pull away, but I tighten my grip refusing to let her go.

Freeing one of my hands from around her back, I snatch her chin roughly and tug her eyes back to mine.

"You may not have run this time, but I told you before, I will *always* find you."

Her defiant nature runs wild, I can sense it before she does. She rips her chin from my fingertips and shoves with her entire strength against my chest, making us both stumble apart.

"You shouldn't have come for me." She steels her emotions, pushing them down deep, but I'm too attuned to her to miss the way her chin quivers slightly like she wants to cry before she locks it down.

My jaw tightens and I shove my hands deep in my pockets to hide the rage clenching through them. I close the short distance she's tried to put between us, leaning down into her space. I catch her scent and my body instantly craves a deeper hit, like a smokers need for nicotine after a meal, but she's trying to cut me off cold turkey.

My lips glide against her ear. I feel the small shiver she tries to still, but it's futile.

"We can do this the easy way, sweetness. Or if you want to keep trying to push me away, I'll kill every fucking person in this building and drag you out kicking and screaming. Your call."

She stills next to me, the quick shift of her weight as she rubs her thighs together pulls a smirk from my composed muscles.

That's what I thought.

"Oh, I hope I haven't caused a lover quarrel," the feminine lilt purrs sarcastically, as heels click against the floor toward us. That voice causes my entire body to ice over. Keira's heat shifts away from me, but I'm cemented to the floor. I can't follow like my heart yearns to because my logical brain wins this war.

Slender manicured fingers wrap around my bicep pulling me from the fog.

"Hey baby, did you miss me?"

My eyes slide from the giant diamond ring on the hand to the face of a ghost.

She's alive?

THIRTY-SIX
KEIRA

See You Bleed – Ramsey

My entire world tilts on its axis and crashes down around me as I watch him take her in. I told myself I wouldn't get between their reunion, but my heart is crumbling, and I don't think there's enough super glue on this planet to piece it back together. He was finally mine. His attention, his touch, his heart, it was mine and now that she's back, I'm not confident it will stay that way.

He's stiff. In shock. Much like I was when she walked into this office earlier with my long-lost father. I was reeling from the news of our connection, and he came in with the one-two punch. I went from having no family to speak of to two blood relatives standing in the same room. Finding out my late twin was alive should have been a monumental event for me. But the possibility of a tight-knit sisterhood was nothing more than a figment of my imagination for all those years.

Because the only thought flooding my mind when she walked into the room was how it would affect my relationship with Harkin. Now she's standing here with her hand on my man, even though it's hard to miss the gaudy ring on her finger.

Harkin still hasn't uttered a word; his silence is killing me. I want him to rip her slimy fingers from his arm and march in my direction. I want him to show her she doesn't get a piece of him anymore. That he's moved on and is mine. That I finally get to be the chosen twin and one-up her. She never knew about me, but knowing about her my entire life set us up for a one-sided sibling rivalry. I wait and wait, but he doesn't do any of that. He just stares at her.

The smile plastered on her perfectly done-up face makes me want to punch it and watch the blood trickle from her surgery-altered nose. How do I know? Because we used to have the same one. Now hers is thin and petite, like the rest of her. I never thought we'd be in the same place at the same time so I could compare our similarities and differences.

She might be my twin, but you can tell our personalities are on two different ends of the spectrum, our looks following suit. Where she's little miss elite clubs, high-end everything, she's the light to my darkness. The Louboutins to my Docs. We're not comparable, at least that's how I'm hoping Harkin feels.

"What a reunion," Domenico—my father says, clapping his hands before sitting behind his desk. The thrill of the reveal bolstering his confidence stifling the room.

His interruption finally breaks the trance Harkin's been standing in since Alina waltzed in here, resurrected. I watch as he stumbles away from her, finally breaking the contact I haven't stopped staring at since she had the nerve to initiate.

"What the fuck?" His voice is quiet but strong, it doesn't waiver or break. "How?" he adds.

"It's a long story, baby, and I want to tell you all about it when we can get away and have some privacy." Her gaze moves my way me, and I swear she sneers. My fists clench on my chest behind my crossed arms.

Yep, I definitely want to break that perfect nose of hers and send her back to whatever plastic surgeon gave it to her.

"Alina, I don't think that's a good idea," Domenico tells her from across the room.

"But, daddy!" she protests, in the whiniest tone I've ever heard come out of a grown woman. She can't be fucking serious.

"Mr. Greyson, please, come take a seat. We have a lot to discuss regarding your relationships with my daughters." For the first time since our bodies separated, he finds my eyes, ready and waiting for his attention. He's always had it—for years now—and that'll never change.

Stuffing the emotions I'm feeling deep down, not wanting to stoop to Alina's level of spoiled demands to get my way. I need him to see past the façade I'm throwing up, like he has every other time in the past couple of months. I need him to command them from me, like we both crave.

I don't know how their relationship was, but I know he's not the same man she used to toy around or used as a back-up plan when she was bored. The Harkin she knew died in that car accident, just like we thought she did. Except, she obviously didn't and nothing about her has changed. If I'm being honest, she seems to be the same girl I watched online, but worse, and that has to be Domenico's doing. But Harkin? No, he's changed. His blackened soul matches mine. The other side of some fucked-up coin the universe handed us. It's weighed down with tragedy and trauma that only happens when you lose someone in the blink of an eye, right in front of you.

"Keira, you too. Come sit." I shift in his direction, but I don't make to move. I don't trust myself not to send Alina back to where we though she was, six feet under.

"I'm good," I tell him and lean against the table next to my hip.

Harkin's lips pull to the side, but he schools it before walking toward the sitting area in the center of the office. Alina traipses behind him like a little puppy, all too excited for another person to give her attention. I always thought if we could have spent time together, we would have been close. That she would have been the sister I never had because our parents separated us at birth.

But I can see the way she's soaking up every inch of him. She's intrigued by the changes he's made, the new man he's become. The little green goddess in my head is telling me to shut that shit down, claim what's now mine before she can get her claws back into him. But the thing is, I won't fight for his attention. I'm not her. If she can steal him away, then he was never truly mine, and I was just a replacement.

Harkin's shock must be wearing off because his frame drops into the leather chair with a lethal air of disregard for the man across from him. I'm impressed. Domenico is an intimidating man in his own right. But I guess when you're the Don of the New York, Italian mafia with a mini-army at your disposal there's no reason to act otherwise.

Harkin's bulky frame shifts in the chair as he moves to prop his foot on the opposite knee. His hands come to interlock, resting behind the back of his head. I'm momentarily distracted by the bulging of his ink-covered biceps.

"So, you kidnaped my girl for this fucked up family

reunion?" he asks bluntly. A small gasp comes from the unnecessary occupant in the room.

Point for Keira.

If I was the insecure type, I'd walk over to him and let my actions speak for me, but I still don't know what Domenico has up his sleeve, and I'd rather not tip my hand just yet. He told me about his history with my mother.

How no one knew she was having twins until the moment she had me. How his uncle had secured an adoption through Harkin's father for Alina, which could have been me, had I not been born after the men had taken Alina from my mom the moment she drew her first breath. The young woman, who'd stayed back to look after my mom didn't expect her to start laboring again. When I came fifteen minutes later, she quickly got her situated and ready to leave like nothing extra had happened.

They hid my birth from his uncle in fear that I'd be taken away, too. So, my mom took me and ran, not even an hour after giving birth, with the clothes on her back and a wad of cash in her pocket.

I don't think she ever looked back or spoke to her family again. And according to him, Domenico never stopped thinking about us, worrying about us.

What I didn't expect him to tell me was that his uncle eventually found out about what my mom had done. I couldn't tell from his story, if he ever fessed up to his aid in our disappearance.

The emotion of him dropping the news of our relation was overwhelming. For a few minutes, I could picture my future where I had a father. One I could slowly get to know and build a relationship with. I was naïve. The kidnapping should have been the first clue that there was more to this than a father finally reunited with his long-lost daughter. The second sister dearest waltzed through the door in all her resurrected glory. But the breaking point was finding out his uncle was the one to put a hit out on us.

It doesn't matter that his uncle's choice is what ultimately lead to his demise, with a bullet to the brain at the hands of a distraught father. Because that means nothing to me. He had years to step in and help, but now that I'm grown, he pops back up.

I think not.

"Listen Mr. Greyson, my uncle and your father had a business agreement—"

Harkin's hand raises to silence whatever, Domenico was about to share. "Let's get one thing straight, I am not my father. I don't know what he did for your family, but I will not be following suit. My skills are no longer available for hire to your organization."

Domenico scoffs at the interruption. I wouldn't be surprised if the last person who did that is hidden on this property somewhere. He's being tolerant of him.

"Harkin, right?" he asks—like he doesn't already know. "I'm sure we could have a mutually beneficial understanding if you listen to what I have to offer you."

"You have nothing of interest to me."

"Oh, I wouldn't be so sure about that," he taunts. His tone, grates on my nerves. A knot forms in my stomach at the possibilities. My mind is already reeling from all the secrets that have come out in the last few hours. I might lose my shit if he drops another bomb.

Harkin waits, probably weighing his options. I haven't pieced together how we're getting out of here, but that's why I've stayed quite, observing my surroundings. Our best option is to play Domenico's game, find out what he wants and go from there.

Domenico ignores Harkin's silence and continues, "We all have a piece to play here. You, me, my girls. You can make it easy, agree to my proposal. I'll even let you leave here breathing with your choice of sister."

My eyes swing to said sister in question. She doesn't look offended. Instead, her eyes are filled with joy and excitement. She has no doubts that he'll choose her. Well fuck this shit, I'm not a pawn in whatever game Daddy Dearest is playing.

"The fuck he will." The words tumble from my mouth, before my brain can process my sentiment.

Three sets of eyes swing in my direction at the back of the room. My feet pull me into the mix before I slam my hands on Domenico's desk.

"Alina, might play your little puppet, Domenico, but I never needed a man to keep me. If you want my help, you might want to ask me nicely instead of threatening the man I've shacked up with since your men tried to kill us," I spit out.

A rough hand seizes me around the waist and pulls me backward. I lose balance and stumble into a hard chest before my ass meets his lap.

His warm breath caresses my ear as he quietly whispers, "Ahh, there's my girl. I was wondering when she was coming out to play." I elbow him hard in the side, but he doesn't release me. He just chuckles at my attempt to fight him.

"One," He whispers again against my skin and I still. He's got to be fucking kidding me. But I can't deny that single word pulls at my core, even in the middle of everything going on around us.

His hand continues slicing possessively around my waist to my stomach. His thumb moves rhythmically against the thin fabric of the hideous dress, calming my agitation, but lighting something lower aflame.

Now we have Alina's attention. She now understands he isn't hers to pick up like discarded trash on the side of the freeway. She lost her chance, and I wormed my way right into the black hole she left behind. My little green goddess laughs manically in triumph.

"Well, I think you heard the lady Domenico. It's not up to me to choose. This one here might cut off my balls if I even tried. You've sorely miscalculated this scheme if that was your plan to entice me."

"Let's cut the bullshit, Domenico. Tell us what you really need from us." I break their intense stare off. Men and their macho bullshit attitudes always impeding on the resolution to problems.

Domenico huffs. "You know, I might not have raised you but you're certainly my daughter."

His opinion stings. I'm this way because of the fucked-up childhood my situation forced me into because of his family. Any traits he sees of himself in me are from years of abuse and neglect burned into my psyche. From fighting to survive in a world that doesn't give two shits about little girls who lose their only parent in a drive by shooting. We're nothing alike and fuck him for trying to claim that deranged part of me.

Harkin's fingers pinch the sensitive flesh on the inside of my thigh, the sting calms my mind from completely imploding with rage. He knows. We're not even facing each other, and he can gauge my mood. I draw in a deep breath, settling further into his body, relaxing into the powerful force behind me. We've got this.

THIRTY-SEVEN
HARKIN

Give – Sleep Token

The operation to retrieve Kiera has been a clusterfuck. I expected us to come in, possibly drop a few bodies, find her, and get out. I never could have imagined that the ghost of girlfriends past would strut into the same room, like the last few years hadn't passed. She's been acting as if my entire world didn't crumble after the accident because I was under the impression, she'd died that day.

It's clear she hasn't changed. There isn't an ounce of her that shows she cares to know what I've been through. No, but there is that sparkle in her eye that she used to get the moment a plan formed in her mind. When she wants something even though it's not hers to take. Too bad for her, I'm not the same man she knew. Not even close. And the only way she's getting in between Keira and I, is with a bullet.

Keira shifts in my lap, relaxing into me while remaining

focused on her father behind his desk. She became ridged from the moment Alina exposed herself. I could tell she was anxious about my reaction and what that would mean for her. As calm and collected as she may have tried to portray for the room, behind her mask sits an inner child that expects to be abandoned.

When my rough hands gripped her sides and set her in her proper place, that worry dissipated. She needs reassurance. Even in the middle of this fucked up scene, my little one is at the surface begging to be taken care of, no matter how much she tries denying the need for it.

Domenico watches us, observing every shift of our bodies that feeds silently off each other's touch. He may have overestimated Alina's draw for me, but he can see clear as day that there's still another piece on the board. Too bad for him, he sees her as another pawn to be sacrificed for his kingdom. When in reality, she sits on my side coated in black, a crown on her head. He'll never be able to use her against me and vice versa.

He stands from his chair, walking around to the front of his desk, where he can loom over us. He's trying to reassert the dominance that's slipping through his fingers. He puffs out his chest, leaning back lazily and steeples his fingers against his lap.

"I can see allowing him to breech the compound was a mistake," Domenico sneers at me, but Keira shifts to block his view.

"What did you expect him to do after you kidnapped me from our bed, naked might I add." My body tenses under her, my jaw tight and teeth clenching. The thought of the scum of the earth seeing her naked flesh, let alone having their grimy hands all over it, has me itching to reach into my boot and fling my blade into his chest.

"I'll admit, my men may have been a little rougher than I expected. Seems you killed their cousin the other day." Domenico's indifference is aggravating. His men's leash seems to be too long for their own good.

"They brought that on themselves," Keira quips back. "Don't expect me to apologize."

"Oh, there's no need, *mio cuore*, I've already dealt with them. You're losing me good men from your actions, but they should have known better."

Mmm, so he cares about what happens to her.

I store that information away.

"You still haven't said what we're doing here. It's clear you could have kept me and my men out. Which tells me you anticipated my arrival but didn't want to bring us in together. Otherwise, your men wouldn't have waited for me to leave the apartment before they broke in. So, why not cut all the theatrics and move on with it?"

Domenico shakes his head at me, having ever the arrogant air about him.

"Mr. Greyson, your fate's been in my hands since moment I saved my daughter from the hospital after the accident. It's not what I need from you, but I'm the man to make what she needs happen. Keira, on the other hand, is my blood. She will be a part of this family, as it should have been for the last twenty-plus years. How you three work out your entanglement is none of my business."

She shifts ready to throw back an insult, but I flatten my palm against her thigh to stop her. "And what is it you need from me?" I inquire, turning toward Alina for the first time since we've sat down.

She looks small and timid for once, nervous to tell me

whatever is on the tip of her tongue.

"It's not what I need Harkin. Your daughter needs you."

My vision blurs as the room turns red. *There's no fucking way.* She couldn't have been pregnant back then and even if she was, how did she not lose the baby during that accident or from downing pills like they were candy.

"No." The tiny cry leaves Keira's stunned lips as she pops off my lap and heads for the double doors of the office. I doubt she knows where she's going, but Domenico doesn't make a move to stop her even after she's fled through them.

I jump up ready to chase after her. I don't believe Alina's story for a second. Even if the miraculous is true and she was pregnant and didn't lose the baby, I'm not naïve enough to not question the paternity. She was the type of party girl to cheat and hook up with some random guy when my back was turned. So high out of her mind, she probably thought he was me. But I knew, and we fought about it all the time. She'd always deny it, but I knew and yet I stayed. And here she is, trying to pull this shit again. Once a pathological liar, always a pathological liar. Too bad that truth is just dawning on me now.

Her claws clutch my arm as I make to move past her to go after Keira. "Harkin, wait! We need to talk about this."

I shake off her hand and call back over my shoulder. "I want a paternity test." Not waiting to see her reaction, though I can hear it as I break through the doors at a jog.

"Keira!" I roar through the compound, not sure which way her feet took her. Stopping down the hall, I pause, training my ears for anything that might tell me which way she took to escape.

I don't hear feet pattering against the marble floors, but the longer I stand there the rise of angry voices and shouts come from around the corner. A scream pierces the air and I take off at a run. When she comes into view, the picture isn't what I was expecting. There's no one else here, man handling her like I anticipated. Instead, she stands in front of floor to ceiling windows that look out onto a courtyard, screaming at the top of her lungs, bent over and pounding against the glass.

I slow my pace, sliding in behind her, cradling her body back into mine.

"Shh, little one. I'm right here." Her body collapses against my embrace and then fights to be freed.

"Let me go Harkin. I can't do this! It's always her. She always wins." She's not only screaming but big fat tears roll from her eyes down her rosy cheeks.

"Baby, shh. I don't know what you're talking about." I try to calm her, but my statement only seems to bring tears on faster.

"She got the fancy house, the parents that loved her, you." She whips around in my arms to face me. "Harkin, she got you. The only thing I've ever wanted for myself in life she got. And not only then, but she gets you now too. How am I supposed to compete with your flesh and blood. Jesus Christ, Harkin, you guys have a child together."

"Woah, slow down." I try to implore her, but she lost in her head. Not listening to a syllable, let alone a word coming out of my mouth.

"I should have known. I should have known you'd never be mine. That we were too good to be true. I should have stayed away!"

"Keira, stop this." She struggles against my hold, but my arms tighten refusing to let her go.

"You were always hers, Harkin. I may have gotten you for a few stolen moments in real life and it was better than I could have ever imagined." She draws in a deep breath, hiccuping on top of another sob. "All those nights I spent thinking about what it would be like to take her place with you—" She cuts herself off, clamping her eyes shut at the realization of what she's finally shared.

I grip her chin, until our faces are only centimeters apart. "Open."

She doesn't listen shaking her head.

"Open those beautiful eyes for me, baby, or I swear to God I will thrash that ass right here in the middle of your father's hallway for all his men to see." The threat hits its mark as she opens them slowly.

"Did you really think I didn't know." Her glossy honeycomb eyes widen.

"Maybe not at first, but when I saw you that day on the curb you woke something in me."

"But how?" she asks settling down enough to listen to me.

"Babe, computer genius, remember?" I joke and the small sad smile that pulls at her lips leaves a sharp pang in my chest.

"I'm serious Harkin, what do you know exactly?"

"You know, I'm flattered." I smile down at her. "You spent years following me online." I brush a stray piece of hair behind her ear. "I can't blame you, sweetness. You found Alina, and it's only natural that you'd be curious. Curiosity can spin into a wild of obsession if left unchecked. Trust me, I know."

"So, you've known this entire time, and you didn't tell me? You don't care?"

"If I did, we wouldn't be here right now." I shuffle us to stand up against the window, it's progress from the scene I found her in. "We can talk about this later. All of it if you want to know, but what's important now is getting us both out of here."

"Out of here?" She looks shocked. "What about what Alina said? You can't just run out on that, not for me. I won't be the reason another little girl grows up without a dad, Harkin."

"Yeah, Harkin you can't just run out on your responsibilities," Alina's voice mocks from the other end of the hallway.

Her tiny heels clack against the marble floors as she slowly makes her way toward us. She's living for this moment of being the center of chaos. Her ugliness hides in plain sight, under a thick veil of makeup and designer clothes. Taking her in again after the last couple of years, it's clear to me now that she was never more than a placeholder in my life.

Keira's entire demeanor shifts the closer Alina gets to us. Gone is the girl on the floor in shambles. Now, her back stiffens as she steps away from me, but my body automatically follows, refusing to let her stand on her own.

The tension between the three of us is suffocating. "I already said everything I need to say to you, Alina."

"Mhm, but I don't think you did." She plays with the giant diamond on her finger, drawing my attention there.

"What is it you want from me exactly?" I ask her.

"I told you, Harkin, your daughter needs you. She's sick. I got tested but I'm not eligible to donate to her. But you might be what we've been praying for."

"Wait." Keira pipes in. "Were you a match?" she asks Alina.

"Yes, but I'm not able to donate."

Keira's eyes swing to mine, a look of apology under the surface. "I'll do it."

THIRTY-EIGHT
KEIRA

Crazy Girls – TOOPOOR

The longer I'm here, the more I realize I don't want to be. Wanting a family was never supposed to be this convoluted. Alina's too focused on one-upping Harkin to get under his skin. She's overlooking the obvious answer. I don't know if it's because she never mentioned me to her daughter's doctor, or she would rather rope Harkin in and tie him down, even though she's already attached to someone else.

"I didn't ask for your help," Alina snarks back.

"God, have you always been such a stuck-up bitch, or has it gotten worse with age?"

She rolls her eyes, but I can tell my words don't affect her like they would anyone without her confidence.

Harkin stands quietly next to me. He gets it, but he's waiting for me to put the offer on the table.

"Listen, you two have your own problems to work out. But as much as you seem to hate me for whatever fucking reason, all I'm hearing is that your daughter, my niece, needs something. You must have skipped high school biology when they explained identical twins share exact DNA, meaning whatever you could have donated, I should also be able to."

The air sucks from her lungs, a look of surprise and realization washes over her features.

Jesus Christ, she really didn't see that option coming.

"Harkin will get tested too." I throw a look in his direction and see the quick smirk before it disappears when Alina's attention falls on him.

"We can do the paternity test at the same time," He asserts, no emotion behind it and I understand. There's no doubt in my mind that if that test comes back positive, he'd step in. But from everything he's told me, she's given him no reason to trust what she says.

"What is wrong with you, Harkin? Of course she's yours. You know you never would have questioned me before her." She throws a disgusted look my way, but it doesn't phase me. I feel the same way about her now.

"You've been dead for almost two-years Alina, things change." He's not giving into her emotional whims, only stating facts, and keeping things short between them.

"And this change happened way before Keira came into the picture. But you keep blaming her if that's what will help you sleep at night."

She huffs in irritation, nearly stomping her foot again like before. "Whatever." A rush of feet comes battering down the hallway. Rounding the corner, is a group of men in black suits, all carrying a variety of assault weapons strapped around their chest. One man stands out. He's tall, suave, with thick, slicked back black hair and olive skin. His eyes are hard and menacing, the air around him screams danger. He leads the group to a stop a few feet away, breaking from formation to step in closer to us.

Harkin moves quickly blocking him from getting any closer to me, but it's not me he has his eyes set on.

"*Mia Tesoro.*" He stops next to Alina, his hand coming up to cup her face. The giant rock on her finger makes a whole lot more sense now. His eyes soften briefly as he takes her in. But I don't miss the way her body tenses when his skin draws against hers. The feelings between them don't seem mutual, but that's not my problem. She made her bed. Now apparently, she has to lie in it with this guy.

"Your father had a business issue to deal with." His eyes swing in my direction, though the majority of my body is still behind the wall of man muscle in front of me. I shove my way forward, not missing the quick shake of Harkin's head or the finger signal he flashes me.

Two.

I scowl back, knowing I'd rather these men see me as the force I am, instead of writing me off like my twin. I'll deal with Harkin and his delicious torment later.

"When will he back? I need to talk to him," I ask calmly. The man stares me down, a light of intrigue in his hollowed eyes.

"When he gets back. You'll wait in your room. Follow me," he orders, expecting my unyielding cooperation. He turns and heads back in the direction he showed up from, not checking to make sure I'm following behind.

I don't make to follow, but Alina does, falling in line just as I expected. She's all bark, no bite, or backbone.

"How long until you think he notices," I whisper, leaning

into Harkin. His light chuckle warms my body that's still fighting the shock from everything that's happened today.

"You're just a glutton for punishment today, huh, baby?" He sighs back. The warmth from his breath sends a shiver down my spine.

"You think we can just back away slowly and make a run for it?" I ask, ignoring my bodies response to having him so close.

That thought disappears when a deafening explosion shakes the house. The dry wall crumbles from the ceiling as a crack from the stress forms above us. "Yes, now we can." Harkin says, grabbing for my hand. "Run!" He instructs before turning and running to one of the many doors along the wall of windows looking out into the walled-in courtyard.

"How are we supposed to get out of here?" I yell over the blaring sirens, as we run down the narrow paved walkway outside.

"Just give them a second," he calls over his shoulder.

"Give who a second?" As soon as the words leave my tongue, a second explosion sounds from the direction we're heading. For fuck sakes, for the first time since I woke up on the couch, I'm hoping we're nowhere near civilization.

The cascade of gunfire sounds in the distance, getting further away as we run to the corner of the compound. A small section of the cement wall now lies crumbled on the ground. I dig my heels in, jolting Harkin back, when two men in blacked out military gear and skeleton masks stand waiting on the outside of the ruins.

"They're with us," he placates.

I hesitate for a few seconds looking back at my father's home.

"Harkin, wait." I tug at his hand again.

"I can't do this. I promised Alina." He huffs in irritation at my sudden onset, conscious.

His rough hand finds my cheek, cupping it softly. "You can help her, without being a prisoner in a house full of men who want to kill you. Your father won't always be around to protect you. I won't leave you here. So, you either take that fine ass over those bricks and into the woods or I'll throw you over my shoulder and carry you."

I roll my eyes at his over-the-top bullshit. Unfortunately, for me, he's right. If I stay here, it's just a matter of time before my life is on the line, regardless of how much Daddy Dearest wants us to be a family.

Heaving out an exasperated groan, I stomp past, shoulder checking him as I go. His annoying laughter follows behind me.

THIRTY-NINE
HARKIN

Switchblade - Neverwaves

My eyes drill into the scratches marring her legs as she climbs up the embankment to the rough trail above. Her head keeps swinging back in my direction and over my shoulder to the compound disappearing into the thick woods. The alarms and shouts are audible through the calm forest, a warning we're still too close for comfort.

Keira's foot slips on the uneven earth, her ill-prepared footwear giving her zero traction or protection. Her knee hits the ground hard, and her frustrated groan meets my ears. I bet she's missing her signature Docs right about now.

My hands reach down, scooping her body back up and helping her up the last couple feet until we're once again on even ground. She looks down at the white summer dress coated in dirt, a small smile of defiance lights her face. Forever my obstinate, shadowed beauty.

"Where's James?" I ask the man leading our little group.

"He stayed back, told us to get you both out of here. We lost track of Domenico."

Rage burns through my veins at not knowing where he is now. He might have left for business like his security guard said, but I doubt it. That's not information one of his standing would offer freely. If I had to guess, he left because he had an inkling of what was coming.

Men like him weasel away, breaking from the chaos like cockroaches who scurry into the dark for safe hiding. He can run and try to hide all he wants. I know him now; I watched the way he interprets information and uses his reputation to move his pawns. He's cocky and cocky men always slip up.

"Fine, tell him to get in touch with me when he's finished. He'll handle the rest of your team's payment."

He shrugs off a black backpack and hands it to me, dropping an old school flip phone in my palm, before pointing off into the trees.

"Head east about four klicks, you'll find a compact sedan. Keys are in the wheel well. You know the rest." I nod as Keira shifts uncomfortably beside me.

"Let's go." I tell her, slinging the bag onto my back and gripping her hand in mine, interlacing our fingers. The warmth from my skin cools against her chilled fingertips. Fuck, she's freezing.

We stumble along through the muted night. The trees are thick blocking the moon from beaming down to light our way. Keira trips jolting forward, but I yank her up.

"Fucking useless shoes," she hisses after righting herself.

I flip the burner phone open, using the small screen to illuminate the ground right in front of her next step. "There. Just keep an eye on your feet and let me lead you."

"I'm not a fucking dog, Harkin."

"Jesus Christ, woman. Do you want a broken ankle?" I can't see her face, but I have a feeling that signature eye roll just passed between us.

I pause, pulling her shivering body flush against me. "Was that three, little one." The shiver intensifies and her throat clears.

"I—I don't know what you're talking about," she plays off.

My hand meets the curve of her ass, giving it a little tap. "Mhm, but I think you do, baby. You're lucky we need to hurry and move out or I'd shove down into the wet earth and fuck you right here. Watch that pure little white dress coat with filth, while you scream my name into the night." A hushed moan rumbles in her throat. My cock twitches at the scene and how much she'd enjoy it. I'll file that one away for a rainy day.

I drop my lips to hers quickly, before pulling her along again. "We're almost there."

The trees thin as we come up on another dirt road. A small black Honda sits on the side of the road, a note tucked under the windshield wiper I run my fingers along the back wheel well until they bump against the key box hidden there.

Popping the trunk, I ditch the backpack and pull out the other I already stored there. Keira stands by watching the quick exchange. I pull out a change of clothes for her and reach back to find her Docs waiting.

"Change, quickly. I'll get the car started." I move to the front, stealing the note waiting on the windshield, before dropping into the car and blasting the heat for Keira.

Harkin,

If you're here, things didn't go as planned. But like I taught you, that's why we have a backup plan ready to execute. And plans that backup those plans. Continue to do so. You know where you're going. Keep her safe. She's important to him. I'll get in contact when things are done and settled. You've got this, kid.

James

THE DOOR POPS open and quickly shuts. "God, this feels much better." She says under her breath, getting settled before turning to me. Her eyes find the small slip of paper in my fingers, and she snatches it, reading over James's message.

"What does this mean?" she asks, and I shift the car into gear, taking off down the beaten path.

"It means I just stole something valuable from one of the most powerful underground men in America and he won't stop until he has it back."

"You can't really steal me if I came willingly," she jokes trying to break the growing tension while my mind calculates what our next steps will look like. When I don't reply, she huffs and turns on the radio. The music comes through full of static, it'll stay that way until we get somewhere with better reception, but she leaves it anyway.

The broken melody of some old love song fills the car. Her head leans against the window, her body tucking in under itself on the seat.

"Where are we going?" she asks sleepily.

"Somewhere far away. Sleep. You'll wake again before we're there."

THE CAR COMES to a gradual halt in front of a small log cabin surrounded by more woods. The sun is just peeking over the horizon through the trees. A thin layer of undisturbed snow coats the ground for as far as the eye can see.

My hand reaches over finding Keira's knee, I give it a soft squeeze. She rouses from the fitful sleep she's been in and out of over the last couple days as we traveled across half the U.S. Her back arches like cat, arms stretching above her head, while a yawn parts her lips.

"My turn to drive?" Her question is laced with sleep that's still hanging on.

"No, sweetness, we're here."

Her eyes cast to the front of the car, taking in our surroundings.

"Where the hell is here?"

"Colorado."

Her eyes bug at the answer.

"What the hell are we doing in Colorado?" she asks.

"Regrouping. Come on, let's get inside. We're due for another storm tonight, and I need to get things up and running before we possibly lose power."

She doesn't look impressed by that possibility. But that's the reality when you've sequestered away in the remote reaches of the Rocky Mountains.

The thick wooden door creaks, opening without a key. The entry's cloaked in shadowy forms of furniture draped in fabric cloths. James said this place has been in his family for generations, but with his work taking him all over the world, he hadn't been here in ten plus years; it shows.

The stench of stale air permeates the further we advance, while looking for a light source.

"I've got it," Keira calls before the dim glow of a lamp clicks on illuminating the space.

"Well, I've stayed in worse," she says shrugging and takes off to explore. That fact kills me. The detachment with which she shares it makes me want to pay off James to take care of everything back home. Spending the rest of my days showing her what life without abandonment and abuse would look like. Where she'd never have to want for anything or worry about vengeful twin sisters and power-hungry, long-lost fathers.

But that's not our reality. Our reality is this: fleeing across the country to a safe house where we can lie low and rally. Where I can use all of my skills and contacts to hunt her father down, figuring out what he really has planned and why exactly he needs his daughters back in his life after twenty-plus years.

Alina's sob story was nothing more than icing on the cake for him, a wedge he thought would cause irreparable harm between Keira and me. But he underestimated the tether that binds us, he doesn't know his daughter as well as he would like to think.

A crash comes from the other room and my feet tear out from under me as her screams hit my ears. I round the corner, stilling in place. Keira kneels, hunched over with a mess of boxes around her still settling from their fall.

"What happened?" I ask, my heart still racing in my chest.

When she turns, two sets of the biggest eyes train on me.

"Oh, no," I declare, "we have too much going on right now

to worry about another living thing," I remind her. But then she brings the small ball of fluff up to her nose and cuddles it in closer.

I'm fucking screwed.

"Well, we can't go drop her off, now, can we?" she says confidently, knowing she's going to get her way. What was I just saying about wanting to give her the world.

"And she'll never survive if we put her out in this weather." She pleads her case.

"I wonder where she came from? It's not like a pup of her age to get separated from her mom," she says to herself, solidifying that we do, in fact, have a dog now.

"That's all you, babe. I'm going to get my stuff set up. Bedroom should be down the hall to the right." I motion in that direction. "And, for the love of God, don't yell like that unless someone's here to kill us." I smile after her as she takes the small bundle in her arms and disappears again.

The shower turns off, the old pipes creaking as the last bit of pressure subsides. Fire warms the living room where I sit working, engulfed in the beginnings of a plan. A small snoring fluff ball, Keira's named Cinder, lays curled up in between my feet on the floor.

Light feet pad down the hall, coming to a stop behind the couch. Her warm arms engulf my neck, laying lazily on my chest as she peers over my shoulder. "Did you get it all figured out?"

"Not all of it, but it's a start." My lips find hers, soft from the steam of her shower. A small hum of contentedness echoes in her throat. Her hands dip lower across my stomach, heading further south.

I reluctantly break our kiss, "It's going to take time. I hope you don't mind the cold because we might be here a while."

"I can think of a few ways to stay warm." She winks. Her fingers reach the metal of my belt buckle and halt their journey.

"Miss. Fitzpatrick are you trying to distract me?" I tease.

"Hmm, I think I remember you saying something about a punishment, Mr. Greyson," she drawls with a wicked smirk.

"Punishment, huh? That's what you're looking for?"

Her pale cheeks flush the most exquisite shade of pink. I move my laptop to the side, reaching over my shoulder to hook under her arms and drag her over the back of the couch. She lets free a loud squeal of excitement, but she won't be beaming once she sees what's in store.

My fingers find her chin, pinching to guide her focus, as she settles straddling my lap. "Is that what you crave, little one."

Her throat bobs with a hard swallow. The striking hazel slowly disappears taken over by the blackening of her growing pupils. "Yes, sir."

"And why is that?" I ask.

"I want to let go. Help me forget, even if it's just for tonight," she begs breathlessly.

"Stand."

She does, careful to avoid her new best friend still sound asleep below us.

"Drop the towel."

She makes a show of untying it from between her perfect breast, before tossing it in my direction.

I point toward the crackling fireplace, dancing behind the grate. "Kneel; facing me."

She doesn't hesitate, following my instructions to the T.

"Good girl," I praise, watching her body relax further into the correct position before I pick my laptop back up.

My fingers clack against the keyboard as I type away, digging through the information I backed up to this computer from my hard drive back at the apartment. There's not much I can do, until I hear from James, but I dig anyway, searching for even the smallest thing I may have missed.

Labored breathing snags my attention, and I still my typing. I check my watch, noticing the twenty minutes have passed. I look over to her, still surrendered in the same position I set her in.

Powering off my work, I set the laptop on the coffee table and walk toward where she waits for me, holding out my hand for her. Her delicate fingers reach for my support to stand. Her legs will be asleep from the extended punishment.

"I've got you."

The lust filled haze crumbles at my words, mixing with something more, something that looks a lot like unfiltered love.

"I know," she confesses, everything still not said between us within those two words.

To be Continued…

THANK YOU READERS

If you've made it this far, I hope you enjoyed the ride that is book one in the Shadows and Secrets duet. If you've enjoyed The Shadows We Keep, please leave a review on your favorite review platforms and retailer. Your support and feedback is important to me.

ACKNOWLEDGMENTS

Where to start because this book is the culmination of my blood, sweat, and tears. When I started this project, I envisioned a story much darker than it became but I absolutely love who Harkin and Kiera turned out to be.

While the story might be my be my baby, it wouldn't be what it is today without the help of some very special people in my life.

To my alpha reader, Diana, thank you for basically living inside my brain and knowing my characters just as well as I do. The way they're basically our imaginary friends at this point is amazing to me. You are the biggest support and always there when I need an ear to listen to my crazy ideas, even with a six-hour time difference.

To my betas, Kylie and Marykate, Shadow's is such a better story because of your feedback. The time and effort you put into your notes did not go unnoticed, and I hope the end results show that.

To my street team, you guys are the absolute best hype team. I was blown away by how many new readers wanted to join the team and help me get the word out about TSWK. And to those who have been with me since the start of my author career, thank you for coming back, time-and-time again to support me and read my work.

Lastly, to the woman who made it possible for you to have this book in your hands, KM Mixon. I'd use her legal name…

but then I'd have to enroll in WITSEC. Since the moment I shared Shadows with you in all it's rough draft, unfinished written-while-intoxicated glory you've been such an amazing support. Not only did you help build my confidence to finish their story, but you also helped bring it to life as we collaborated on the cover. THANK YOU, for ALL of the hours you put into editing and formatting this baby. I'm forever indebted to you with books, endless hours of ridiculous chats, and pictures of "your" dog.

ABOUT THE AUTHOR

Hello Readers,

I'm Cindy Dawson, the author of The Shadows We Keep and two other romance novels That Night and A Christmas Deal: A That Night Novella.

I live in Central Texas with my husband of nearly ten years and our four incredibly rambunctious dogs. When I'm not writing, I'm reading and if it's not those two things I'm likely spending time with family. I run on caffeine, smutty books, and puppy cuddles!

If you're interested in my everyday life as an author and reader come follow me on Instagram: author_cindydawson or Tiktok: author.cindydawson.

Lots of Love,
Cindy

ALSO BY CINDY DAWSON

That Night

A Christmas Deal

Made in the USA
Coppell, TX
18 January 2026

68620136R00226